THE GRAVE ROBBERS' CHRONICLES

VOL 4

Palace of Doom

BY XU LEI
TRANSLATED BY KATHY MOK

The Grave Robbers' Chronicles: Volume 4
Palace of Doom
By Xu Lei
Translated by Kathy Mok

Copyright©2013 ThingsAsian Press

Edited by Janet Brown and Michelle Wong
Illustrated by Vladimir Verano

ThingsAsian Press
San Francisco, California USA
www.thingsasianpress.com
Printed in China

ISBN-13: 978-1-934159-34-7
ISBN-10: 1-934159-34-4

TABLE OF CONTENTS

CHAPTER ONE

THE THIRD FISH

I felt drugged by winter, so lazy that I didn't even have the energy to take a nap. Lying on my couch in a warm and stuffy room, I hovered between sleep and wakefulness, a hot water bottle tucked firmly between both feet. A tap on my office door snapped me out of my lethargy. "Boss, there's someone here to see you," Wang Meng, my shop assistant, announced.

"Who's crazy enough to come out on the coldest day of the year?" I grumbled as I stumbled toward the door of my shop. There was a young girl, shivering in the winter wind.

"You're Lao Hai's niece," I said, grabbing her by the arm and pulling her inside. "What are you doing so far from home? Wang Meng, get this poor girl some tea."

Lao Hai was one of Southern China's leading antique dealers. Ever since the day I brought him Uncle Three's most precious discovery, a jade shroud from the cavern of the blood zombies, we had been business associates.

His niece and assistant, Qin Haiting, was only seventeen but was already well-known among antique dealers for her knowledge and acumen. I led her into my office and made her sit on the sofa I had just left. I handed her my hot water bottle along with a cup of steaming tea and watched her shuddering subside.

"What brings you to this frozen city? Why did your uncle send you north at this hellish time of year?"

"He didn't want me to come, but I heard that Hangzhou is beautiful so I ignored him. I'll know better next time. It's business that brought me here as well as curiosity. Here's a check for that fish-eye pearl you brought from the undersea tomb."

I glanced at the sum before pocketing the check; Fats would be pleased when he found out what his treasure had yielded him.

"That's not all," Qin Haiting continued, taking a letter from her handbag. "My uncle is coming to Hangzhou the day after tomorrow to go to an antique auction; he would be delighted if you would go with him. He has something he needs to talk to you about face-to-face, in private."

"The day after tomorrow?" I asked. "I don't know if I have time. Can't your uncle and I talk over the phone? What could possibly be so important?"

Qin Haiting leaned close to my ear and murmured, "My uncle said he has news about a bronze fish like the ones you and your Uncle Three discovered. If you don't find time to see him, you'll always wish that you had."

I met Lao Hai at the train station two days later and drove him to his hotel. "What's going on?" I asked bluntly. "Don't lie to me, Lao Hai. I'm too good a customer for you to try to bamboozle me with some wild story."

Lao Hai was shivering as hard as his niece had when she first arrived here. "No lies between us. But first let's get something hot to drink. I'm dying from your winter weather."

After I bought him some mulled wine, he looked less like a hypothermia victim and more like the successful businessman that he was. "Now that you're going to live, tell me what's going on here."

"Look at this," he said, pulling an old newspaper from his bag. I picked it up, careful not to tear the brittle, yellowed pages, which bore a date from 1974. An article had been circled on the front page, accompanied by a large black-and-white photo. It was a picture of a bronze fish with snake brows, much like the one I'd found in the puzzle box and its twin that Uncle Three handed to me before he disappeared.

I had seen three fish in the bas-relief carving within the undersea tomb and was certain there was one that I hadn't yet found. Did this picture show the missing fish that would complete the trio?

"How did you find this newspaper? What's the story here?" I asked Lao Hai.

"I found it in a rich man's collection," he told me. "Read it; you'll find it's very interesting."

When an ancient pagoda collapsed, it was discovered that it had been built above an underground palace. Within the palace walls were many old books and documents and while they were being carried out, the bronze fish turned up. Experts believed it dated back to the Northern Song dynasty.

How about that? I asked myself. The first fish that I knew of showed up in a noble's tomb from the Western Zhou period. My uncle found the second in an undersea tomb from the early Ming dynasty—and now this one came from a pagoda built in the Northern Song dynasty.

1. THE THIRD FISH

And there was no relationship between any of these historical periods.

"Terrific," I snorted. "This is useless. I still don't know anything about these damned fish."

Lao Hai patted me on the arm. "Don't be discouraged. I haven't finished. Wait until you hear the rest of the story."

"What are you talking about? Tell me what you know."

The old man smiled. "Have you ever met a man named Chen Ah-Si?"

"You mean the famous grave robber from Changsha who disappeared after he went blind? The one my grandfather said would commit any act, even murder, if he would profit by it? He must be over ninety years old by now. Is he still alive? Did you meet him? What does he have to do with the fish?"

"He's the man who found the fish in the ruined pagoda. Listen. It's a long story."

CHAPTER TWO

FINDING THE PAGODA

"Chen Ah-Si was almost sixty years old in 1974 and hadn't yet gone blind. This was during the Cultural Revolution and his reputation as a grave robber put him in danger. So he became a bandit, hiding far from any town where he might be recognized and turned over for execution.

"This was when the Four Olds were under attack: Old Customs, Old Culture, Old Habits, Old Ideas. Many historical sites were being destroyed and so when Chen Ah-Si heard that a pagoda had collapsed in a place called Reclining Buddha Ridge, he wondered if it might have been a victim of the Red Guard's campaign against ancient buildings.

"He had heard about this place. The pagoda was part of a temple that had been built in a basin surrounded by mountain cliffs. A Hmong village had been built on the top of one of the cliffs, more than three hundred feet above the temple site, which was obscured by a thick forest. No road led to the basin; it could only be reached by descending the cliffs on ropes. It was said that anyone who ever tried to explore this spot would never come back.

"The villagers knew there was a pagoda only because its spired top protruded from the green canopy of trees below. One morning there was a thunderous explosion and the spire disappeared. Eerie cries rose up from the basin and the villagers knew something terrible had happened.

"Chen Ah-Si knew that the destruction of this pagoda could hold some benefits for him so the next day he set off for Reclining Buddha Ridge. When he got there, he was amazed. The pagoda had been huge; where it had once stood, there was now only a deep ravine surrounded by tilting trees. Yet he could see something within the ravine, a building only partially revealed by the pagoda's collapse.

"A 'mirror palace,' he thought, one of those underground structures that was a reflection of the building above it. It was the first he had ever seen and it made his palms twitch. What would he find there? A sacred relic, a golden statue of a famous monk, Buddhist scriptures recorded on silk? Any one of these things could keep him in comfort for the rest of his days.

"And yet he was a wanted man and had to approach this place without arousing local suspicions. He needed to find a local guide, pay him well, and tell him a convincing tale of woe, that he was a professor who had been traveling with one of his students. Tragically the young man fell off one of the cliffs into the area of the collapsed pagoda and it was up to his mentor to recover his body and take it to his parents.

"The Hmong guide he hired was moved by this sad state of affairs and agreed to take Chen Ah-Si down into the basin. Villagers produced a large wicker basket, large enough for two men to squat in, tied it to a long rope, and lowered it—with its human cargo—along the side of the cliff.

"Although they reached the basin in broad daylight, the moss-covered trees blotted out the sky and the sun. Chen Ah-Si took a step and then fell to the ground. 'I'm too old to explore this dark and frightening place,' he told his guide. 'You go look for my young friend. I'll sit here and wait for you to come back.'

"The minute the guide disappeared into the forest gloom, Chen Ah-Si switched on his flashlight, took out his compass, and walked off in the direction of the collapsed pagoda. If my guide returns before I do, I'll just tell him I went for a walk and got lost, he decided.

"He walked for four hours without reaching his goal. He was ready to sit down for a rest when something flickered at the corner of his vision. There sat a corpse, leaning against a tree, its stomach quivering violently as though there was something inside it, trying to get out.

"Dead men were nothing new to Chen Ah-Si; he'd brought more than a few of them to death's door himself. He walked to the corpse and prodded it with his foot. The body was dressed like the Hmong villagers he had just met and looked as though it might have been dead for several years. But why was there still flesh on its bones and what was moving within its dead belly?

"Quickly, he drew his pistol and fired three shots into the stomach of the corpse. It split open under the force of the bullets, revealing a large clump of eggs wrapped in a coil of intestines. Some of the eggs had hatched and out of them slithered masses of white worms. He gagged, turned, and ran.

"Then before him, in the distance he saw pieces of a massive tower, covering the ground ahead. Shattered trees surrounded a crater as large as a canyon; it was in the middle of the broken portions of the tower. When he approached the huge hole in the ground, he saw a wall extending deep below. It was the foundation of the pagoda he had come here to find. This was the pathway to the 'mirror palace' that lay underground.

"It was probably so far underground, he warned himself, it would take him six months to dig his way into it. And now the forest, which was dark enough during the day, was almost pitch-black; his flashlight was too dim to show him the way back to where his guide had left him. I'm truly lost, he thought, and built a bonfire so its leaping flames and smoke might bring someone to his rescue.

"Quickly he began to reconnoiter while the bonfire blazed high; the ground was spongy and uneven. The soil was soggy with moisture; it would be much easier to excavate than he had thought. It was bound to be as soft and yielding as a steamed dumpling; half an hour, he thought exultantly, and I'll be within the underground palace. Why not do it now?

"Like all grave robbers, Chen Ah-Si couldn't restrain himself when he knew that treasure was close at hand. I have to dig, he decided, it's my discovery, no one else's. If my guide finds me here and tries to stop me, I'll kill him.

"Taking a folding shovel from his backpack, Chen Ah-Si began to dig, staying close to the foundation of the pagoda. Within minutes his shovel struck the roof of the mirror palace. It's not stone, he laughed silently, it's made from a whole tree trunk—what luck!

"The wood was old and rotting. It was easy to dig through it with his shovel and soon he shone his flashlight into the opening he had made.

2. FINDING THE PAGODA

"The palace was a long and open space with no walls to partition it into rooms. As he swept the flashlight into its depths, he saw something white and vaporous. Could this be fog? Or the breath of a legendary monster that might be living in this place?

"Time for my gecko imitation, he decided. Removing a golden hook from his pack, he jammed it into a portion of the roof that seemed undamaged by rot and hooked both feet around it. Suspended upside down in midair, he peered at the underside of the wooden roof. There was writing all over it, in characters he couldn't read, inscribed with red lacquer. The letters were curved, with some placed above and below other characters. It looked like a drawing he had once seen of a temple in India that was covered with this sort of writing; could it be Sanskrit? And why was it placed where no human would see it? Was it a spell to ward off demons or the monster he had recently imagined?

"He looked downward again and saw a crowd of statues, each the size of a man and each wearing monk's robes. Beneath him the palace consisted of ten separate floors, each surrounded by ten of these statues. One hundred holy men—arhats—he shivered, this is no place for a brigand like me. But why am I afraid? They're only statues.

"He continued to sweep the flashlight across the palace, hoping to see something other than these eerie sculpted figures. A face appeared in the darkness, a deathly white countenance with eyes that stared directly into Chen Ah-Si's. Oh hell, he thought, it's a ghost—maybe of one of the many men I've killed in my lifetime.

"When he looked closer, he saw that the face belonged

to just another statue, yet one positioned so carefully that it seemed as though it were meant to frighten away intruders. And it could certainly harbor a deadly trap. Pulling his gun from his pack, Chen Ah-Si fired two shots straight into the statue's pallid face, leaving two hollow sockets where its eyes had been. 'Stare at me now, will you?' he taunted the disfigured face, his voice echoing through the silent darkness.

"Removing another golden hook, he attached it near the first and then tied a rope to it that was almost as strong as a cable, made from the hide of an elephant seal. He securely fastened the rope to his ankle and swung into the air, letting his body slip down the leather strand, which he knew would extend thirty feet.

"But the mirror palace was over thirty-six feet deep. Even though his rope was stretched to its limits, Chen Ah-Si was still far from the bottom floor. However he could see it.

"The palace ended in a floor made of white marble. In its center stood something that looked like a miniature pagoda made either of ivory or the palest white jade. It was shrouded with a curtain made of finely woven white fabric that made it look as though it was covered with mist."

At this point in Lao Hai's story, I had to interrupt. "Didn't this barbarian know what was beneath this tiny pagoda? Didn't he know about the Eight Treasures? Even a village bumpkin would know that there should be eight boxes, each holding either a bone from the Buddha or precious replicas of holy relics, made of the finest jade. But then, he couldn't have found them or that news would have been in the article you showed me."

2. FINDING THE PAGODA

"Quiet," Lao Hai said sternly. "There is no way to rush a story like this.

"After Chen Ah-Si had finished peering at the tiny pagoda, he wanted more than ever to reach the bottom, but it was impossible. He swept the area below him with his flashlight and suddenly noticed a mound of dirt lying on the white marble floor. His hopes died when he saw it. It was a gigantic hornet's nest, capable of holding enough hornets to kill him, serving as a barrier between him and the lovely little pagoda.

"Since I can't climb down, I have to figure out how to bring that treasure up to my level, he decided. It's time for the Hook with Nine Claws.

"Chen Ah-Si had been brought up in a fishing village where he had learned to catch sand crabs when he was hungry. To do that, he learned to use a special claw made from nine hooks, all placed in a tight circle, with a rope tied to it. He became so skilled with this tool that he could hook an uncooked egg in its shell that was over sixty feet away from him and retrieve it without breaking—or even cracking—it. Now, even though he lived far from the sea, he never traveled anywhere without bringing this claw with him.

"He stretched down toward the pagoda as far as he could and threw the hook to catch the gossamer material that covered it. That was easily done. Then he hooked a portion of the pagoda; it wouldn't budge no matter how hard he pulled.

"Damn it, what does this thing weigh—half a ton, he cursed to himself. He swept his light across the pagoda and saw its foundation was based upon four pocket-sized columns. These supported the weight of the tiny building and in the middle of them were eight boxes—the Eight Treasures, he thought and his pulse quickened.

"To hell with this, he told himself and fired two bullets that struck one of the small columns. He leaped down upon the pagoda, breaking the other three columns. He grabbed the boxes beneath it with his claw and then attached the other end of its rope to one of the nearby statues, pulling himself and the treasure boxes back up from the floor and the hornet's nest.

"He was fast but the statue couldn't bear his weight. As soon as he was safe, the statue plunged straight down, pulling row after row of its fellow arhats with it onto the hive of hornets. I'm dead now, he thought.

"And yet no hornets crowded toward him. Is it an abandoned nest? he asked himself."

CHAPTER THREE

THE FIRST PUZZLE

"He scrambled his way back to the uppermost floor of the palace, clutching his treasure. There was the statue of the arhat whose eyes he had damaged, its white face still gleaming in the darkness. No reason to be alarmed; it's not real, he told himself, and at that moment, the face of the statue twisted into a contorted expression of rage.

"It's not an illusion; it could be a zombie. I really saw its face change, Chen Ah-Si screamed without words. Racing away in a panic, he saw an exit lit by leaping flames that lay just beyond it: his campfire. As he plunged toward its safety, a knife touched his throat, and hands removed the treasure boxes from his grasp. Before him stood his guide with another Hmong from the village, both looking disgusted and furious.

"Chen Ah-Si reached for his gun but a popping sound filled his ears and a rush of strangely cold air swirled around him. 'My finger, my trigger finger,' he howled. It was gone.

"Before he could react to the pain, the man who accompanied his guide stepped forward and Chen Ah-Si again felt a billow of frigid air sweep over his body. The man raised his knife and slashed it across Chen Ah-Si's left eye. The blade sliced across the bridge of his nose, stopping only after it had passed through his right eye. In his agony, Chen Ah-Si vividly noticed the calm, clear stare of the man who had disfigured him, along with the tattoo of the prancing qilin that covered his assailant's torso. That was the last thing he ever saw.

"At least the men didn't kill him," Lao Hai concluded. "They turned Chen Ah-Si and the treasure boxes over to the local police who felt his blindness was enough of a punishment. The treasure boxes were sent to a museum; when they were opened, all they contained was this bronze fish." He tapped the newspaper with two fingers. "So strange, but there you have it. Chen Ah-Si always claimed that someone else opened the boxes after he brought them to light and removed everything, leaving only a fake antique fish."

"Why did he think the fish was fake?" I asked.

"I don't know. Chen Ah-Si later became a monk at a temple in Guangxi. I learned about all this from some old acquaintances of his and the information didn't come cheap. If you get anything from it in the future, don't forget about me."

Of course Lao Hai wasn't helping me just from the kindness of his heart, but I needed more details if either of us was going to profit from his story. "Why are you going to this auction here?"

"Although nobody knows where this fish is, everyone seems to want it and it's in the auctioneer's catalog of things to go on the block. I thought you'd want to see who submits the winning bid for it."

"Look at the suggested opening bid for it—eighty

million yuan. Hell, I have two identical fish—I should get an easy one and a half billion for them. Who'd be willing to buy this fish—the Sultan of Brunei?"

I took Lao Hai back to his hotel and tried to relax at home. But the story I'd just heard made me restless and I went to my Uncle Two's teahouse to calm myself down a little.

As I sipped my tea, lit a cigarette, and stared vacantly at a magazine that my uncle kept for his customers to read, I puzzled over the three fish, each from its own dynasty, and each from locations that were far from one another. How did they all get to the places where they had been found and why? And why in the hell wasn't my Uncle Three here to help me figure this out? He was the instigator who brought this puzzle to light, after all.

I suddenly smelled something burning and saw that as I pondered, my cigarette had burned holes in a map that was bound into the magazine. I put out my cigarette, put down the magazine, and felt relieved that my uncle wasn't there to scold me for my carelessness.

Before I could make for the door, an elderly man picked up the magazine I had ruined and began to chuckle quietly. "Whoever would have damaged such a valuable map? What a barbarian!"

Not wanting to appear guilty by rushing away from the scene of my crime, I stayed at my table and watched the old gentleman. He was short and bony and looked as though he might be around seventy. He wore glasses with lenses as thick as the bottoms of beer bottles and he carried himself with the erect posture of a military man or a martial arts expert.

He carried the magazine to another table that was filled

with middle-aged men, all of whom seemed to regard him with the respect they would give a leader. Curious, I picked up my tea and moved closer to be within earshot.

"Look at this." The old guy held the magazine toward his companions. "Tell me what's special about this map? Pay attention to the feng shui that's been accentuated by the burn marks from some idiot's cigarette."

None of the other men offered an answer and the old man laughed softly again, as he said something in a dialect that I couldn't understand. The men who sat with him all scrambled to look at the map, and I began to feel curious. Whatever language this old guy spoke, it bore no relationship to Chinese.

Putting on my most humble expression, I shambled over to their table. "Please, could a poor student ask you gentlemen, where are you from? What language are you speaking with each other at the moment?'

The men looked surprised and then burst into laughter. "My boy," said the elderly gentleman, "of course you don't understand; we're speaking the Hmong language. Not more than a thousand people in this country can speak or understand it."

"But none of you look Hmong," I said, which sent them into paroxysms of laughter again. Taking advantage of their jollity, I blurted, "Oh please. I just heard this gentleman talk about the burned map. I was the oaf who did that. Why does this map interest you so? And what do you mean about a feng shui formation?"

"What interests you about feng shui? You certainly aren't a student of it, are you?" The elderly gentleman frowned as he spoke.

"I only know a little and I want to learn more. Please tell me what you know so I can be a little less ignorant."

The old man exchanged glances with the others and smiled. Then he said, "It's actually no big deal. It's only that the positions of those three burned holes on the map are significant. Link them together with an imaginary line and then look at them sideways. Do you notice anything interesting?"

I followed his suggestion and then felt my mouth go bone-dry. The burned spots were on the places where the three bronze fish had been unearthed: the tomb found in the cavern of the blood zombies at Mount Qimeng, the undersea tomb in Xisha, and the mirror palace in Guangxi. All fell along the line the old man told me to imagine. It curved in the shape of a dragon.

The old man saw my surprise and knew I had an inkling of what the connection between these places was. With a note of something that sounded almost like comradeship in his voice, he said, "It's the shape of a water dragon—but one thing's missing. Where's his head?" and he poked his cigarette into the map, burning a small hole on the site of the Changbai Mountains.

"Sir," I stammered, "what do you mean?"

The old man chuckled and said, "You may know that all of China is linked by an interconnection of underground dragon veins. This particular one links a number of separate mountain ranges with one end in the water, so it's called a water dragon."

As I listened to him, I knew he followed the school of feng shui developed by Wang Canghai. Was Wang Canghai the connection I had been seeking? The hexagonal bells found both in the carcass cave and in the undersea tomb, the puzzle box showing up in a tomb of the Western Zhou, the bronze fish in three different locations—were they all in these places because Wang Canghai had once been in each of these spots? Were they all somehow part of his plan for his palace in the clouds of heaven, the one I saw pictured in the undersea tomb, the palace that was now buried under an avalanche? And whose corpse occupied the tomb that rested beside the Palace in the Clouds, under heavy blankets of snow?

The old man saw how fascinated I was. He signaled for his companions to get up. Then he put the magazine in my hands, paid his bill, and walked out. I hurried after him; as I came out of the teahouse, he was taking off his glasses. A hideous scar ran from one eye to the other, making a deep ravine across the bridge of his nose.

I stood stock still as he and his friends climbed into a car and drove away.

Impossible, I thought, how could I hear the story of Chen Ah-Si and then run into him by chance several hours afterward? It was too strange to be a coincidence. What kind of deal had been struck between this old man and Lao Hai? And was this man truly Chen Ah-Si? He was supposed to be blind but this guy could see—and he looked much younger than the ninety years that the blind grave robber had been on this earth.

Yet whoever he was, he had shown me a connection that I had been struggling to discover for myself. That was enough to allow me to sleep better and longer that night than I had in weeks.

I slept so late the next day that I missed the auction

altogether and when I called him, Lao Hai told me nobody had bought the bronze fish, since the opening bid was too high. As soon as I hung up, there was a call from Uncle Three's shop manager. "Someone is here asking for you," he said. "Please come and find out what he wants."

Afraid that it might be Lao Yang and his ghostly mother, I forced myself to go to the shop. The minute I walked in the door, tears began to run uncontrollably down my face. "Panzi, you're alive!" I gasped as he stood up and grabbed me by the shoulders.

CHAPTER FOUR
PANZI'S RETURN

Panzi was in good shape for a man who had looked like death when we got out of the cavern of the blood zombies. He had been flat on his back in a hospital bed for nearly a month. When he finally recovered from his wounds and got out of bed to look for us, all of us had gone.

"Who died?" I asked him, noticing a mourning band on his right arm.

"You know, Big Kui and I worked together for years and he was like my brother. I was unconscious for the first seven days after he died so I couldn't mourn for him at the right time. But I'm making up for it now."

Since I felt responsible for Big Kui's death, I felt ashamed as Panzi spoke. I turned my head away and Panzi patted my shoulder. "It's all part of our business; we have to take these things as they come. There's no blame coming your way in any of this. Death comes to all of us when it's our time; you need to remember that."

Easy for you to say, I thought, it wasn't you who had to kill Big Kui after he became a blood zombie.

Trying to shake those memories from my head, I began to tell him what I'd gone through since we had last been together, along with my doubts about my uncle's truthfulness.

Panzi frowned. "I've known your uncle for years and he's never lied to me. Don't listen to other people's malicious bullshit, Young Master Wu."

I knew he was loyal and devoted to my uncle; there was no point in discussing what I'd learned about Uncle Three with Panzi. "Enough gossip," I said. "What do you plan to do now that you're strong and healthy again?"

"At first I thought I'd go back home and do the work I've always done. But now that I know that your uncle may be in danger, I want to do whatever I can to find him. In fact there are some people I need to call right now. May I use your mobile phone?"

I nodded and handed it over. Panzi knew people I didn't and his help wasn't something I'd ever turn down. I listened as he made a few phone calls, each one ending with grateful thanks that the person on the other phone had promised to call him back soon. I was sure we'd hear nothing for a week or more but within five minutes, my phone rang. It was for Panzi.

Handing me back the phone as the conversation ended, Panzi frowned again. "Young Master Wu, there's another trip waiting for us to take together soon."

"What do you mean? What did you find out about my uncle?"

"Your uncle left a message with someone in Changsha but the man entrusted with it will only give it to you, face-to-face. That person has asked me to bring you there as soon as possible."

"A message from Uncle Three?" I jumped to my feet. "I know people in Changsha! Why didn't anyone tell me my uncle had been there?"

"Those answers wait in Changsha. Can we leave now? The last train of the day will go in an hour."

Panzi hustled me to the train station and whisked me onto the night train to Changsha without an explanation. It wasn't until we were seated and the train began to move that I asked, "Is this a joke? If this journey is so urgent, why didn't we fly to Changsha?"

"You'll find out soon enough. Don't be impatient, Young Master." Panzi looked nervous; he was actually sweating. Is he still ill? I wondered. Not wanting to agitate him more than he was already, I decided to wait in silence.

We weren't on an express train; this was the slowest, most dilapidated hard-seat train I'd ever had the bad fortune to ride on. When it lurched to a stop in the middle of nowhere, three hours after our departure, I wasn't at all surprised.

Panzi leaped from his seat, tapped me on the shoulder, and gestured for me to get up. I stood and asked, "What's going on?" Without a word, he turned, threw open the window, and leaped out into the night.

I stood in complete confusion while all the passengers in our car clustered around me, looking out the window to see why someone would jump from it. Then I heard Panzi yell, "What are you waiting for? Get off the damned train right now!"

I jumped, landing on my back. Panzi helped me up and pulled me along as he ran through the nearby fields, up a small hill, and onto a road. There was a pickup truck; Panzi pushed me into the seat of the cab and jumped in beside me, and a man behind the steering wheel barreled off into the night.

As soon as I caught my breath, I shouted, "Will you tell me why in the hell we didn't just take a plane?"

Panzi smiled. "Don't be angry. I've never been caught like this before. Who the fuck knows how we were found out and who knows if we can outrun the guys who are out to get us."

I instinctively looked behind us for the sight of headlights but there was nothing in the darkness. "Tell me what you're talking about before I throttle you, Panzi."

He lit two cigarettes and handed me one. "There were police on that train. Your uncle isn't in Changsha now and our business there is completely fucked up. There's an undercover agent working against us." He said this in the Changsha dialect and looked quickly at the driver as he spoke, as though to indicate that the man wasn't to be trusted.

I knew enough to stop asking questions but my brain was boiling with them. Running from the police? Was I a fugitive now? Not for the first time, I cursed my Uncle Three; he'd turned me into a grave robber who hobnobbed with zombies and now I was running from the law. Damn, this was just a bit more exciting than I'd ever wanted my life to be.

The driver took us to a small town near a railway station where we bought some cheap, poorly made clothing. When we put on our new purchases, nobody would ever guess that only a few hours before we'd come from a city. We bought tickets for the same train we'd escaped from, which had just now reached this station. This time we had tickets for a sleeper car and when we entered it, Panzi took a quick look through the other carriages.

4. PANZI'S RETURN

"The cops are gone," he muttered. "They never would have thought that we'd get back on the same train. We're safe for now."

"Panzi, please," I whispered, "can you tell me what's going on? Why are we under police surveillance?"

"I don't know," he replied. "When I called my black-market contact in Changsha this afternoon, once he heard my voice, he had only two things to say—first to bring you there immediately because your uncle left you a message and second that things are screwed up so watch out for cops. This man has worked with your uncle for thirty years and he's absolutely reliable. When I heard what he said, I knew we needed to get to Changsha first and then figure out our next move. Then I saw cops in plainclothes as soon as we got to the station so I made a quick call to a friend and asked him to have a truck follow our train. When the train made that stop, I knew it was time to make our move. Don't worry, Young Master Wu. I think the police are after the big guys in our business—not the likes of you and me."

Just as I began to feel better, he added, "I'm really not sure of what's waiting for us in Changsha and I don't understand how things got so bad. We can't go there directly, I know that much. We'll have to get off the train near Zhejiang and then take a bus to the mountains outside of Changsha. Your uncle has done a lot of business there and it's my home. We can hang out there in safety while we wait for the black-market guy to show up."

I nodded. The train had stopped for more passengers and one of them joined us in our sleeper compartment. Panzi changed the subject and I began to chatter out of sheer nervousness.

"Have you ever heard of Chen Ah-Si?" I asked.

"Everyone has, especially in Changsha. He's a dangerous man. He uses people who then are the ones to get caught and put to death while he walks free. Keep your distance if he's ever in your area. He may be blind but he still has a lot of power."

I thought of how Chen Ah-Si had looked and walked and carried himself. He certainly wasn't completely blind; something about him wasn't living up to his legendary status as a disabled mastermind.

We reached the mountains by morning. I could see why Panzi chose to live there; it was quiet, green, and peaceful. He led me into a dusty little store that looked as though nobody had ever shopped there. He pushed upon the back wall; it swung open and there was a small room filled with shelves holding treasures from tombs.

A man emerged from behind the shelves. "Panzi!" he boomed. "What took you so long? The gear's all ready for you. When do you plan to set off?"

"Gear? What gear? Set off where?"

Looking confused by Panzi's response, the man asked, "Didn't you know?"

Panzi turned to stare at me and I glared back. It's your town, asshole—what are you looking at me for? I asked him silently.

"Captain Three left behind instructions for you. He has a job for you and arranged for me to put together equipment for a crew of five," the man said. "Didn't you know?"

4. PANZI'S RETURN

CHAPTER FIVE
A NEW GANG

"Why didn't you call me?" Panzi exploded. "When did you last see Captain Three?"

The man looked at us skeptically, shrugged, and smiled. "Quit messing with me. Of course Master Wu would have told you; this is a huge enterprise he's put together."

"Why the hell would I lie to you?" Panzi sputtered. "Exactly what did Captain Three say to you and when did he say it?"

The man looked at us again and realized we really didn't have a clue about anything my uncle had told him. "You really don't know, do you? I don't know anything specific myself. I just got the order from Boss Chu at the black-market currency exchange. He's in the back there, go ask him."

Panzi grunted and led me down a narrow hallway. An unlocked iron door at the end opened when he pushed on it. In a rundown office a bald middle-aged man was sprawled on a sofa, smoking. As we entered, he tossed the cigarette butt on the floor, stomped it out, and stood up.

"Brother Chu." Panzi's attitude instantly became respectful and I was sure this was the man with the message Uncle Three had left for me.

The man nodded at Panzi and then turned to me. He

said, "What took you so long? We've been sitting on our thumbs waiting for the past two days."

Panzi gave a quick account of our journey and then asked, "Brother Chu, what's going on here? What did we do to piss off the police?"

Brother Chu stretched lazily and said, "First of all, calm down. Nothing's wrong here. This was your Captain Three's idea—to leak a bit of information to an undercover police team. It looks like he's trying to screw up the activities of a rival business group. As a result, the entire antique market is fucked. Everyone who ever bought from Master Wu is being watched; nobody is able to sell their goods. I think he did this to buy some time for you guys."

I glanced over at Panzi. "Time for what?" I asked.

Brother Chu shrugged. "Who can predict what sort of plot your uncle has in mind? Certainly not me, and I've worked with him for years."

Panzi asked again, "Old Ninety-four outside said that the equipment is ready and that you had told him to prepare it. Now what's that all about?"

"Listen carefully. Once it's public knowledge that I have an expedition to get supplies for, people do their best to fuck it up. So your uncle did all the preparations to get the gear and then I put down the money when everything was ready. Otherwise the clampdown would have been in place and I wouldn't have been able to buy so much as a single shovel."

I asked, "But why buy the equipment? We don't have any plans for a job."

Brother Chu explained, "That's why your Uncle Three left you a message." He let us sit down before he continued. "In fact, he originally didn't plan for you to take part in this; one of the five sets of gear he had originally intended to use himself."

He paused to light another cigarette and then continued, "He's not the only one who's getting ready for this enterprise, there are others who want the same thing, and they're by no means to be underestimated. If he doesn't show up when it's time to set off, you have to take his place. You can't let this other group get there first."

Another group? I suddenly thought of that company Ning worked for. Could Uncle Three have concocted the whole undersea tomb disappearance to distract them from what he was doing here?

Panzi asked, "Did Captain Three tell you who the other group is?"

"No, but I think he may have possibly fallen into their hands. Otherwise he would have returned a long time ago. Unfortunately we don't know anything right now, not one shred of information that would help us figure out what's going on."

Hell, I thought, this sounds way too familiar.

"All I know is you're being sent to the Hengshan Mountain Range of the Changbai Mountains in Jilin. I've arranged for a local guide to take you guys there."

Mount Changbai? I immediately thought of Wang Canghai's Palace in the Clouds, which was reputedly somewhere in the Hengshan Mountains. But why did I have to go there? And why in the hell did this have to take place in midwinter?

Seeing my confused expression, Brother Chu shrugged and said, "To be honest, I'm pretty bewildered by this plan myself but there's only one thing to do. You guys have to follow the plan in order to find out what's going on—otherwise I'm sure that your uncle is going to die."

Panzi gripped my shoulder for a second and then asked, "What's the first step in this plan?"

"Tomorrow you'll take a train to Jilin, with all of the gear. You'll meet the crew your uncle's put together and then you're all set to go. I have every detail taken care of. You just hit the road and keep a low profile. This is your uncle's plan—and you know he's an expert at this sort of thing, so don't worry."

We went out the same way we came in. I saw a lot of secondhand computer monitors being carried into the outer shop and Panzi told me they were used to conceal the tomb treasures when they were sent to their purchasers. A lot of our gear would be hidden in the same way when it was put on the train.

As we left the store, Panzi looked preoccupied and was quiet for a while. When we made our way down the street, he said, "You know, that company that arranged for the undersea tomb expedition seems not quite on the up-and-up to me. Do you think they might be the group that your uncle is trying to outrun in this journey we're about to make?"

"I have the same idea myself, except I think there's a larger group behind that company that's directing operations. But my concern is can we trust Brother Chu?"

"I've worked with him for a long time and so has your uncle. You don't need to worry about him," Panzi assured me. "But the other three guys in our five-man team? I wonder who they are and what kind of guys they are."

5. A NEW GANG

"Uncle Three picked them out, so they have to be okay," I said.

Panzi shook his head. "Not necessarily. Captain Three used to say that you have to spend no less than three hundred and sixty-five days with someone before knowing them at all. People change. You don't see a man for a week, and the next time he shows up he could be planning to kill you, especially the barbarians in our business. There aren't many of us whose hands aren't bloodstained. If they're desperate enough, they'll bury their own mothers alive. Who knows who's waiting for us in Jilin?"

The next morning Brother Chu took us to the train in his own car. As we got in, an old man was already sitting in the backseat. "He looks familiar," I remarked to Panzi. "One of our undercover policemen perhaps?"

I peered at him as I sat down and then felt my throat close up. It was Chen Ah-Si.

Panzi recognized him at once and greeted him by name. The old man was resting with his eyes closed and only nodded in response.

Panzi hissed at Brother Chu. "What the hell is he doing here?"

"Master Three hired him to work with you. It's all his idea—don't ask me," Chu whispered back.

"Impossible," I muttered. "He's almost a hundred and he's blind. What good can he possibly be? Who's the next team member going to be—a woman in her ninth month of pregnancy or maybe someone in a wheelchair? Is my uncle testing our powers of compassion?"

When we entered our sleeping car on the train, there

was a fat man sitting with a cup of noodles, slurping his meal. He looked at me, raised his eyebrows, and said, "What the hell, it's you again?"

My head began to throb and I felt dizzy. Why did my uncle hire Fats? I looked up at the sleeper above and a pair of cool, unemotional eyes stared back at me. As I grinned with relief, Poker-face, good old Zhang Qilin himself, squinted at me for a second, rolled over, and fell asleep.

5. A NEW GANG

CHAPTER SIX

THE COFFIN CARRIED BY NINE DRAGONS

Brother Chu's plan was for us to take a train to the mountains, about a two-day journey of over a thousand miles. Fats, Qilin, and I had a lot of catching up to do, it was true—but whether those accounts would be truthful was anybody's guess.

I gave Fats the check for his fish-eye pearl that he'd brought back from the undersea tomb. That cheered him up enough that I was able to ask him why and how he ended up on this adventure.

"We need teamwork to carry off this job," Fats blustered in his typical fashion, "and we needed someone like a general contractor to pull it all together—that was Brother Chu's job. He has a friend in Beijing who is also a good friend of mine, so when my buddy was asked to recommend someone for the job, of course I was the first one to come to mind. Who else? But I was told nothing except it was a big job—customarily the details are kept secret until we reach our destination. Otherwise who knows what sort of mutiny would take place along the way?"

"Did you know that the job was the brainchild of my Uncle Three?"

"No way in hell," Fats replied. "If I'd known your uncle

was involved in any way, I wouldn't have come if he gave me all the money in the world."

No answers here, I thought. My best hope of information was going to be Chen Ah-Si, but he was snoring and had been for hours on end. So was my outgoing, chatty, poker-faced old pal, Qilin, who rarely gave up anything he knew. "He's been sleeping ever since he got on the train," Fats told me.

To kill time, Fats, Panzi, and I played cards and I wondered about Old Chen. He had finally awakened but said nothing except for a mumbled response to a couple of Panzi's polite questions. Soon after that, he wandered away from our sleeper car and disappeared. "Who is that skinny old coot?" Fats asked. "He looks so exhausted and bored with us all."

When Panzi told Fats about Chen Ah-Si, Fats looked a bit sick. "He's over ninety and he's going to climb a mountain with us? Whose bright idea was that?"

"He's tougher than you think," Panzi muttered, "and he's a killer. Don't underestimate this old man."

I remembered the feeling I had when I first saw Chen Ah-Si at the teahouse, that he was like a mystical and unfathomable great master, surrounded by his disciples. Why had he come alone to work with strangers?

I mentioned this to Panzi. He smiled and said, "Who knows if he's alone? He's a crafty old devil; he may have arranged for his gang to be nearby. He could be sitting with them now; we'll never know."

Fats slammed his fist against the wall. "I really don't get it. Why did your uncle ask ask this guy to come along? If this old man is really that dangerous, I think we should strike first. We can just tie him up, strangle him, and push his body off the train."

Panzi glanced at the hallway. "I'm warning you, don't cause any trouble. Captain Three definitely has his own reasons for recruiting this man. Let's just give him a little respect. He's old and he had rotten luck when he was young and strong. If we have to get rid of him, at the right time…Shit!"

Before the thought was completed, Qilin's arm whooshed down from his bunk. He grabbed Panzi by the shoulder. Under his grip, Panzi crumpled into a heap, moaning with pain, just as Chen Ah-Si returned to his seat nearby. Qilin released his grip and slumped back into sleep. He stayed that way until we reached the station where we would change trains for the last leg of our journey.

We had a two-hour wait between trains so the five of us went out to the waiting room to stretch our legs. It was a holiday and the station was packed with bodies. We soon were caught up in a river of people and got separated. I was with Panzi; I looked for the rest of our group, saw Qilin and Chen Ah-Si, and raised my hand and my voice to show them where we were. Panzi grabbed my arm and pulled me into a crouching position.

"Stay quiet," he hissed, "the police are everywhere."

I sat on the floor, hidden by the people milling around me. As I peered about, I could see policemen checking people's identity cards at the front door.

I lowered my head and said softly to Panzi in the Hangzhou dialect, "It's all right. It happens in Hangzhou all the time. They're just checking people's IDs. We don't have any equipment with us, and we're not fugitives. What are you so afraid of?"

Pointing with his chin, Panzi indicated a few ordinary-looking men in the crowd. He said, "Those are only the gatekeepers at the door. The plainclothes guys are scattered about in the crowd and they're looking for people. Keep your head down. Don't let them see you."

I looked up and in a flash, I saw someone familiar looking right at me. I was trying to recognize who he was when the person struggled as though trying to free himself. He pointed at me and shouted, "Over there!"

I could see he was handcuffed and flanked by two men who held his arms. "Holy shit, I gasped, "it's Brother Chu. What's he doing here? And why is he shackled?"

"Move!" Panzi rasped. He yanked at me, pulling me to my feet, and we started running. A group of plainclothesmen dashed toward us from behind, yelling, "Stop!"

Weaving and swerving, we forced our way through the crowd. Panzi mowed people down like a bulldozer but I wasn't big enough to make the same impact. Bodies blocked my escape in front of me and the police were fast approaching from behind.

Then there was a sudden loud pop. A fluorescent light fixture on the ceiling of the waiting room hall exploded into tiny pieces. People screamed. Another pop and one more lamp went out. I took advantage of the confusion; hunched over, I squeezed my way through the crowd, fighting my way to the door.

A man caught me and pulled me aside. It was Panzi. He forced me to a stop as all the lights above us broke, one after the other. The waiting room was dark now and a continual shower of broken glass pelted the crowd. Children were screaming, and people shoved their way to the exit; in the chaos, we were forgotten.

I could see Fats waving at us and we rushed in his direction. I was just about to yell, "Where's Poker-face?" when Qilin suddenly appeared out of thin air, like a ghost.

"So your contractor is useless now; what are we going to do?" Fats asked.

"That son of a bitch," Panzi was white with rage. "If I ever see him again, I'll kill him."

"What good does that do us now? We need to know where to go and how to get there. He's the only one who knew what that crazy Master Three had planned."

Panzi shook his head, glaring at Fats. Qilin stepped between them and said, "Follow the old guy."

A few feet away was Chen Ah-Si, with several men near him in a protective half circle. Qilin walked toward him and we followed. As we came near, the old man gestured toward his companions and they disappeared into the crowd. Then he turned and led us out of the station.

We walked until we reached a park where we all collapsed on the grass, silent and shaken. Chen Ah-Si looked and laughed harshly. "What the hell?" he croaked. "You're the ones chosen to dig up the Dong Xia Emperor's Coffin Carried by Nine Dragons, are you? Has Wu Sansheng lost his mind?"

CHAPTER SEVEN
YINGSHAN VILLAGE

We were already in bad moods and Chen Ah-Si's remark didn't cheer us up. It was certainly too much for Fats, who let out a long stream of descriptive profanity and then explained, "Sir, you don't understand what's going on here, and neither do we. This was Young Master Wu's uncle's plan, and nobody knows what that madman had in mind. All I know is, after decades in this business, this is the first time I've been chased by the police—and I don't like it."

He was going too far—Panzi would kill him if he badmouthed Uncle Three. I shot a warning glare at Fats and he shut up.

Panzi swallowed his annoyance and turned to Chen Ah-Si. "Grandpa Chen, you can see we're in trouble. You have the most experience of any of us; please tell us your thoughts and we'll listen to you."

Chen Ah-Si squinted at Panzi and looked him up and down. He was silent for a long time before he said, "So you understand some of the rules. I'll let it go this time. Let me remind you guys. You can't take trains. I've arranged for a car and those who want to come with me are welcome. Those who feel otherwise can go back home. But I have to warn you guys in advance. The place we're going this time is no beginner's playground. When Wu Sansheng came to me, he said I was the only one who would be able to take you there safely. As far as I know, no one else in the world can get to this place except me."

Fats sneered. "Hell, don't try to spook us, old man. We've seen a few things ourselves. We've gone up to heaven and touched the moon; we've gone down into the ocean and caught soft-shelled turtles. We've even pissed in the urinal of the Jade Emperor. Your goal is only a Coffin Carried by Nine Dragons. How terrifying can that be? I can go to it and slap the zombie inside until it jumps out to escape my blows. And this one here—do you know who he is? He's the grandson of the King of the Changsha Dogs; why I remember…"

I pushed Fats aside and smiled. "Please don't listen to this nonsense, sir. You have to break whatever Fats says in two and throw half of it in the toilet before you can pay attention to what comes out of his mouth."

Chen Ah-Si glanced at me and said, "I know you're Old Dog Wu's grandson. Don't deny it. I went to the feast celebrating the first month of your father's time on earth when he was an infant. In fact, you should call me Granddad."

Old Dog Wu was a name for my grandfather that was used only by a handful of people who had worked closely with him. And as my grandfather had said several times, he had worked with Chen Ah-Si in the past.

I nodded respectfully. "Grandpa Chen, thank you."

The old man flashed a wolfish grin in response as Panzi asked, "So Grandpa Chen, what should we do now? Should we find a place to spend the night or—"

Before he could finish what he was saying, he was interrupted by the sound of a car's horn. "My car has arrived," Chen Ah-Si said. "Decide whether or not you're going with me. You have one second to make up your minds. If you're ready to tackle the mountains, then follow me." He walked in the direction of the honking car without looking back to see who went with him.

Panzi whispered, "It seems as though this old guy was well prepared for what just happened; I'm sure he's the one who tipped off the cops about Brother Chu, and he's probably taken care of whoever was waiting for us at the end of the line. Who knows what's become of the equipment Master Wu had ordered? We have no choice but to follow this old bastard if we want to help your uncle and find out what he had planned for us to do. I'm going with Old Chen—you suit yourselves." He set off toward Chen Ah-Si's car, with Qilin at his side.

Now there was only Fats and me. We looked at each other and Fats asked, "Just what is this Coffin Carried by Nine Dragons and who is the Dong Xia Emperor?"

"Damned if I know."

"Well, why don't we go along and find out?"

"Lead the way, fat man." I laughed and we ran to catch up with the others.

We all climbed into an ancient vehicle, piled high with bags and boxes. I immediately fell into an exhausted sleep and woke up the next day at noon. It was cold and we were still half a day from our destination. I shuddered uncontrollably, envying Old Chen's heavy coat. Panzi was right; this old man was well prepared.

"Here's what we're going to do," Chen announced. "A

7. YINGSHAN VILLAGE

guide will be waiting for us when we arrive in Dunhua, along with the equipment we need. The plan was to go straight to the Lizi Valley but the cops are probably waiting for us there. So we'll head for our destination in another direction, stopping in a few villages along the way. Once we get to where we want to be, we'll be on our own. But it's not going to be a cakewalk. Changbai Mountain is so huge that part of it lies over the border in Korea. I'm sure we want to be near the Lizi Valley since that was our original destination, so we'll head for a nearby village and then begin our search."

Everything proceeded as he told us. Boxes were waiting for us but when we opened them, I began to wonder about just how sane our new leader was. Among a few ropes, some shovels, chocolate, and a big bag of chili peppers was a gigantic supply of women's sanitary napkins.

"What the hell is this?" Fats exploded. "Are we going to provide charitable supplies for peasant women?"

"You'll find out what these are for all too soon. Meanwhile shut up," Chen growled and amazingly, Fats obeyed.

Three men joined us as we set off on our four-day journey to the mountains: the driver, Lang Feng, who was almost as big as Panzi; Monk Hua, whose glasses gave his viciously scarred face a scholarly appearance; and a man who never stopped talking, Ye Cheng. The road was rough; at times we were inches away from sliding off it, plunging over the cliffs, and becoming a huge pile of muddy blood and bones. When we came to a village in the middle of the Hengshan forest, we were all grateful to put our feet on the ground again.

I looked at the surrounding mountains, trying to spot

the one I'd seen in the undersea tomb painting, but they all looked the same under their shrouds of snow. What exactly were we looking for and how would we ever find it?

There was no guesthouse in the village and we had no choice but to knock on the door of the village committee head. He was a hospitable man who put us in an empty makeshift wooden house that was normally used by the forest guards. We settled in for a few days, rented some horses, and found a veteran who'd fought in Korea, a local guy named Shunzi who was willing to be our guide.

"Most people refuse to go to the mountains at this time of year," he told us. "The roads are hard to follow once the blizzards strike and then there's nothing to see when you get to the top. I only climbed there when I was in the army on patrol. I'll take you, but once we reach the snow zone, you have to listen to me."

He gave us a list of supplies to purchase before we left and a couple of days later, the nine of us marched into the forest, with fourteen horses to carry us and our gear.

The mountain scenery was breathtaking, and it was easy to make Shunzi believe we were sightseers as we gaped at the beauty of what we saw and stopped to take frequent photos. But when we reached the foot of the mountain range, our path became steeper, and we paid less attention to the glories of the landscape. Our horses' steps now followed a sixty-degree incline and we clutched at our saddles to keep from landing on the ground.

"We're coming to a deserted village, where the border sentry used to be," Shunzi told us. "We'll spend the night there, and then we'll cross over the line into the snow zone."

7. YINGSHAN VILLAGE

We had just reached a viewpoint, with a lake below us, looking like a small pond from the height we had reached. Then Fats cursed, "Damn it, look at that. We have a problem."

Near the lake was another train of horses, at least fifty, with about thirty people bustling around, setting up a camp. "Give me your binoculars," I said to Fats and trained them on the group below.

"There's a woman in that group, one we've met before," I muttered. "Lucky us. We're going to have another delightful encounter with our girl, Ning."

CHAPTER EIGHT

TROUBLE BREWING

"At least she proves one thing," I muttered. "Panzi, we were right. That shipwreck salvage company in Hainan is out to rob tombs in the mountains; they're the group that my Uncle Three is trying to outrun in this adventure he's sent us on."

Chen Ah-Si took one look and smiled. "Well, we know we're headed in the right direction—and we're in the lead. Forget about them. Let's get moving."

I scanned the group below one at a time, hoping to catch a glimpse of my uncle but with no luck. Of course if he was being held prisoner, he wouldn't be roaming around with the others. What I did notice, and what made me very uneasy, was at least half of the group below had automatic rifles.

Fats saw the same thing and growled at Chen Ah-Si, "Sir, you told us not to buy guns but you can see these people are armed. If we get in a fight with them how are we going to hold our own? By using our washbasins as shields while we bludgeon them with our sanitary napkins?"

"We need no more than we have, young man. You'll understand after we reach snow country."

We continued our trek until some dilapidated wooden

houses behind steel-wired gates appeared ahead. A sign written above announced "The sacred territory of our motherland is inviolable."

"This supply depot is the last shelter we'll have until we reach the abandoned outpost in the middle of the mountains," Shunzi told us. We made ourselves at home, slept soundly, and awoke the next morning to snowfall. It was frigid as we entered snow country, and all of us were southerners except Fats and Ye Cheng. The two of them gloated as we shivered and turned pale blue with cold, but there was worse to come.

The snowdrifts grew higher and the trees smaller as we climbed. Everything that surrounded us was dazzlingly white and the pathway was invisible. Without Shunzi, we'd be lost, we all realized, and gratefully followed in his footsteps.

The sky darkened well before nightfall, the wind became a gale, and falling snow whirled before us like fog, cutting into our faces in sharp little jabs. "We should camp here, right now," Shunzi said. "This blizzard will only get worse."

Old Chen nodded and we made camp rapidly. We were on a low foothill of the mountain range, overlooking the forest we just had traveled through.

"When tombs were built in ancient times, they were located close to building materials," Grandpa Chen observed. "You probably noticed the forest we passed through was sparse and easy to traverse; I'm sure it was logged many times over the centuries and there's probably a grave site nearby. We're on the right track but we still have some miles to cover before we reach our destination."

8. TROUBLE BREWING

Ye Cheng asked, "Sir, there are a dozen peaks above us in this range. How will we know which is the right one?"

"We'll keep looking as we travel along a ley line, which will lead us to the Dragon's head. The place where the ley line stops is where the heart of the Dragon is. There are many hills here but there's only one ley line. We're walking along it right now, so I'm not worried we'll miss it. At the worst it'll take us longer is all; but we have no time to waste. We have to go on now."

I followed his gaze and saw nothing but clusters of scraggly trees. I'm out of my league here, I told myself.

"If you insist on going further, you have to understand you can no longer ride horseback," Shunzi announced. "We need the horses to pull your equipment on sleds. But if the storm gets worse, you must listen to me. If I say stop or even go back, you must obey."

We all assured him of our future obedience and put the gear on the sleds we had brought with us. We jumped onto the sleds ourselves; Shunzi shouted, whipped the lead horse into motion, and began to climb, with our horses falling into step behind him.

At first I thought this was fun, like riding on a dogsled, but then as the wind gusted harder and my body turned numb with cold, our journey turned into a nightmare. The horses moved slowly through the heavy drifts and their snail-like plodding grew even more hesitant as the wind took on the sound of a howl. Snow blew off the surrounding peaks and would have sliced our eyes to ribbons had we not been wearing goggles. I tried to say something but when I opened my stiffened lips, the words froze in my throat as the icy wind blew straight into my lungs.

Suddenly Shunzi's horse came to an abrupt stop. We forced our way through the gale to reach his side; his face was a mask of concern and his eyes looked troubled. "The wind is too strong and there's been an avalanche that's dumped snow in our path—too much for the horses to get through. They'll founder; it's going to come up past their bellies. We're in trouble."

"Then what do we do now?" Panzi looked up at the sky. "This type of weather doesn't look too pleasant. Can we go back?"

Shunzi glanced at the sky and then at us. He said, "I can't say for sure, but once the wind starts blowing really hard, it won't stop for at least two days and two nights. I think it's too late to go back now. We're not far from the next outpost; we can take shelter from the blizzard there. We can trek over there on foot; it should only take an hour or so."

We put on our snowshoes, braced ourselves against the wind, pulled the sleds ourselves, and advanced in the snow, leaving the horses to face the storm. We were between two ridges that made a natural wind tunnel and turned our walk into a hellish one. After four hours, we still hadn't reached the outpost.

Shunzi stopped, looking bewildered. Then he shouted, "Oh hell. I know what the problem is. This avalanche was worse than I thought; the outpost is buried under our feet—no wonder we can't find it."

"What the hell do we do now? Fats barked. "Stand here and die?"

Shunzi pointed ahead and said, "There's still one last hope. There's a hot spring nearby. If we can get there, we'll survive for a few days. If we can't find it, then only our willpower will keep us alive."

He took out a long rope and tied us together in a human chain. The snowstorm had stripped away our senses of sight and sound; in a white and howling world, only the rope let us know we weren't all alone. Did my uncle doom us with this plan? I wondered, are we going to die?

When I looked toward Shunzi, my fear died down; although he was invisible in the swirl of snowflakes, his grip on the rope was unquavering as he led us into the storm. He's used to this weather, I told myself, if we were in real danger, he'd stop in his tracks and work out another survival plan. I trudged on and then in the funnel formed by the windblown snow, I saw a shadow waver and then collapse in front of my feet. It was Shunzi.

Qilin was beside me in a heartbeat. Together we raised Shunzi to his feet and supported him as we waited for the others to join us.

Fats went out of control when he saw what had happened. "God damn it, what kind of guide is this? He gets us lost and then passes out on us—now what are we supposed to do?"

There was no point in responding. The blizzard had already obliterated our tracks behind us so we had no way of retracing our steps. The wind blew the flakes in front of us into the shape of a horrible flower that made me feel sick and dizzy when I looked into its center. I drooped my head to keep from being suffused by vertigo and around me I saw everyone else was doing the same thing. The wind had become so strong that if we didn't have the rope to cling to, with our combined body weight anchoring our feet to the mountain, we would have been blown over the edge of the surrounding cliffs that were now invisible.

Chen Ah-Si had lost his air of command and looked as though he were in a walking coma. There was no use in depending upon him now.

"The old man is gone," Panzi said. "If we don't find the hot spring that Shunzi talked about, we're all going to become as hypothermic as he is. We need to go as far from each other as we can while still clutching the rope. If any of you find the hot spring, yell as loud as you can and tug on the rope as a signal in case the wind keeps us from hearing your voice."

We spread out as far as we could. But the blowing snow hypnotized me as I wandered into it; my body felt numb with exhaustion and all I wanted was to sink into sleep.

I had seen movies where people became sleepier and sleepier as they walked through the snow; once they succumbed to that feeling, they never woke up. I struggled to keep going but my eyes wouldn't stay open and my legs felt like pieces of lead as I moved them through the drifts.

Then I heard Fats. His words were swallowed up by the wind and I could barely make out his shadow ahead. Then he vanished and the rope began to jerk violently. "Release the rope!" Qilin yelled. "Fats has fallen into a crevasse and he'll pull us in after him."

Then his body disappeared into the snow, rapidly followed by the man who stood next to him. That was me.

One by one we were dragged into the snow by Fats's weight, entombed in whiteness and silence. We rolled head over heels as we plunged downward and then suddenly came to a stop.

8. TROUBLE BREWING

All I could see was white, all around me, but I could still breathe. I could hear Panzi's muffled voice saying, "Nobody move. I was the last to fall. Perhaps I can get to the surface and pull us all back up."

"No. Stop!" It was Ye Cheng's voice. "There's something nearby—can't you see it all coiled up in the snow?"

CHAPTER NINE

THE DRAGON WITH ONE HUNDRED FEET

I could see nothing; I was in a daze, only aware that my back was pushed against a rock and Ye Cheng was shouting below me. Then I slowly realized we weren't buried in snow. Our backs were against the mountainside and our rope was caught on a huge rock that had broken our fall. We were about twenty feet from the base of a steep slope which had been covered with heaps of snow and gravel. From under that pile emerged several long, thin, black claws.

I began to choke and pressed my back closer to the rock wall behind me. Beyond the claws I could see a coil of black curled in a nest of snow. Part of its segmented body was visible and that part was covered with scales like a snake or a gigantic insect. It lay motionless; I could see neither its head nor its tail.

"What the hell is this? Is it dead or alive?" Panzi whispered. "Those look like the claws of a centipede—but much bigger. I'm going down to get a closer look."

"No!" howled Ye Cheng. "Don't wake it up!"

Fats hurled a snowball at his head, hissing, "Shut the fuck up. You're going to wake it with that blubbering, not Panzi. He knows what he's doing. Better him than me—or you."

As he spoke, Fats took a step forward, broke through the crust on top of the snow, and plunged through it closer to the coiled creature, taking us all with him, one by one, each of us still holding the rope.

This fall took us away from the gusts of wind and finally I could breathe without difficulty. We were at the base of the slope and it was easy to take steps now that we were sheltered from the blizzard. Panzi and Qilin released their hold on the rope and stealthily crept toward the snow-covered coils.

As they drew near, they both stood to their full heights and beckoned for us to join them. As we approached, they brushed the snow from the covered body—it was carved into the rock, a coiled dragon with many legs carved under its body.

As Chen Ah-Si stumbled toward it, his face took on signs of life. "Help me get close to whatever you've found here," he commanded Monk Hua and soon was exploring the carving with both hands.

"What an ugly carving," Fats said in disgust. "It's truly hideous, like a worm I could crush under my foot—it doesn't have the nobility and grandeur of a dragon at all. Why waste our time over such bad workmanship?"

"Don't display your ignorance, fat man," Monk Hua replied, "this is something you've never seen before—it's a Centipede Dragon, carved in the early Dong Xia period, not one of your common water dragons. When artists first began carving dragons, they would put the head of whatever animal they chose on a snake's body and call it a dragon—I've even seen some with the heads of pigs. Then as carving evolved, the dragon as you know it came into being. This one that we've found has a dragon's body supported by the legs of a centipede."

Fats smiled. "Why Brother Scar-face, who would ever guess you were so educated? So this rock dates from the Dong Xia Kingdom? How interesting."

"That's right. But the question is where did the rock come from that this dragon rests upon?"

We each turned on our flashlights and wiped away all of the snow from the carving. It was formed from a huge flat slab almost nine feet wide and fifteen feet long, very smooth, and as black as obsidian. It was completely different from any of the other rocks nearby and it leaned against the wall of the mountain, distinctly not part of it.

"Look," I said, "there are some cracks on the slab close to the dragon's head. It could have fallen from a higher part of the mountain, which means we have to climb even higher to reach our goal. And notice, the dragon's body isn't symmetrical—this is one half of the Two Dragons Playing with Pearls. Usually this was carved on a door, with the second dragon carved on the opposite side."

Chen Ah-Si coughed and then gasped, "Stop farting— you eat a bit of knowledge and then release a lot of nonsense. There's no stone door involved here—this is the rock that seals off the passage that leads into the tomb."

He pointed toward the open mouth of the carved dragon. Monk Hua immediately walked over to it, reached inside the opening, and pulled out a black chain as thick as his forearm.

Chen Ah-Si said, "This is the chain used to pull the rock into place when the tomb was sealed off. The side you see is the one that faced into the tomb."

9. THE DRAGON WITH ONE HUNDRED FEET

I flushed red with embarrassment. "I see I was wrong—but how did this rock end up here?"

Monk Hua pulled on the chain. The rock didn't even quiver and Chen Ah-Si looked puzzled for a second.

You're not as sure of your facts as you want us to think you are, I thought as I stared at the old man, You know that if this sealing rock collapsed from above, the entry corridor to the tomb may be badly damaged. Even if we're fortunate enough to find the entry, we may never be able to go inside. Yes, we were lucky to find this carving but who knows if we'll ever find the Palace in the Clouds.

Above us we could hear the wind shriek and the blizzard obscured the night stars. "We'll stay here tonight," Grandpa Chen ordered and we all nodded with relief.

As we set up our camp, Monk Hua checked on Shunzi. In a second, he was back, shouting, "Our guide has almost stopped breathing."

Sure enough, Shunzi was completely unconscious. We shook him and slapped his frozen face but he only muttered something unintelligible. "Hypothermia," Panzi growled. "If we don't get a fire going and warm him up, he's going to die soon."

Our sleds, which had plunged down with us, were the only wood to be seen. If we burned them, we'd never be able to carry our equipment. Monk Hua turned to Old Chen and asked, "What should we do?"

"Don't let him die just yet," Chen Ah-Si ordered, "I still have something to ask him."

Monk Hua began to break the sleds into chunks of firewood as we all watched, doubting that the snow-covered wood was still flammable. Suddenly I caught a whiff of sulfur, like the stench of rotten eggs in the cold air.

The others raised their heads and began to sniff; Monk Hua stopped his destruction.

"My friends," Fats announced, "I smell a hot spring."

Chen Ah-Si jerked his chin at Ye Cheng and Lang Feng. "Check it out," he commanded.

"Stop," Panzi said. "We have our secret weapon with us," and he stared at Qilin.

Without a word, Qilin extended his two abnormally long fingers and touched the ground at his feet. He frowned, muttered to himself, and turned to the carved dragon.

Pressing upon its head, he said, "How strange. Behind this head is a hollow space."

CHAPTER TEN
A FISSURE

"You all know that Changbai Mountain is a dormant volcano, don't you?" Qilin told us. "It hasn't erupted for a thousand years, but it still generates a lot of heat from an internal lava pit. There's probably a crack, a fissure, behind this carving and that's where the sulfur stink from the hot spring is coming from. It's good news but our dragon friend here weighs probably twelve tons. We'll never push it aside without some sort of magic."

"Let's all try," Fats yelled, and together we pushed with every fiber of strength we had. It was hopeless.

"Why the hell didn't you bring dynamite instead of those fucking sanitary napkins?" Fats yelled at Chen Ah-Si.

"Oh shut up," Monk Hua replied. "Dynamite would only produce an avalanche, you fat moron. Do you want to be buried alive? Let me know and I'll help you on that path anytime you want."

"Wait a minute," I said. "Look at the different sizes of rocks under the base of our slab. Maybe we don't need dynamite—let me try something."

Taking a small sledgehammer from a bag of gear, I walked to a corner of the slab and examined some of the larger rocks underneath it. Taking careful aim at the biggest one, I brought the hammer down upon it with all of my might. Under the pressure of the slab and the force of my blow, the rock split, a crack appeared, and as it separated in two pieces, the surrounding rocks began to move. Slowly the dragon slab began to slip downward for a few inches before it came to a stop. Still we could see a crack in the mountainside that was now exposed to view. There was just enough space for us to come close to the crack which was as wide as Fats's head.

"I think we can squeeze into this," I said. Fats stuck his head in, directed his flashlight into the opening, and took a look.

"It's warm in there—feels great! But where we'd enter is at a weird angle. And there are words on the walls but I can't read what they say."

He leaned forward and tried to squirm through the opening. Slowly and with a little pain, he squeezed himself inside the mountain.

One by one, we followed him, with Chen Ah-Si ordering Ye Cheng, Lang Feng, and Panzi to guard the opening from the outside.

Within, the ground tilted steeply downward in a passageway that was dark, narrow, and looked very deep, as though it ran all the way to the heart of the mountain.

To walk along it we would have to go in single file. The rotten-egg stench of sulfur was almost overpowering and the temperature had to be around ninety degrees Fahrenheit. The rocks that surrounded us were glowing warm as we touched them.

"Look at those words," Fats said, revealing them with the beam of his flashlight. "Can any of you read what they say?"

I peered into the darkness. The words weren't carved on the

walls but on a rock lying nearby; they were carelessly engraved and seemed to be a mixture of Korean and Chinese script.

Monk Hua came to my side and said, "This is written in Jurchen, the language of the people who were conquered by the Dong Xia."

"What does it say?" Fats asked.

"Hold on, I'm not that brilliant. I'm going to have to puzzle over this. Give me a second to copy the words down."

We waited for a moment while Monk Hua copied the words into a notebook and then, with Fats in the lead, we filed our way down the passageway.

It was an uncomfortable descent and we had to crawl on our hands and knees in some parts of the tunnel-like passage. But at least we were warm—in fact we began to sweat. It felt good.

"Grandpa Chen," Fats asked in humble tones, "don't you think that slab blocked our entrance by design, not by coincidence?"

After a long pause, Chen Ah-Si said, "Building a tomb within a mountain takes a lot of local materials. This may have been a stone quarry for the construction of a mausoleum. Workers could have found this crack when they were quarrying stones. But I don't know why they would need to block it with a sealing stone when they finished working here."

Less than three hundred feet down, the smell of sulfur became stronger and the rocks took on a darker color, with a glazed shine to them. That had to be caused by mica melting at a hellishly high temperature. Had we reached a crater of a dormant volcano? If it suddenly became active again, we'd all die in an inferno. Damn you, Uncle Three, I thought, you've sent us into death's kingdom one more time.

Fats stopped suddenly and pointed his flashlight forward; we all did the same. The passageway had narrowed to a pinhole opening, with rocks scattered about everywhere. Squatting down, I pointed my flashlight inside the gap; the passage ahead had collapsed, leaving a tiny entrance that would be difficult to squeeze through.

"Grandpa Chen will never make it through here. You guys go ahead; I'll stay with him," Monk Hua said.

Qilin, Fats, and I all took off our outer garments to allow us to squeeze through the tiny gap, Qilin in the lead and Fats cursing his way in at the end of our line. On our hands and knees, we crawled for a long time down the narrow tunnel, rocks cutting into our exposed flesh and ripping our few remaining pieces of clothing.

The temperature within the tunnel rose steadily and it was hard to breathe. "We should have thought about the air quality in this place before we plunged in," Fats gasped. "Stupid of us—Qilin, usually you would have warned us about that."

I turned around to take a look. The space was so small we could never manage to turn around. There was no way out without crawling backward. "Let's go up a little further. If we don't see the end, we can make our way back."

"Right," Fats grunted, and then Qilin made a sound that I couldn't understand.

When I looked for him, he was gone. All I could see ahead was a dark, narrow tunnel with no end in sight.

CHAPTER ELEVEN

THE TUNNEL

How could Qilin disappear in five seconds? I tried not to panic. Then suddenly in the next instant, there was that poker-faced bastard, crawling in front of me again.

I yelped and Fats asked, "What's going on with you?"

I sputtered incoherently as Qilin turned to us, called "Come on!" and crawled ahead at a faster pace.

All that I had seen—and not seen—had happened in less than a minute. Had I been hallucinating from lack of oxygen?

There was no time to think this over. Fats was pounding on my legs to get me to move; all I could do was look for places that Qilin could have plunged into for a couple of seconds. I saw nothing and I had a distinct feeling that something was very wrong.

We crawled for another ten minutes; then Qilin slowed down and his body stretched forward. I could see the tunnel had become wider and I was certain we had reached its end.

We found ourselves in a large chamber. Fats peered about with his flashlight and said, "Strange—there are murals here. Obviously we aren't the first men to step into this place."

He was right; there was a mural, but it was so faded that

all we could make out was the shape of something that looked like a flying fairy or a ghost.

There was an entrance to another room that was blocked by a huge sealing stone. What on earth was this place used for? I wondered.

As we walked along the tunnel, hot springs bubbled up through the rocks, all very shallow, scalding our hands when we touched the water. The tunnel narrowed as we went deeper into it; hot air blew from it and when we pointed our flashlights it looked as though it was bottomless.

"Let's stop here," Fats suggested and we agreed. The air was fresh and easy to breathe, so Qilin went back to tell the others that it was safe to join us.

Soon Monk Hua and Ye Cheng appeared, followed by Panzi who carried our guide. Shunzi's face glowed with heat but his arms and legs were still like blocks of ice.

I wasn't at all certain he'd survive and wasn't sure we could make it without him. But even more strongly, I didn't want him to die because he had agreed to guide us to the end.

Monk Hua soaked a cloth in hot water from a spring and let it cool for a few minutes before using it to scrub Shunzi. When his ministrations had turned Shunzi's white and frozen limbs to a blazing scarlet, Monk Hua poured hot water over the unconscious man, who began to cough uncontrollably.

"He's going to be okay," Monk Hua told us, as Shunzi's eyes opened, flickered, and then closed as he fell into an energetic snoring. We all relaxed.

Panzi disappeared and then came back, supporting

Chen Ah-Si. Now that we were all safe and together once more, we began to settle down, drying our clothes on the hot rocks and cooking some food by boiling it in the waters of the closest hot spring.

As I ate, I examined the faded murals. I was still unsettled by Qilin's unexplained disappearance and tried to distract myself by trying to figure out why someone had painted a flying fairy in this weird place. As I stared, Fats came over and began to poke at the painting with his fingernail.

"What are you doing? This is ancient, even if it isn't particularly interesting. Why destroy it?"

"You really think I'd thoughtlessly damage something? I'm not one of you southern vandals. Come take a look— there are two layers to this painting."

Sure enough there was a painting under the first that was completely different. "Good work, Fats," I said as I looked closer at his discovery. "Whatever you've found here someone had tried hard to conceal."

I joined Fats in peeling away the top layer, which came off easily. Soon the bottom mural was visible and we could make out a horse-drawn carriage floating on top of the clouds, carrying a fat man who was being attended by several women wearing Mongolian clothing. It was obviously a painted narrative, much like the paintings on the jars that we had found in the undersea tomb. Was this also an account of the Palace in the Clouds?

Carefully, we all began to remove the outer painting, hoping to uncover all of the original mural and the information it might contain. Sheets of paint fell from the wall and an inch at a time, the painting revealed its secrets.

CHAPTER TWELVE

THE SECRETS OF
THE MURAL

We all stared in silence. Monk Hua began to pace back and forth; finally he spoke. "This mural is in three parts. The first shows the battle between the Dong Xia Emperor and the Mongols, the war that annihilated the Dong Xia kingdom. Here is the emperor's army; you can see how outnumbered they were by the Mongol forces."

I stared at the army he pointed at in bewilderment and Fats obviously felt the same way. "Why do all the troops of the emperor's army look like women?"

"That's just the style of painting," Monk Hua explained. "Legend says that the Dong Xia people never grew old. They kept their delicate good looks all of their lives and painters exaggerated that as they depicted them."

Fats looked unconvinced but continued to study the mural without argument as Monk Hua pointed to the second segment. "This shows the ferocity of the battle, with each Dong Xia soldier fighting three Mongols at a time. The emperor's troops were eventually all massacred in a total bloodbath."

I shuddered as I stared at the scarlet-infused mural; it showed group after group of soldiers drowning in their own blood; the Mongolian soldiers rode past them to slaughter the next battalion and put villages to the torch.

"The third part of the mural is obscured by the sealing rock into the next chamber, but it will simply show more of the carnage," Monk Hua told us.

"But this isn't right," I interrupted. "The Kingdom of Dong Xia only existed for seventy years and during that time they were constantly at war. They could never have been the ones to build a tomb as magnificent as the one my uncle hopes to find."

Monk Hua turned to us and smiled. "I know what your doubts are, but your thoughts are misguided. The information you guys have read about the Dong Xia was probably based on a few incomplete ancient texts. In truth, the facts and records left behind by the Dong Xia Kingdom are so scarce that foreign countries don't even believe it ever existed. Most of the information about it isn't at all factual."

Fats objected, "What proof do you have that your information is valid?"

Monk Hua said, "Look. We have direct information." Then he took out a piece of white silk cloth from his pocket and spread it out before us. Within the silk was the third bronze fish with snake brows.

How did he get that? I frowned. If no one had bought the fish at the recent auction and it was now in the hands of Chen Ah-Si, did that mean the old man had the fish in his possession all along, from the moment he first picked it up? Were he and the old antique dealer in cahoots somehow?

I did my best to keep my face from showing my shocked surprise but my thoughts were racing like mad dogs chasing their tails. Monk Hua continued, oblivious to my change of mood.

"This bronze fish was obtained by chance by our old leader. I believe it was made by someone who knew the inside story of the Dong Xia Kingdom, because he very cleverly hid a top secret message inside this bronze fish. Watch this—"

He put the bronze fish next to the lantern. The gold-plated fish scales reflected a golden light and many fine bright spots were projected onto the mural. Monk Hua rotated the body of the fish and the spots began to change form. Then gradually they turned into something that resembled text.

"This is the secret. There are forty-seven Jurchen words concealed in the scales of this fish."

I involuntarily tightened my grip on the two bronze fish that I always carried with me in my pocket. Trembling slightly, I asked, "What…what does it say?"

"I haven't been able to decipher all of it because I don't have all the information. But I'm sure that the person who made the fish recorded things that he didn't want others to find out. This is a record of the actual Dong Xia history." Monk Hua continued in a condescending voice, "In fact, I'd already concluded after years of study that the Dong Xia Kingdom was more than a mere legend long before I saw this fish. They reigned in the depths of the remote mountains, and for several centuries managed to hold onto their sovereignty even though they were placed between an extremely powerful Mongolia and a covetous Korea. I've read Korean news accounts that said ginseng collectors have identified people in odd clothing moving about in these mountains. I think they could be surviving remnants of the Dong Xia Kingdom."

Then he pointed to the bronze fish and said, "The records here confirm my theories. After their decisive battle with Mongolia, the Dong Xia Kingdom retreated to the border between Jilin and Korea, and managed to remain alive in secret for hundreds of years. There were a total of fourteen emperors. Mongolia and Korea wanted to destroy this small country more than once, but for some odd reason, all attempts failed."

"Why?" Panzi asked. "Monk, can you be a little less obscure?"

Monk Hua shrugged. "I don't know. The information on the fish is incomplete. I'm sure the rest of the history is recorded on other objects, but with the words I have in my hands, I can say that something very astounding took place in order for the Dong Xia Kingdom to survive for so long. I have no more information, however; we've been looking for other objects that might contain more facts but with no success." He paused and then said, "Do you guys know what the last sentence of this Jurchen text says?"

We all stared stupidly as Monk Hua looked at us and said, "It says that the Emperor Wannu of the Dong Xia dynasty wasn't human."

"What was he then?" Fats asked.

"It says he was some sort of monster that crawled out from underground!"

"It can't really say that," Ye Cheng protested. "Can't it be a kind of metaphor that means the emperor was a heavenly being and therefore not human?"

"I also thought he was referring to the Dragon of Heaven metaphorically, but after I studied the text, I realized the writer was trying to objectively record Dong Xia history, so he probably wouldn't have used such respectful language. Besides, do you think anyone would talk about an emperor like that—imagine wishing the emperor happy birthday by saying, 'Your Majesty, you're truly not human.' You'd be chopped to pieces before you had the chance to begin your next sentence." He smiled. "If I could only get my hands on the rest of the history, I might be able to discover what the writer meant."

Both Fats and Qilin knew that I possessed the remaining two fish, but neither of them said a word. I gripped the contents of my pocket as though I held my own heart there. Suddenly the fish felt extremely heavy.

Why don't I reveal them? I asked myself, what use are they to me? I can't read Jurchen; I'll never decipher their secrets. But, perhaps in honor of my Uncle Three, I couldn't bring myself to hand them over to Chen Ah-Si and this condescending, learned monk.

Panzi stared at the mural while muttering to himself, "If the person on the mural is the Wannu Emperor, he looks human, not monstrous at all. What is this monk saying? What sense does any of this make?"

Fats patted him on his back, saying, "Calm down, it's all right," then turned to Monk Hua, "Brother Scar-face, what are you talking about? I say we're all real people here; don't play intellectual games with us. When we open the coffin, then we'll find out if your emperor was a man or a dog."

Monk Hua smiled mysteriously and said, "What I meant was that it's always best to know all sides of a story."

We rested and slowly recovered our mental equilibrium. While we slept, Chen Ah-Si ordered his men to take turns keeping watch outside and to tell us when the blizzard had stopped.

When I finally woke up, Shunzi had also regained consciousness and couldn't stop apologizing to us. Fats ignored him and I gave him some food, saying, "Rest because we'll need to continue this ascent."

Without being able to see the passage of either the sun or the moon, we had no idea how much time had gone by but we figured we had probably been within the mountain for two or three days before the storm cleared and we were able to go back outside.

We emerged into a world of blinding whiteness that stabbed at our light-starved eyes.

As we reassembled our supplies, Panzi remarked that we had eaten far more than we should have during our time of recovery. "We'll have to hurry to reach our goal," he told us. "Shunzi, we need to find a faster route to the tomb. What can you do for us?"

"There's only one way to get there," our guide stammered. "Either we go back for more supplies and return or we move on and eat less than we would like."

Nobody was happy to hear this and to make matters worse, after the heat we had been basking in, the cold was insufferable.

"Look," Chen Ah-Si announced, "you laughed at these but now you'll understand why we need them." He lined the inside of his boots with sanitary napkins, saying, "Follow my example. These will absorb the sweat from our feet, keep our socks dry, and our bodies will stay warm."

He was right; the trick worked. But as time went on and we discarded our old napkins for fresh ones, I felt embarrassed, wondering what those who followed us might think when they found our castoffs. When I mentioned that to Fats, he stared at fresh hoofprints in the snow and said, "No worries. It looks as though Ning and her group aren't behind us anymore."

Two hours later, we almost caught up with our rivals. They had made camp on a hill not too far from us and they had apparently gone through hell in the blizzard. Half of their horses were gone and at least ten of their men. None of us could see Uncle Three among the group but I could see Ning peering through binoculars into the distance. I followed her gaze and blinked hard at what I saw.

There in the clouds soared a familiar peak; it was the same one I saw painted on the murals of the undersea tomb, the one that held the Palace in the Clouds.

"We're there!" I shouted. Turning to Shunzi, I asked, "What is the name of that mountain? How can we get there—and fast?"

Shunzi grabbed my binoculars and stared for a minute. Then he scowled at me, his teeth bared in what looked like a snarl. "Forget it. You can't go there; I'll never lead you to that place. If I'd known that's where you were headed, I would never have come with you."

12. THE SECRETS OF THE MURAL

CHAPTER THIRTEEN

THE FIVE SACRED MOUNTAINS

"The mountain you want to go to is over the border, in Korea," Shunzi explained as he saw our stunned faces. "It's in a different mountain range, the Trinity Peaks. It's over seven thousand feet above sea level. And it marks our border with Korea."

"What in the hell are we going to do?" I asked, "Three of the most guarded borders in the world—India and Pakistan, Israel and Lebanon, and this eight-mile border here at the Trinity Peaks. What was my uncle thinking?"

"Smugglers manage to cross over on the western slope of Changbai Mountain. And I've heard there are tunnels under the Trinity Mountains that lead from China to Korea, but they're quite heavily guarded," Fats said. "We don't have enough food to do anything other than go straight across the border here and then scale the mountain where our tomb is buried."

Suddenly the hazards of our journey were no longer the expected ones of zombies, vampires, or carnivorous insects. Now we faced the possibility of bullets from assault rifles, aimed at us by well-trained army battalions, rows and rows of them.

"Take it easy, guys," Panzi reassured us. "There have to

be paths along the border that we can pass through without detection—that's what we're paying Shunzi for—and we'll pay him even more once he gets us to where we want to be. You know the secret trails, don't you, old comrade?

Shunzi frowned and shook his head. "No way in hell do you have enough money to persuade me to do that. Those trails are all heavily patrolled. You can't even get close to the sentries on our own side of the border. When I was stationed there, my orders were to shoot if anyone came close—the first bullet went into the sky, the second into a kneecap."

"Why don't we buy some fruit and dress up like local residents who have come to convey our respect and appreciation?" Fats asked.

Shunzi grinned. "You've got to be joking—where are you going to find the fruit? We'd only look all the more suspicious if we came bearing fruit in this frozen, snow-covered country."

"Then what do we do?" Fats argued. "Are you saying there's no way we can get over the border? I don't believe you. Even the Macedonian defense line was breached by Alexander—could this broken old border line be stronger than the Macedonian one once was? Are we paying you too little? Are you holding out for more money? How much do you want? Give it to me straight."

Shunzi shook his head in some embarrassment. "Aiya, this isn't about the money. If there really was a way to get there, why would I make life difficult for myself like this? If you told me earlier that you guys were heading for Korea, I wouldn't have taken you along on this route. Now that we're at this point, I don't know what to do."

Monk Hua began talking with Chen Ah-Si some

distance away as the rest of us fell silent, lost in our separate thoughts. My feeling was that we had no choice but to cross here, where we stood right now. Our food supplies wouldn't last if we took a more circuitous route, and to go back to the beginning and then repeat this same journey was only wasted effort. We have to keep going, I told myself, if only to rescue my uncle from Ning and her group—I'm positive he's in their clutches. Once we find him, I'll be ready to say the hell with the rest of this little scheme.

Over in the corner, Chen Ah-Si scowled, sighed heavily, and said nothing. I knew this old mobster from Changsha had no problem with committing murder or arson to get what he wanted. Government officials, however, were another story and I could tell he was reluctant to come up against bureaucracy.

I glanced at Poker-face, but Qilin had pulled his usual trick of pulling away from the matter at hand, staring off into the mountains as if nothing we had discussed had anything to do with him at all.

Our silence was broken by Ye Cheng calling, "Look at this!" Over on the next hill, Ning's group was moving on, in the direction of the Trinity Mountains. They'd jettisoned most of their supplies, tossing bags and boxes into the snow, and were moving quickly without that weight to bog them down.

"Strange," Ye Cheng observed. "Don't they know they're headed for the border? What the hell's wrong with their guide? Doesn't he know what Shunzi does? Is he willing for his clients to become target practice for the border troops?"

"No," I said. "That's off base. These people are professionals and they probably have hired more than one local guide, the best they could find. I'm sure they researched the terrain and planned their route before they got started. They know what they're doing."

"So what's up with our guide?" Fats growled. "Speak up, man—are there roads that other locals know about that you don't? Are you a professional or a fraud?"

Shunzi squinted at the group ahead of us and replied, "There's only one way for them to go—they're probably trying to go around another mountain in the pass ahead, enter Korea from that portion of the border, and then backtrack toward the Trinity Mountains. It's risky but it's a better idea than crossing the border here. Obviously they have more food than we do and that allows them to make a long-distance trek."

"Then what should we do? Stop talking and follow them?" Ye Cheng turned to ask Chen Ah-Si.

Chen Ah-Si shook his head without saying a word. Suddenly he pointed to a small hill on one side of the Trinity Mountains and asked Shunzi, "What hill is that?"

Shunzi looked through the binoculars and replied, "That's the Small Sacred Mountain, on our side of the border. The Trinity Mountains, this Small Sacred Mountain, and the Big Sacred Mountain over there— together they're known as the Five Sacred Peaks."

"Can we get to the Small Sacred Mountain from where we are now?" the old man asked. We all stared at him, wondering what his plan might be.

"No problem at all," Shunzi replied. "We could make it in a day. And it's far from the border sentries; it's a rough route but it's not beyond our capabilities."

"Okay," Chen Ah-Si ordered, "take us there then."

"What's going on? Are you sure? It's a waste of time to go over there—our food will be gone before you know it," Monk Hua sputtered.

Chen Ah-Si waved his hand and pointed to the mountain range on one side. He said, "These mountains stretch in three directions and are never free from snow. This is a rare Three-Headed Dragon. To those who know feng shui, this is called the Spot Where the Dragons Rest. The Trinity Mountains are dragon heads, key locations for royal tombs. If this Palace is located on the cliffs of the middle mountain, the queen and other members of the royal family should be buried on the two smaller dragon heads next to it. The layout of the Three-Headed Dragon is very peculiar. All three heads must be connected, or each one would fly separately and there would be no set direction for the dragon. This would cause chaos and warfare among the children and grandchildren that are buried here, so these tombs are always connected with hidden passages that lead to the Palace in the Clouds."

Although I knew little of feng shui, I knew Grandpa Chen was correct. Other mausoleums had been excavated where the tombs were linked by underground passageways that led to the middle tomb. How he had arrived at this conclusion, however, I had no idea.

As soon as Chen Ah-Si finished his speech, he turned to Qilin and asked, "Young man, am I right?"

For the first time ever, Poker-face responded to someone else's question. He turned to look at Chen Ah-Si, then without saying a word, turned around again and continued to gaze into the blindingly white mountains in the distance. With his apparent agreement, we all began to feel a little better about our new destination.

When at last we reached the spot where Ning and her team had camped, we noticed they had left no food or anything useful. We followed the hoofprints of their horses into a valley where Shunzi began to lead us toward the Small Sacred Mountain.

It was a world of whiteness all the way to the horizon, broken only by the pale blue of ice. We found ourselves walking along a glacier, a river of ice punctuated by deep craters, some containing small lakes and others appearing to be bottomless pits. At other times, statuesque ice formations blocked our way, taking on weird shapes and sending out waves of chill that pierced us to our kidneys as we clambered past them.

It was nightfall when we reached the base of the Small Sacred Mountain; we set up camp in a cave. We were now high above the valley and close to the sky that was thick with glittering stars.

"Where are those damned hot springs when we need them?" Fats grumbled.

"We're up too high," Shunzi told him, "but if you're bored, you can always try to find one. And there's a small burial ground not too far away that might interest you gentlemen."

"Burial" is a word guaranteed to get grave robbers on their feet. We all followed Shunzi, except for the exhausted Chen Ah-Si and Monk Hua who remained with him. The rest of us made our way to a cliff overlooking the valley below.

Throwing a flare into the darkness, Shunzi pointed out curled-up human shapes packed beneath the glacial ice. "People practiced glacial burial right up until Liberation," he told us. "Even today old people come to perform ceremonies for their buried ancestors. See those specks in the ice? Those are bodies buried over a thousand years ago."

There were more specks than I could count—perhaps hundreds of thousands of them.

"Do you suppose any of those specks were slaves who helped to build the Palace in the Clouds?" Fats asked nobody in particular.

"It's possible," Qilin answered him, and we all gaped at the sound of his voice.

The light from Shunzi's flare died. We returned to our camp, ate, and then fell asleep quickly. I awoke in the middle of the night, roused by the echoing snores from Panzi, Fats, Monk Hua, and Lang Feng, all together in a ghastly chorus.

Wide awake and knowing I was going to stay that way, I left my tent. "Go to bed," Shunzi," I said, "I'll take your watch for you."

Shunzi handed me a cigarette. "Just keep me company," he told me. "I'm being paid to do this, after all. I can't slack off on the job."

"You've got it," I said. "I'd rather chat with you than listen to those four walruses over there in the tent all night."

"I'm used to the mountains after dark. I used to gather plants to make herbal medicine before I joined the army. Rest easy; I know what I'm doing up here."

I felt a little dubious. How come you fainted before we even began to climb the mountains? I asked him silently, but continued to listen even though I didn't believe anything he said.

As the night went on, we became more relaxed and suddenly Shunzi blurted, "Tell me just what you guys are really doing here, won't you? What do you want from the mountains?"

He caught me off guard and I thought carefully of how to respond. If I told him we were looking for the Palace in the Clouds, would he believe me? I certainly couldn't tell him we were here to rob a tomb and we were obviously not sightseers. I had to tell him the unvarnished truth: "I can't tell you."

He smiled. "That's okay. I was just curious."

"Well as long as we're playing Twenty Questions, why did you stop being an herb gatherer to become a mountain guide? You can make a lot more money from herbs and you don't have to put up with asshole clients like us. It has to be safer too."

I didn't expect an answer but the one he gave me almost made me cough up my guts and spit them out on the snow.

"I'm not a guide; I'm still an herb gatherer. Once in a while I've taken some people into the mountains but only as far as that big lake we passed on the first day. I've never brought anyone this far before."

"Stop kidding around."

"I'm telling the truth. There aren't any professional guides who would take you into the mountains in winter. If I didn't do it, you would have had to come here by yourselves." He smiled at me. "It's too dangerous. If it weren't for the blessings of the Buddha, we'd all be dead by now. It's a miracle we've come all this way without losing anyone in the group. But don't worry. Although I haven't brought anyone here before, I've come here by myself many times. I'm very familiar with this territory; I wasn't lying when I told you that. Everything will be okay."

His expression was serious and I realized this was no joke. "Damn it, if it's so dangerous, why did you bring us? Are you that short on cash?"

"Money's the least of why I came. The big reason is…it's because of my father. He…he disappeared ten years ago when he was taking a group into the mountains in winter, along a route more or less the same as the one you guys are taking right now. But they all vanished, never to return. I vaguely recall that the people he took were dressed a lot like you guys and they had the same determination to get to the mountains. So when you came, I felt as though I needed to follow in my father's path. For one thing, I didn't want you to die here like my father did. Second, I have a very naïve idea that perhaps your reason for coming here is the same as the group had ten years ago. Then maybe I'd be able to find out what on earth happened to my father. Of course, this is only my daydreaming getting the better of me." He smiled in a self-mocking fashion. "My father and his group probably got swept up in an avalanche and are buried deep in the snow somewhere."

"So that's why you wanted to know why we're so insistent on going into the mountains."

Shunzi nodded. "You'll never understand how it feels to be sure that your father is buried up here when you can't verify this for yourself."

My feeling about our guide changed completely as I listened to his story; he wasn't trying to bilk us out of our money at all. He had a reason more compelling than our own to reach the Sacred Peaks. When he looked at the bodies entombed in the glacier ice, did he wonder if he was looking at his own father?

13. THE FIVE SACRED MOUNTAINS

Then there was the group his father had tried to bring here—were they searching for the Palace in the Clouds too? No, that was too huge a coincidence, I told myself.

I was interrupted by Shunzi. "Master Wu, I think you're different from the others, which is why I told you all those things just now. Please don't tell your companions. I'm afraid they'll become upset."

Upset is one way of putting it, I thought, Who knows what Chen Ah-Si would do to you if he found out this was the first time you brought anyone here—but it's a damned sure thing that Fats would beat you to a bloody pulp.

"Don't worry," I said, just as Lang Feng crawled out to take the next watch and Shunzi and I went back to our tents.

Surrounded by deep and deafening snores, I dozed into a half sleep, dreaming of Shunzi's father and his group of explorers. I know these people, I thought in my dream state. Where have I met them before?

Our climb of the following morning was more difficult than the previous day. The cliffs above us carried tons of snow—avalanches just waiting to happen. We spoke infrequently and then only in whispers. Drifts along the trail covered the craters we had been able to see and avoid on our first day; occasionally one of us would break through the hard crust of snow that covered the holes and would sink in up past the waist. We began to probe the terrain ahead of us with long icicles as if we were making our way through a minefield.

Fats was the fastest and most agile of us all and soon took the lead from Shunzi, who lacked his stamina. The rest of us felt our tongues begin to tingle and go numb. "Altitude sickness," Shunzi told us grimly. We moved as quickly as we could through a world so silent that it seemed as if it were dead. The only sound we could hear was the noise of our own panting.

The steep trail evened out and we found ourselves in a valley surrounded by giant cliffs that blocked out all light. "Here it is," Old Chen announced. "This is the first dragon head, the approach to the first tomb," and he gestured to a steep incline leading up from the flat ground we stood on. We all cursed quietly as we used our ice axes to pull ourselves up the face of the cliff, one by one.

The Small Sacred Mountain stood alone, facing the Big Sacred Mountain that was directly opposite, separated by a valley. They both stood in front of the Trinity Peaks as if they guarded them like a coiling dragon and a tiger poised to spring. As I stared, I could feel a powerful current of energy sweeping over the mountains and was sure that we were approaching the tombs my uncle had sent us to find.

The route we followed was punishingly cruel and Chen Ah-Si collapsed, unable to move. "Come, Grandfather Chen," Lang Feng sighed and pulled the old man up onto his back, which slowed our ascent even more.

We slogged onward for three more hours. My mind was empty and my shell of a body tottered behind Fats in a robotic determination.

Fats was the first to reach the mountaintop, almost sobbing with relief as he fell flat on the snow, arms outstretched and motionless. One by one, we followed him, gasping for breath as we stared at our surroundings.

We were in a huge field of snow, so clean and pure it was almost blue, sparkling with crystals of one hundred twinkling colors. Black rocks jutted through the snow and the setting sun cast a blue haze over the surrounding Trinity Peaks. The Big Sacred Mountain loomed above us like an enormous monster. None of us could speak; it was as though we were in the middle of a painting that was spiritual, sublime, and sinister, all at the same time.

Of course it would be Fats who broke the mood. Jabbing me with his fist, he hissed at me, "Is he out of his mind?" And there was Qilin, on his knees, bowing his head toward the Trinity Peaks. His face, no longer impassive, was twisted in a mask of sorrow.

CHAPTER FOURTEEN
SUICIDE BOUND

None of us said a word as Qilin completed his silent gesture of respect, rose to his feet, and resumed his customary detachment from everyone and everything around him. We knew better than to ask him to explain himself.

It was more to the point to concentrate on regaining our strength, so we sat, drinking cups of hot tea and staring at the mountains as they turned purple in the twilight.

Shunzi began to chatter as his energy returned. "In ancient times, the Five Holy Peaks were united as one huge mountain, until a supernatural being passed by and split it into five separate pieces with a magic sword. My grandfather told me that behind the Trinity Peaks was another mountain called the Ladder. Legend had it that at the top of this mountain was a ladder that led first to the Palace in the Clouds, and then became a link between our world and Paradise. However, this peak is shrouded in clouds that make it invisible. Only when the weather is at its very best, then beams of rainbow-colored light appear in the space between Ladder Mountain and the Five Holy Peaks, and Ladder Mountain shines out from behind the rays of light, looming high above all of the other mountains, unearthly in its beauty."

"Bullshit," Fats interrupted. "The Palace in the Clouds lies within the Trinity Mountains, not on Ladder Mountain. This legend is absurd."

Monk Hua broke in, "I've heard this legend before. My theory is that when the Palace in the Clouds was built, its reflection was cast on the snow of Ladder Mountain and created a mirage. Because of the fog that surrounds Ladder Mountain, people who saw the reflection believed the palace was truly built in the sky."

"But mirages occur in deserts or near lakes, not on snow-covered mountains," I argued. "I think this is a deliberate part of the feng shui that Wang Canghai put in place when the palace was built, to hide its entrance from anyone else forever."

"Believe whatever you choose," Shunzi said "It's almost nightfall and we still have to find level ground so we can make camp." He began to gather up the teacups and I glanced at my watch. We had about an hour before darkness fell; Shunzi was right about moving on.

But in what direction? We clustered around Chen Ah-Si, asking him to make that decision. The old man was still in bad shape after the long climb, but he pulled himself together enough to give us an answer.

"There should be a clue to our destination right beneath our feet. Let's just put down a few shovels and see what's under the snow before we decide what to do next."

The snow was much softer than the mud we usually dug our way through to reach a tomb, so it was an easy matter to plunge our shovels through the drifts. In a matter of minutes we had managed to make over a dozen preliminary tunnels; but then twenty feet down we could go no further. We pulled up our shovels and found there was nothing clinging to them, not even snow crystals.

"Damn it," Fats exploded. "We've struck glacier ice and that's as hard as concrete. We can't break through that. It's been snowing here for thousands of years and the snow has been compressed into even more ice. The first tomb, the one with the bodies of dead workers, is probably encased within this glacier, don't you think?"

We all nodded. This seemed plausible, but how could we get to it through the barrier of solid ice?

"Too bad we don't have some dynamite with us," Panzi said. "Just one blast hole would make it easy to break through—and it would clear away the snow so we could see what's beneath the ice."

"I have dynamite in my pack," Monk Hua told us. "But take a look above our heads. Wouldn't it be suicide to blast a hole considering what surrounds us?"

We looked up. Above us was a mountain range with towering cliffs, blanketed with snow and stretching far beyond the horizon, while we stood below it like ants waiting to be stepped on. All we needed was a little bit of snow sprinkled over us and we'd sleep here forever.

"What choice do we have?" Panzi boomed out. "Either we get past this problem or we go back home, failures. Let's use your explosives, Brother Monk. We'll be fine."

"It's too big a risk, Panzi," I said.

"Stop arguing and listen to some expert advice," Monk Hua barked as he pointed at Lang Feng.

Panzi and I both shut up—this little shrimp an expert? We looked at Lang Feng skeptically.

"Do it," he said.

14. SUICIDE BOUND

"Are you sure?" Fats asked. "This is like setting off firecrackers in a pot of tofu—can you make a hole here without setting the surface into motion?"

Lang Feng nodded. "When I was a miner, I blasted at least ten thousand holes. This is nothing."

Monk Hua looked at us and grinned. "Although he doesn't talk much, Lang Feng was a miner for twenty years. He's been blasting holes since he was fourteen and he's flattened at least twenty hills. Our old man took a liking to him and introduced him to our line of work about a year ago; now everyone calls him the Dynamite God. There's nobody better than he is."

"So you're the Dynamite God?" Panzi gaped. "I've heard about you."

Lang Feng looked a little shy and embarrassed. "The others came up with it. It's only a nickname."

Monk Hua turned to us. "If Lang Feng says this is safe, I say we should do it. Do any of you have an objection?"

"Go ahead," I said and nobody spoke up to dispute the decision.

Since we were all of the same mind, Lang Feng and Ye Cheng pulled out a Luoyang shovel and began twisting a special spiraled head onto the end. Then they drilled a few trial holes in the snow.

Next, Lang Feng blended a few different types of powder to create a unique form of dynamite and buried a few low-powered detonators deep inside the holes. I knew that he had lowered the power of his explosives to less than the power of ten cannons; this guy knew what he was doing. This was enough to make a hole for us to pass through but not enough to disturb the tons of snow lying above that threatened our lives.

At the sight of Lang Feng's preparations, Shunzi went berserk. Rushing over to Monk Hua, he yelled, "Stop this man! He's going to desecrate the Sacred Mountain!" He lunged at Lang Feng, who calmly knocked him out with a nearby pickax and then went on with his work.

Fats poked at Shunzi's unconscious body with his foot and asked Monk Hua, "What should we do with this jerk?"

"Let's forget about him right now. We still need him in order to get back down to safety when we're through. We'll take him into the underground palace, prop him in a corner until we're all done, give him some more money, and he'll leave us in peace. What damage can he cause anyway? He can barely do the job we hired him for," Monk Hua replied.

Lang Feng was indeed a professional, quick and precise. When all was ready, he waved his hand, signaling for us to take cover.

I expected the exploding detonators would be very loud and send a wave of snow into the air but instead, the smooth and level crust of snow began to crack without making a sound. Huge billows of drifts began to pour down like waterfalls and the ground beneath our feet shook violently.

But the collapse didn't last. The cascades of snow quickly stopped. A huge layer of mud mixed with snow and ice appeared below us—the surface of the glacier.

Fats was sitting near my side, his eyes tightly closed, unaware that the blast had already occurred. I shook him lightly. Surprised, he looked around and exclaimed, "Holy shit, he really didn't make a sound."

I had no idea whether Lang Feng's skills were really

that perfect or if this was a fortunate fluke, but other than the brief snowslide, there seemed to be no threat of an avalanche. We waited for a minute, felt nothing loosen and fall, and slowly began to relax.

I put both thumbs up in Lang Feng's direction and Panzi patted him on the back;

Lang Feng looked relieved. But before he could say a word, snow began to crash around us.

"Hush!" Fats hissed.

We all looked up and saw a black, bone-chilling crack spreading slowly across the slope above our heads, splitting into many smaller fissures that spread across the snow. More and more waves of snow rolled down around us, getting larger and larger.

God damn it, I thought, looks like Lang Feng lost his status as Dynamite God today.

"Don't say a word—don't even fart," Fats whispered almost inaudibly. "Everybody look for a big rock or a crevasse for shelter—we're all fucked."

"It's impossible," Lang Feng whimpered, "I measured exactly the right amount."

Monk Hua clapped his hand over Lang Feng's mouth and Fats pointed to a huge walnut-shaped boulder, with an opening that would cover us. He tied a rope around his waist and threw one end to us. Slowly, his jaw clamped so hard that it turned white, he stepped onto the glacier ice that lay between us and the sheltering rock. Placing his feet as though they were made of glass, he reached the rock in three steps, held the rope tight, and beckoned for us to follow him.

First Panzi and Qilin, then the others, all tiptoed across the glacier ice as quickly as they could. Lang Feng carried Chen Ah-Si on his back and Ye Cheng bore the unconscious Shunzi. When I saw them all on the other side, safe and secure, I took my first step onto the ice.

My balance has always been bad ever since I was a little boy; I sucked at riding a bicycle and was never able to ice-skate. I was sure the ice would dissolve under my feet as I crossed or that I would fall and break every bone I had. My legs began to shake so badly that I could barely stand and the panic that engulfed me was clear to everyone who looked at my face.

"Come on," Fats urged me. "Don't think about it. Just take three steps and you're safe. You can make it in one jump."

I stepped back to coil myself for a leap and my feet skidded forward. In one second, my body strained against the rope that held me and I was hanging over the cliff. Fats and Panzi tugged at the rope; I felt myself rise several feet toward safety. Tearing my ice axe from my belt, I buried it into the cliff and hauled myself up higher. Then I felt it—a quiver of vibrations above my head. A mass of fog descended around me; I could see nothing but whiteness and knew I was trapped in an avalanche.

All I could hear was Fats shouting, "Hold onto the pickax! Cling to the surface of the ice!" Then darkness caught me; my body sank as if twelve men were pulling on my clothes, dragging me down. The rope around my waist cut into my skin and a rush of air flooded my lungs, making me choke. A powerful force struck every part of my body; I couldn't even raise my head. Soon my throat began to tighten and I knew I was beginning to suffocate. My nose and mouth were full of snow.

I caused this, I realized, with my ice axe I'd loosened the layers of snow that were now burying me alive. My body was spinning within my snow shroud as though I were in a whirlpool. I tried to grab my ice axe but I couldn't even figure out where my own hands were.

Then I felt the rope lift a little and my body came up with it. My God, I thought, Fats and the others are rescuing me. I tried to swim my way up through the snow, pushing myself in the direction of the tugging rope. My ears filled with a roaring sound and brightness stabbed at my eyes. I was free; Fats and Lang Feng loomed above me, yelling, "Are you still alive?"

I gulped down a breath of fresh air and nodded. I looked down and saw the valley wrapped in the white hazy mist of my avalanche. Fats grabbed my shoulders and yelled, "Kid, you really lucked out. Be grateful this was just a little snowslide, not a real avalanche. Otherwise, I would probably have been dragged down along with you."

Staring straight ahead, I saw a gigantic glacier, scoured clean of the snow that had covered it. Ye Cheng murmured beside me, "Lang Feng's cannon wasn't completely fucked up," and Monk Hua pointed his flashlight into the depths of the ice, hoping to see some traces of a tomb.

Fats had the eyesight of a hungry falcon. He yelped something, grabbed a flashlight, and redirected its beam. Within the pale blue depths of the glacier was an enormous shadow that was only partially visible, curled up like an infant with an oversized head.

CHAPTER FIFTEEN
THE KUNLUN EMBRYO

We stood staring at the frozen shape, its eerie gigantic head and its body covered with spiky hair. What the hell was this thing? It looked as though it was as tall as a five-story building. Could it have been a sea creature lifted from the depths of the ocean, when a volcanic eruption raised these mountains out of the water?

Striking our axes into the ice, we lowered our ropes to reach the surface of the glacier so we could examine the figure more closely.

"What are we doing?" Chen Ah-Si demanded. When we explained what we saw, he gasped, "My God, could we have found a Kunlun Embryo?"

"What are you talking about?" Fats demanded.

"A Kunlun Embryo is a rarely seen natural phenomenon. At places where the aura of heaven and earth concentrates, often in rocks, glaciers, or forests, some bizarre infant-shaped things are formed, called 'Kunlun Embryos.' As legends have it, some of these earthborn embryos hold evil spirits."

"I've read about this," Monk Hua interrupted. "Some Tibetans once discovered a mammoth frozen embryo in the Kunlun Mountains. It was as big as a mountain itself with all its face clearly identifiable as a very lifelike baby girl and was named the Kunlun Embryo. A temple called the Temple of the Kunlun Child was built right on the baby's belly button. In the realm of feng shui, the Kunlun Embryo marks a treasure point determined by heaven, different from those that are made by men. They can be found only by chance. When they are excavated a tomb is built inside it, in which the most royal of all men can be buried."

"Something that weird actually exists?" Fats crouched down and peered at the shadow. "But this thing is inhuman, isn't it?'

Chen Ah-Si nodded. "Of course this is only a guess on my part. If this really were a Kunlun Embryo, there would be a tomb built inside it. However, if that were really so…" He faltered, looking bewildered.

"I think I understand," I said. "This Kunlun Embryo marks a treasure point—but then why isn't the Palace in the Clouds constructed here instead of in the Trinity Peaks? This spot should be the most sacred one of all."

"That's right, there isn't any feng shui better than the Kunlun Embryo; it's where heaven and earth converge. There's only one place that could be better—if the Palace were truly built in the sky."

Chen Ah-Si was dead serious and that gave me chills. "Impossible," I muttered.

"It is impossible, which is why the appearance of a Kunlun Embryo in this spot definitely poses a problem. What is it doing here?"

"Could it be man-made? Symbolic tricks are among the most common designs in ancient tombs. It could be a trick to throw us off the track. I deal in old books and antique objects in my business and I see fakes every day—it's quite commonplace."

Chen Ah-Si's attention was fully focused on the surrounding mountains; he heard nothing I had said. I turned around to look at Poker-face; he looked as puzzled as the rest of us. Monk Hua was the only one who answered me. "You may well be right. Look at the color of this thing; there are different shades of brightness within it. It doesn't look real to me."

"Holy shit," I gasped. "This thing's shaped like a baby. Did someone make it so it would attract an evil spirit? Could it have been built by the man who built the Palace in the Clouds, that master of feng shui secrets, Wang Canghai?"

"Let's not make any wild guesses," Fats said. "The only way to learn about this thing is to dig it up. Let's get started."

"How?" Monk Hua asked. "If we use our ice axes, it will take us at least two weeks to get into that thing."

Fats stared into the ice below his feet, waved in a dismissive fashion, and said, "How difficult can it be? Just leave it to me."

"Exactly what do you have in mind this time, Fats?"

"Are you questioning my judgment, Young Wu? I've been to the Kunlun Mountains, after all. Have any of you? I know what I'm doing; I've done it before."

"So why don't you tell us about your unparalleled experience? Don't be so modest," I taunted, knowing Fats could never resist telling a good story.

"Fine, okay," he groaned. "In the Kunlun Mountains, the glaciers often crack into gigantic fissures and within them are strange things—ruined buildings from past civilizations lie in shattered pieces within the ice. They had been destroyed by avalanches, my guide told me. Now if this thing below us had been built above us and swept into the glacier below, it would no longer be in one piece. This thing was built where it lies now, which means the ice it's encased in isn't that of a true glacier. This ice will be thin and easy to break through—believe me. Just look at how clear and transparent it is, like window glass and almost as fragile. What we're looking at is just like a normal burial mound, made from thin ice. Now do you agree with me, Young Wu?"

I nodded; his theory was sound. Fats puffed up proudly and announced, "See, no need to doubt me. I know more than you would ever think possible. You want a simple solution to our problem? We blast our way down."

"I don't want to be trapped in another snowslide—or worse, thank you very much, fat man," I said. "Nor do we want to collapse the protective shelter of ice and destroy the embryo or the tomb or the monster or whatever the hell we're looking at. I wouldn't even dare use shovels to reach this thing."

"You damned bookworm," Fats sneered. "Think we can't even use a shovel? Then what do you suggest—a spoon? All you're good for with your college education is to exaggerate things and come up with contrived stories to scare us and create more problems."

"I'm as worried as you are, Fats," I told him. "If you don't believe me, then go ahead with your plan and test it out. But as far as I can see, solving this one problem your way will just lead to a bigger problem."

15. THE KUNLUN EMBRYO

As we glared at each other, Qilin silently picked up our little camp stove and placed it on the surface of the ice. We all heard a series of popping sounds as the stove's heat melted small portions of the glacier. "What about this?" he asked quietly. "Fire?"

"Of course," I agreed. "We can weaken the ice's surface, chip our way through, then heat the next layer and chip some more."

We each took out our little camp stoves and lit them all. Placing them at our feet, we waited a few minutes and began to chip away at the ice. Finally we made a wide crack that led us further down into the glacier's core, but it took forever. After three hours we had finally made enough of a tunnel that Fats was able to push himself into it. He struck at the next layer of ice. There was a loud popping sound and before him opened a large hollow space, big enough for him to stand up in.

"I was right!" he shouted.

We crowded down around him, flashlights streaming into the opening. There was a domed space, like a glass bowl turned upside down. From the walls of the dome wooden beams covered with spiky icicles intertwined to form a scaffold that supported the bowl of ice—they had formed the "thorns" we thought we had seen on the body of our embryo. Lying beneath the dome was an abyss, dark and terrifying.

And in the steep slope of the dome three hundred feet down, we could see what our embryo really was—a gigantic cave shaped like a baby. As we stared at it, Fats let out a howl. "Look—there's a fucking palace right there!"

Fats was right. A palace supported by wooden pillars

with attached platforms seemed to be floating in the air above the cave. "It's the shrine where burial items for the dead are kept," Monk Hua told us. "We'll find the first tomb that we're looking for below this palace, within the mountain."

Fats began to laugh and the rest of us joined him, pushing and jostling each other in our excitement at approaching the first part of our goal. "Stop," Monk Hua scolded. "Look at the snow above us. Another avalanche would swallow up us all."

Few grave robbers are ever given the chance to enter an imperial tomb. If I could just look and then come back out to tell the tale, I'd be grateful—to hell with whatever treasures might be there.

"Grandpa Chen, should we go to the tomb now or wait until morning?" Monk Hua asked and the old man looked at him sardonically. "How many of you could stand to wait until tomorrow?"

Swiftly we gathered our gear together and then hovered about the opening, looking at the terrain we would soon walk on. None of us wanted to take the first step. From where we stood there was a three hundred-foot drop and a sixty-five-foot gap that separated us from the embryo-shaped cave. Our ropes were long enough to get us three hundred feet down but it would be impossible for us to swing over the gap to reach the palace.

Chen Ah-Si elbowed his way past us all. "Get the hell out of my way, you imbeciles. Damn my luck for teaming up with a bunch of know-nothings like you." He crouched down with Ye Cheng beside him and the two of them talked quietly together. Then the old man stood up and bellowed, "One of you morons get some rope and climb down to the tiled roof of that shrine."

"I'll go," Panzi said. "It can't be any worse than making my way through a minefield and I did that when I was in the army."

We tied a rope around his waist and handed him some lightweight tools in a backpack. Chen Ah-Si made him gulp down some wine as he cautioned, "Don't get too excited. This is only the first step toward our goal."

Panzi nodded, inhaled deeply, and began his descent. As he reached the first pillar that stuck out over the abyss, we all heard the popping sound of breaking ice and we stopped breathing for a second, hoping the frozen wood would stay in one piece. It held together; we released our breath in one big gust of gratitude.

Panzi continued to move forward, walking as if he were dancing to a song with an extremely slow beat. Our hearts kept pace with his careful steps as he reached the end of the protruding pillar. The cave lay far below him.

Lighting half a dozen flares at once, Panzi tossed them into the abyss; they floated down like shooting stars, becoming brighter and brighter as they fell. Uncoiling his rope into the darkness, Panzi followed the streaks of light, down to the tiled roof on the lower level of the palace shrine. He made it, gesturing to us that we should follow. One by one, we joined him on the rooftop.

We lowered ourselves down to the doorway of the palace shrine. Standing before it like a silent sentry was a big stone turtle. It guarded a door made of gleaming snow-white marble that was covered with carvings of birds with strange faces floating through clouds. Brass tiger heads glared menacingly from its top.

It was Fats who broke the spell that held us all motionless as we stared at the palace's entryway. Grabbing a crowbar, he began to pry the door open, wedged open a crack, and then stopped dead as we all pointed our flashlights into the shrine. The darkness within was so absolute that we could see nothing at all.

With a surprising touch of humility, Fats turned to Poker-face. "Would you please use your superior skills to check for traps, Zhang Qilin?"

Carefully Qilin ran his fingers over the door's carvings and looked puzzled. "I can't tell if there are any," he admitted. "All of you follow me. Don't get in front of me and don't talk."

We all knew that when this guy took the trouble to open his mouth, it was in our best interests to listen. We fell into single file, following as Qilin stepped over the high doorsill and entered into the shrine. We may be the first people to enter this place for the past thousand years, I thought, what could be waiting for us here?

15. THE KUNLUN EMBRYO

CHAPTER SIXTEEN

THE GRAND HALL

We had entered a grand hall with columns on either side, each about fifteen feet in diameter. Beyond them we could see a lamp, pitch-black, shaped like one that would be used by a genie. Our flashlights detected nothing else in the darkness that lay ahead of us.

"Let's get that lamp going," Fats whispered, taking some matches from his pocket. "No!" I hissed back, "Don't touch anything until Qilin tells us this place is safe."

We tiptoed cautiously, making not a sound except for our deep and heavy breathing. Soon we were at the center of the hall, where a jade platform sat, surrounded by giant copper pots shaped like birds with human heads. Above the platform was a huge black statue that was neither a man nor a Buddha, only a pillar covered with moss that grew in spirals. We all felt uneasy; only Chen Ah-Si and Qilin maintained any sort of calm.

What was this statue supposed to represent? I wondered. Why didn't this shrine have a statue of a god to worship or an image of the owner of the tomb? Instead, high above everything was something that looked like a worm. And then I remembered the words encoded on Monk Hua's bronze fish, that the Emperor Wannu of the Dong Xia was not human, but a monster. Was this thing what the fish referred to? If only I knew what information was encoded on my two fish, but somehow I was reluctant to bring them into public view.

"Look at what I found," Panzi called to me. He had climbed to the top of one of the copper pots and had found something inside it, which he held carefully in both hands. It was a little statue of a monkey, with a green face and long fangs, like a small demon. "It's made of bronze," he said as he held it out for our inspection.

We peered into all of the copper vessels and found that same monkey in each one. Obviously it was of personal importance to the tomb's occupant; why, we would probably never know.

"If this moss-covered pillar was worshipped by the people of this area, maybe these monkeys were intended to guard it," Monk Hua said. "It could all be explained by local legends if we could only hear them for ourselves."

Finding nothing else near the mysterious pillar, we moved further into the darkness. Fats began to curse quietly as we walked. "So far this trip has yielded nothing but headaches. I'm sure there's something we failed to notice—probably behind that lamp you wouldn't let me touch. Can't I go back and take a look at what might be there? I just have a hunch that it's the place we're looking for."

Qilin shook his head in refusal but took a flare from his bag, lit it, and tossed it behind the lamp Fats yearned to explore. As soon as the flare landed behind the lamp, it went out, as though it had been covered by a piece of black cloth.

"What the hell is going on?" Fats asked and Qilin whispered, "I have no idea."

"I tell you, I need to check this out," Fats argued. "Tie a rope around my waist if you think it's dangerous; anything I find I'll share with everybody."

"Don't be such an asshole. We're a team and we're going to stick together. It's what my uncle wanted and why he chose Grandpa Chen to lead us. Stick with us and shut the hell up, Fats," I told him.

"Great, you have everybody else on your side, even if you don't have any ideas that are worth a damn. I'll toddle along with you, Young Wu," Fats sighed. I watched him grin at me, knowing full well I couldn't trust this guy. Keep an eye on Fats, I told myself, which was something I'd been saying ever since I first met him in the cavern of the blood zombies.

At the end of the hall was a jade door inlaid with four white marble tablets. Carved centipede dragons coiled around the hinges and two guardian figures stood in bas-relief on each side. We pried it open and found yet another jet black tunnel that we were sure would lead us to the rear hall of the shrine.

Fats's eyes lit up when he saw the two dragons. "I saw dragons like that at an auction once. They went for two hundred million Hong Kong dollars. You know, this door doesn't look very heavy to me…"

"Forget it," I said firmly. "That was back in the days of the financial bubble. Now the most we'd get for this would be four hundred thousand—not worth it, Fats. Come on."

The two bronze fish in my pocket were worth twenty million dollars, I thought. But when the time comes to sell them, who's going to pay that kind of money? Nothing is going to sell for what it's worth anymore; our business is

16. THE GRAND HALL

going to go straight to hell. If we don't follow our trade for the love of adventure and discovery, we might as well give it up and start picking pockets instead.

Fats looked shattered by what I'd just told him and stared at the door, stupefied. We ignored him and walked down the tunnel toward the rear hall, where an entrance to the tomb is usually found. In other halls in the past we'd found a decorative coffin with longevity candles burning with a perpetual flame or sometimes a large number of burial offerings. Since this had been a tomb from an insignificant border kingdom that had been constantly at war, we didn't expect to find anything worth looking at in the hall, but we had to walk through it to get to the tomb.

The walls on both sides of the tunnel had been painted with murals that were now covered with ice. I turned my flashlight upon them to see what information these frigid pictures might hold. When I got a good look at them, I felt as though I'd been suddenly enveloped by the ice that held them in its grip.

Spiraling, twisting, soaring, coiling all over the walls, trapped under the ice, were paintings of centipede dragons soaring through the sky. The murals were packed solid with them, some accompanied by troops of soldiers who bowed down to the dragons, looking very small and insignificant in comparison to these flying monsters.

"Who do you think is buried here, the emperor's wife or one of his relatives or his closest minister? And why would the emperor choose to have so many dragons painted in these murals that lead to the tomb?" Ye Cheng asked.

None of us answered because none of us knew. But we

did know that in tombs of this sort, the murals usually depicted the life of the royal family or scenes from the emperor's court. If the emperor's tomb had murals of dragons in its hallway, that would be expected, but for his family or his ministers? It wasn't right; it didn't add up at all. And besides, there was no picture of the person who occupied this tomb. The only people shown were soldiers or slaves; there was no leader in any of the pictures—and that was so wrong it was absolutely eerie.

Fats suddenly asked, "Could these murals also be double-layered?"

I touched the wall. Some of the murals here had already eroded under the ice, and there was nothing beneath them. "No," I said, "that's not the answer."

Then there were no more murals. The tunnel ended with the entrance to the rear hall directly in front of us. No door barred the entrance but a lampstand that was half as tall as any of us, shaped like a crane, stood at the center of the opening.

We walked around the crane and into the hall, which was a small replica of the first one. Its walls were also covered with the murals of Centipede Dragons, scarlet when they were first painted but now frozen into a gray gloom.

The rear hall was absolutely empty except for the center of it where there were three black stone platforms. Each one held cracked and frozen wooden coffins with clouds carved along their edges. Behind the platforms was a slab of stone carved with two birds with human faces.

When the three coffins were carried into this tomb, they were placed here before they were interred. As was often the custom, two living members of the family had probably been buried along with the person who had died. Fats looked around and said, "This Emperor Wannu was so damned stingy. He was willing to spend money to build his subordinates' houses, but he wouldn't buy them any furniture. How were they supposed to be comfortable after death? He must have kept all the good stuff for himself."

Monk Hua snapped, "Don't talk nonsense. If he could build such an enormous tomb, why could he begrudge a few burial offerings? There has to be another reason why this hall is empty."

We searched the hall but found nothing. When we got to the slab behind the platforms, Fats said, "This has to be the sealing stone for the tomb," and did his best to move it away from the wall.

"It's too heavy—come give me a hand," he asked but Qilin said, "Wait, there could be a trap here."

He poked about and then breathed, "Safe." Panzi and Monk Hua joined Fats and slowly they moved the stone away. There was nothing behind it at all, only a depression in the brick floor where the slab had pressed down on it for centuries.

"What's going on here?" Panzi yelped. "All that work just to move a decoration?"

"That's impossible. The tomb entrance has to be here somewhere," Monk Hua said.

"Could it be covered under these bricks?" Ye Cheng asked.

"Oh, come on," Fats laughed. "There's no one here to stop us and imperial tombs don't come our way often. Let's just remove the bricks and see for ourselves."

All of us were sky-high from our racing adrenaline. Finding an underground tomb is exciting but opening a coffin is like being a little kid again, faced with a wrapped present. Even Qilin's eyes glinted for a second or two as he crouched down and pressed on both sides of one of the bricks with his long, sensitive fingers. Rapidly he jerked the brick out of the ground, making a small gap. Immediately we joined him with our pickaxes and began to remove every brick in the floor.

It was easy—too easy. There had to be something wrong here, some kind of a catch, I thought. I glanced at Qilin who was his usual poker-faced self.

We soon dug up the last brick; at the bottom of the pit we had excavated was a black stone covered with a tortoiseshell pattern.

"Is that the tomb-sealing stone?" Ye Cheng asked, red with excitement.

Monk Hua leaped to the bottom of the pit, pounded on the stone, and shook his head. Rapidly he dug all around it, revealing a black double-headed stone carved like a turtle. It was about the size of a square table that could seat eight people.

"Will you look at that?" he said, peering at the pattern on the turtle's shell. "There's a woman's face carved in this thing."

"What's going on here?" he continued. "This should be the entrance to a tomb but all that's buried here is a stone turtle."

"Let's move it away and see what's under that rock," Panzi suggested.

But there was no need to move the turtle. There was nothing under it, only black rock. We had come to the bottom of the cave.

Still Fats was determined to find more than we saw and

leaped into the pit. As soon as he landed, he yelled. The folding shovel that he had hung on his belt became stuck to the back of the turtle; he pulled it away but the minute he let go, the shovel returned to the rock.

"What the hell? Is this thing a magnet?" Fats yelled. He took out a coin and tossed it on the turtle's back. It stuck there as if it had been glued to the spot. "So here's our treasure—it's a giant magnet. We've found the tomb of a scrap metal collector."

"Let me see what's going on here," Chen Ah-Si snapped at Monk Hua. Ye Cheng helped the old man climb into the pit, close to the turtle. Pulling out a compass from his pocket, Chen Ah-Si brought it millimeters away from his eyes; then he cursed violently, dashed the compass to the ground, and crushed it under his foot. "We've been tricked," he muttered. "This entire shrine is one big trap and we fell for it."

CHAPTER SEVENTEEN

THE GAME OF GO

For the first time since I first saw him, I saw anger on Chen Ah-Si's face. The old man was engulfed in fury and it made me nervous. So apparently did this upset Monk Hua, who sidled up and murmured, "Sir, what's wrong?"

Chen Ah-Si kicked his broken compass. "This piece of stone has a magnetic force that has thrown us completely off the correct trail. Don't take my word for it; check it for yourself."

I pulled out my own compass. No matter which direction I turned, the compass needle swiveled in the direction of the black stone turtle. Under its power, the coordinates that our old leader had memorized and followed to guide us toward our goal became gradually more and more skewed by the magnetic force of this damned turtle. We were nowhere near the tomb we were seeking; the embryo cave under the ice dome was a trick to lure us off course.

This had to be the work of the feng shui genius, Wang Canghai, who a thousand years ago or more came up with this plan to keep us away from his Palace in the Clouds. It was as though we were playing a game of Go with a man long dead, who had beaten us before our first game had even begun. All of this time, thought, and energy wasted, I groaned inwardly, could we ever recoup what we had just squandered?

"We're finished," Monk Hua said, echoing my thoughts. "We're almost out of food, and we've definitely exhausted our strength. We'll have to go back to the village, rest, and replenish our supplies. By then, that other group will have already reached the tomb and stripped it bare. This expedition is a total failure and the worst thing is we have nobody to blame. We were outwitted—that's all."

"Well, why don't we just hurry back and return immediately? So we came the wrong way—so what?" Fats argued. "Ning's group is small; they can't possibly carry off everything they find. We can swoop in after they leave and scavenge whatever's left over."

His greed sent me into a rage that was almost as hot as Chen Ah-Si's fury. "Damn you, Fats," I roared at him. "My uncle may have lost his life trying to slow down Ning and her cohorts but that doesn't mean shit to you. My goal is to save Uncle Three if I can but all you can think about is treasure. You greedy bastard, shut up before I tear out your tongue and cram it down your throat."

Fats lunged at me, his hands reaching for my neck, but Ye Cheng grabbed him and held him back. "We have no time for this. Stop it right now."

"We're all disheartened by this failure," Monk Hua said. "But we need to use our energy to find a solution, calmly and without anger. Everybody settle down and start thinking."

"Who knows if we need a solution?" Fats blustered. "Who's to say that Ning and her group haven't fallen prey to a similar ruse? They could have gone off course too and been caught by to the border patrol. Let's hurry back to the village, get what we need, and return, without wasting any more time. So what if we were tricked; let's face up to it and stop blathering."

Panzi immediately shook his head. "Easier said than accomplished, you fat blowhard. Even if we did go back without losing our way, which is quite probable considering that our trail has been erased by the blizzard, how many of us would have the strength to turn right around and come back without a good night's sleep? Young Master Wu is right; the delay that you advocate would turn Master Three's plan into a pointless exercise."

Fats turned bright crimson and exploded like a human volcano. "Master Three! Master Three! Fuck Master Three! You guys don't even know what that old bastard had in mind so stop the bullshit. What do I care about your family problems? I came to find treasures in tombs; I don't give a damn for anything else. When I get what I came for, I'm out of here and the rest of you can go straight to hell."

He threw his backpack over his shoulders, turned on his flashlight, and stormed toward the tunnel. Before he had taken three steps, Qilin stood in front of him, blocking his path.

Fats wasn't so crazed with rage that he was willing to attack the man who frightened us all, but his mouth still ran away with him. "Damn it! Why do you want to keep me from getting rich? Just what's wrong with that? You know I'm a grave robber—we all are, aren't we?"

"Don't you think this is a little strange?" Qilin asked mildly. "Ever since we reached this spot we've all been upset and troubled. Even our quiet intellectual Wu has lost his temper, which I've never seen him do before."

17. THE GAME OF GO

Everyone turned to look at me, even Fats. I felt my anger ebb away. My pulse rate slowed and my fists loosened. Qilin was right. I had lost my temper with Fats only once before when I was under a magic spell in the cavern of the blood zombies. What had caused it this time? This wasn't like me at all.

And for that matter, Fats's own reaction to my anger was way over the top. Never before had he spoken that way about my uncle or about anyone else for that matter. Even when Ning had annoyed him in the undersea tomb, his threats to her were always more jocular than dangerous.

Were we all being affected by where we stood? And what could cause this? We were in a dark and confined place, true, but that was nothing new for a bunch of grave robbers. What was wrong with this place?

"You're right," Fats said to Qilin, in his normal tones. "We really did go berserk over nothing. What's going on?"

"I'm not sure," Qilin replied slowly, "but I don't think this trap is as simple as a strong magnet. I think…" He paused as though searching for the right words. "Wang Canghai spent so much time and effort on setting up this place. I think it's going to be difficult to get out now that we're caught inside his trap."

I could feel the rage rise within me again but took several slow deep breaths before I asked, "What should we do?"

Qilin and Chen Ah-Si exchanged a silent look before Qilin responded, "We need to take this step by step without jumping to any conclusions. But first of all we have to destroy this magnet. Then we have to make sure there are no replicas of it in here, or else we'll never find the correct direction."

We were all happy to have an excuse to be destructive; it was a way to get rid of our fury. We hated this damned turtle and obliterating it would be sheer pleasure.

As we approached it with our axes, Chen Ah-Si shouted, "Stop and think this through. If you smash this thing, all you're going to do is make a thousand tiny magnets, all of them confusing our compasses. If you want to destroy this turtle, fire is the only weapon that will work."

Opening one of our camp stoves, we poured its fuel over the turtle. Fats lit a cigarette, took a long puff, and then hurled it toward the black stone. It was immediately engulfed in fire; the force of the heat drove us back. The flames soared and then began to die down, leaving a red-hot turtle resting on steaming bricks.

Taking out my compass, I found that the needle no longer was drawn in the direction of the turtle; its magnetic power was gone. We all walked through the hall, compasses in hand. No magnets made their presence known and we were sure it was safe to leave.

Qilin's words lingered with me and I wondered what we would find once we left this hall. What would do its best to keep us in here forever? I forced myself to stop thinking this way, and tried to remember that step by step was our plan of action. That my hunches were often accurate was a fact I did my best to ignore.

We began to make our way back down the tunnel when we all heard it. A strange cracking sound stopped us in our tracks. "It's coming from that damned turtle," Panzi said and we cautiously made our way back to it, clutching our axes as weapons.

There was the turtle, cracks all over its shell. As we came

closer, we saw a black vapor ooze out of the cracks, rise into the air, and become lost in the darkness overhead. Suddenly it reappeared as a solid, twisting, wriggling mass that took on the shape of the moss-covered pillar we had seen on the jade platform earlier, when we entered the grand hall.

We stared in wide-eyed panic but before we could react Qilin gestured that we keep silent. We all held our breath and listened as hard as we could. A rustling sound came from somewhere in the dark, so soft a noise that it was impossible to tell where it might be coming from. It was almost as though it was being beamed directly into our brains. We all stood frozen, our eyes fixed on the black shape before us. Our ears were filled by the rustling sound nearby; it grew more and more distinct until it began to echo in the empty hall.

Qilin grew pale, his eyes staring at the black mass of vapor that gathered above our heads. "There's something in that smoke," he whispered.

Monk Hua gasped, "It's Chong Xiang Yu that's come out of that turtle. Wang Canghai wants us dead!"

"Who or what is Chong Xiang Yu?" I asked.

No one answered me, but I knew I would find out very quickly. Qilin pointed to the tunnel. "Run, and don't look back! No matter what you feel on your body, don't stop! Run until you're out of here. Hurry up!"

CHAPTER EIGHTEEN
THE DEADLY CENTIPEDES

In the rare moments that Poker-face took the trouble to say something, I knew I needed to listen and do what he told me. Whatever was going on here seemed to be worse than anything else we'd come up against together. I swallowed my questions and started to race down the tunnel, beckoning for everyone to follow. Fats was already in the lead, far ahead of the rest of us.

We galloped down the tunnel, pushed open the jade door, and came out into the grand hall, where the rustling sounds were louder than ever. The noise was coming from the roof, as if hundreds of feet were creeping over the beams above our heads, but when we directed our flashlights upward there was only darkness. "Let's get the hell out of here," Panzi said and none of us argued with him.

We were all frightened and we fed on each other's panic. We ran for our lives from something we couldn't see, each at a different speed. Fats and Ye Cheng were so far ahead of the rest of us that we could barely make out the dots of light from their moving flashlights. Then they slowed down and when the rest of us caught up with them, we saw that the door that would take us outside had disappeared.

"Impossible," Monk Hua shouted. "We came along a straight tunnel with no diverging pathways. The door has to be right here."

"No," I replied, "Qilin was right. Wang Canghai plainly did not want us to get out of here alive."

"So what do we do?" Fats asked. "Let's search to the left."

"No point. The door has vanished. There's no need to waste our time and effort."

"Are we just going to starve to death here?" Ye Cheng asked.

"Fats, Qilin, and I have experienced these kinds of traps in the undersea tomb and we managed to find our way out," I assured him. "I'm fairly sure we can do the same thing here, if we pool our knowledge and experience. Wang Canghai was brilliant but he was human, not infallible. No matter how precise and careful his traps were, they have to contain a flaw or two. What frightens me is that he might not have intended to trap us, but to kill us. That strange noise above our heads is what we need to worry about—at the very least it could drive us completely out of our minds."

"Standing here is a bad idea," Monk Hua said. "Why don't we split into four groups and run in different directions? That way some of us are bound to get out and we won't be completely annihilated."

"Take a look around," Fats objected. "We aren't all here yet. We can't do anything until the rest catch up with us."

In our terror, we forgot to count heads. Panzi, Qilin, Chen Ah-Si, Lang Feng who carried Shunzi—all were missing and not a single beam of light approached us from the darkness.

I rubbed my forehead and tried to think. Panzi always

took up the rear of any group; it was part of his military training. Chen Ah-Si was an old man; of course he would lag behind and so would Lang Feng with a man on his back. And Qilin? He often disappeared to go off on his own—there was nothing abnormal about his absence.

Monk Hua and Ye Cheng looked lost without their leader, standing silent and confused. Fats of course began to shout with the force of a foghorn, "Panzi! Old Chen! Where are you guys?"

As his voice faded into the tunnel we heard Lang Feng screaming, "Holy shit, turn off your flashlights right now and look up!"

Turn off our flashlights? What sort of insanity was this? We'd already lost part of our group. What if we turned off our flashlights and still more of us disappeared? I glanced at Monk Hua with a questioning stare. He looked as confused as I was. It was Fats who switched off his light and said, "Listen to him. Turn them off and let's see what happens."

We all did and then quickly looked up at the ceiling. Gradually it took on a gleaming light with many small green spots twinkling above us like a sea of tiny stars.

"This is—a Fifty-Star Map?" I heard Monk Hua ask somewhere in the dark.

Fats, Qilin, and I had seen this before in the undersea tomb where the ceiling had been illuminated by the luminescence of pearl-like fish-eye gems. This looked quite a bit like a Fifty-Star Map but in this place, the lights were moving.

"We're going to make a fortune this time! So many glowing pearls!" Fats shouted.

"No, these aren't pearls or your fish-eye treasures either.

These things are moving and alive. They're insects," I said, my lips suddenly stiff with fear.

"Insects? What kind of insects?" Fats was probably thinking of the corpse-eating bugs that nearly devoured us on our first adventure. "Do you suppose they're fireflies?"

"No, fireflies flash. I don't—" Something itchy landed on my neck as I spoke; I reached up and felt a body, pinched it, and killed it. I couldn't see it, but I could feel a hell of a lot of legs. Turning on my flashlight, I took one look at what I had in my fingers and then dashed it to the ground in disgust.

It looked a lot like a centipede, about the length of the palm of my hand, with very long tentacles. Its slender body was divided into nine sections, with a green spot on each. Its legs were much longer than a normal centipede, each almost as long as its entire body, and there were so many of them that they looked like strands of hair sprouting from the insect's torso. I'd seen pictures of this thing before; it was a house centipede that could grow to the size of three feet, and it had always given me the creeps. Now that I saw one in real life, it made me feel even worse. Legend said that if it crawled on a person's body, whatever it touched would rot, and I used to have nightmares when I was young that these things crawled into my ears.

My head itched again—there was another centipede. I killed it quickly as I realized that the damned things were raining down upon us, covering the ground under our feet. They began to surround us from below, climbing up our boots.

Fats took out his washbasin to cover his head while he frantically struck at the ground with his shovel. Ye Cheng held his head and screamed. When I went to help him, I saw that several insects had already entered his ears. "Lower your head and shake it," I yelled at him and killed the centipedes as they crawled out.

The centipedes ran away as we fought them off but more and more continued to drop upon on us from the ceiling. We were crazed and almost overwhelmed when we heard a popping sound. A glow came from the genie's lamp in the grand hall, the insects rushed toward the light, and we could hear Shunzi shout, "Light a fire quickly. These things are attracted to heat. That's why they're falling on you."

Fats and I rushed to the lamp closest to us. Its oil had turned solid and we had to warm it with our cigarette lighters before it ignited. The centipedes clustered to it in swarms, crackling as the flames hit their bodies. Centipedes falling from the ceiling landed on the heat of the lamp instead of on us.

We ran in the direction of Shunzi's voice and found him sitting on the ground beside Lang Feng, who twitched and writhed without stopping. "The centipedes have reached his brain. I tried to dig them out of his ears but they burrowed in too quickly," Shunzi said, as he brushed the remaining centipedes from Lang Feng's tortured body.

"Can we save him?" I asked.

Shunzi shook his head and answered, "I'm not sure. Once someone in our village is hit by these things, we say his life is now in the hands of heaven. But I think he's done for."

Panzi cried out from the darkness, calling us to come to him. "We don't have time to talk right now—just tell me, is your head all right?"

Shunzi nodded. "What made me pass out anyway? All I can remember was you guys blowing up the mountain—hey! Where are we anyway?"

Fats immediately replied, "We were going to fire a salute to that sacred place—whoever expected there'd be an avalanche? Some rocks fell, hit your head, and you were knocked out. Then the snow carried us all to this place that looks like a temple. We're not sure what's going on either."

"We'll talk about this later," I said. "We need to get to Panzi now."

Fats and I tried to pick up Lang Feng to carry him over to Panzi. It was almost impossible for us to move him as he contorted and wriggled; as we struggled with him, I saw Fats frown. I looked to see what was bothering him and saw a gash on the back of Lang Feng's head. It looked as though someone had hit him hard.

What was going on? Had he been assaulted, not poisoned by the centipedes? I looked over at Shunzi, who was carrying Lang Feng's backpack. Before I could question him, Fats whispered, "Shh." Together we hoisted Lang Feng into our arms and trudged in Panzi's direction.

Only Panzi and Chen Ah-Si were there. "Where's Poker-face?" I asked.

Panzi said, "Isn't he with you? I didn't see him anywhere along the way."

Fats shouted into the surrounding darkness. His voice reverberated and circled for a long time around the spacious hall but no one answered. It was as if Poker-face had never come with us at all. When everything returned to silence, we heard no sounds of breathing or footsteps.

I already knew what had happened. Qilin was fine; no

18. THE DEADLY CENTIPEDES

danger would befall him with his power and talents. He must have had a special reason to disappear, as he had in the past. Or perhaps he found something that made him go off on his own. In any case, we couldn't make him return before he was ready, even if we knelt down and kowtowed to him.

Panzi and Fats called out a few more times, then turned on their flashlights and got ready to search. I stopped them, saying, "Don't wander off right now. Let's deal with the wounded first, and then we'll go together."

We all clustered around Lang Feng while Chen Ah-Si checked his injuries. I saw that the old man quickly noticed the wound on the back of Lang Feng's head but although he looked thoughtful, he said nothing. He glanced up at me assessingly and I realized that since Fats and I carried Lang Feng to him, he probably assumed we were the ones who had knocked him out, not Shunzi. Who knew how he would decide to deal with us later?

And what was Shunzi's reason for attacking Lang Feng and then suggesting we give him up for dead? Who was this guy anyway, other than a veteran soldier who served along the border? I didn't feel as though I should confront him; at the moment he was still my ally and I needed that. I was lost and puzzled and had no idea of what to do in the situation we were in now. Damn my uncle and damn Qilin for leaving us, I cursed silently.

Shunzi moved to Lang Feng and placed him on his side, then took some toothpicks from his pocket and poked them into Lang Feng's ears. He picked out the house centipedes that lurked within and threw them on the ground, where Fats promptly trampled them to death.

"Even though I removed those centipedes, there are many more still feeding on this man's brain," Shunzi told us. "Their poison will kill him soon."

"Where do you suppose these insects came from?" I asked.

"They must have been lying dormant in the roof tiles and were awakened by that Chong Xiang Yu smoke," Fats said. "What a filthy trick—but how in the hell could Wang Canghai have known that we would burn that magnetic turtle?"

"Easy answer there," I said. "Since the magnetic turtle was buried under the tomb's sealing stone, he intended for grave robbers to discover it and then destroy it. Whether it was burned or smashed, any kind of destruction would probably make the Chong Xiang Yu smoke volatile and arouse the house centipedes on the tile roof of the palace. But if it were discovered by someone who was respectful to the spiritual shrine and wouldn't wreak havoc on it, the security of the Palace in the Clouds would still be guaranteed by the power of the magnetic turtle."

Monk Hua took out a hypodermic needle and some medicine, which he injected it into Lang Feng's body. "This will keep him alive for a while," he said.

"Grandfather Chen," Panzi murmured, "this is a very powerful toxin that these insects carry. We'd better get out of here as soon as possible. If anyone else is stung, we won't have enough medicine to save them."

Chen Ah-Si frowned impatiently. Ye Cheng sighed and told Panzi about how the door had disappeared, trapping us yet again. "Are you sure?" Panzi asked. "Could we have taken a wrong turn somewhere?"

Before Ye Cheng could explain, Shunzi said, "How

strange." I looked up. The flame he had lit in the first genie lamp had gone out.

"Not so strange," I replied. "The oil in that lamp has been there for hundreds of years. We should be grateful it lasted as long as it did."

"Look again," he said stubbornly. The flame I had lit with Fats flickered as though a breeze had struck it, yet there was no wind in the grand hall.

"Something has walked past it," Shunzi breathed. It must be Qilin returning, I thought and opened my mouth to greet him. Fats clapped his hand over the bottom of my face; there was a shape of a man in the flickering flame and it was much too big to be Qilin.

Chen Ah-Si turned his head toward the figure, as though he heard something. He raised his hand and flung an object in the direction of the flickering lamp. It whooshed past the flame and made it flare into greater brightness; standing beside it was a figure with a neck like a giraffe's.

CHAPTER NINETEEN

THE CENTIPEDE DRAGON

After Chen Ah-Si's missile had whooshed past the flickering flame, the light dimmed again, and whatever we had seen became blurred in gloom once more. We stood in silent fear, hands on our knives.

Chen Ah-Si hissed, "Everyone stay calm" and beckoned to Monk Hua, who quickly extinguished the lamp that stood beside us. We were surrounded by a shroud of protective darkness while the light beside the shadowy figure was now much more powerful.

At first we were sure that what we saw was a man, but one with a neck like a giraffe or perhaps a goose, with tentacles of some sort on his body. The longer I stared, the more convinced I was that this wasn't a man at all but some kind of bird. I remembered the monsters that Wang Canghai had kept for his own amusement within the undersea tomb. Had he brought one here to serve as part of his mountain trap?

Whatever this was, it stood as motionless as a statue, too still to be a living creature. We remained immobile as well and silent until Fats whispered, "This isn't right—are we seeing a hallucination because we're running out of oxygen? Is it a shadow of a statue we didn't notice as we walked through the hall earlier? Or could it be a ghost of some kind, whose spirit is imprisoned in this damned place?"

A year ago I would have scorned any talk of ghosts or evil spirits, but in those days I didn't believe in zombies or sea monsters either. Now I had seen enough zombies to fill up a couple of mahjong tables and I wasn't sure that we weren't looking at a ghost. Fats had a point—if this thing were alive, it would move at least a trifle. Even zombies had to breathe.

And if it were alive, wouldn't the centipedes have attacked it by now? Nothing could stand still under their assault. I pointed this out to Fats who said, "Then let's stop admiring this thing and sneak up on it. If he's human, we'll knock him down and beat the hell out of him." He began to creep toward the light with the rest of us close behind him.

As I drew near the lamp, I felt a strong feeling that something dreadful waited there. Slowing my steps, I retreated into the shadows and moved after my companions at a snail's pace, feeling sure that whatever was near that lamp was something I didn't want to see. Then I did see it.

It was a gigantic centipede with a body like a snake, coiled around the lamp, its jaw gaping open as it inhaled the vapor from the gas that fueled the light. It looked exactly like the carving of the Centipede Dragon that we had seen before we found this place, and like the ones in the murals in the tunnel. Was this creature what the Dong Xia people had turned into a deity and worshipped?

I heard someone mutter, "Move back," and I was more than happy to obey. I stepped back further and further, unable to take my eyes from the monster. I stopped somewhere in the darkness of the great hall with no idea of where I was. I only knew I was alone.

I could hear scurrying legs in the dark, sounding as though they were coming closer each second. I switched on my flashlight and saw Monk Hua some distance away lighting a flare.

"Turn off your flashlights," he called, "and don't anyone light a lamp. Come toward me as fast as you can, all of you."

"If we light the lamps, we'll see where this dragon is— why not take advantage of them?" Fats shouted.

"Because the gas in the lamps is filled with Chong Xiang Yu which these monsters feed on—more illuminated lamps will attract more of these damned things. Do as I say and come here," Monk Hua yelled back.

We all gathered around him, panting heavily. "Here we are. What's your plan?" Fats demanded.

"We have some dynamite left over. We're going to blow this thing to pieces."

"Great idea—who's going to be the bait to lure this thing close enough to the dynamite that will blow it to hell? Will you be the glorious sacrifice, Brother Scar-face?" Fats sneered.

"Don't worry; that's all taken care of. I found a volunteer." Monk Hua's voice turned cold. I looked at the men standing around and me and cried out, "Where's Lang Feng?"

Then an explosion tore through the darkness and a mass of blinding light flashed before our eyes. We threw ourselves to the quaking floor as wood chips rained about us.

I raised my head as soon as the world around us stopped shaking. A cavernous hole was blasted in the floor; within it a fire burned brightly. I could see the twitching body of the Centipede Dragon and its shattered head. Lying close by was a leg, an arm, and some tattered fabric that had clothed Lang Feng. His unconscious body was what our monk had tied the dynamite to; Lang Feng had provided the bait.

I looked at Monk Hua and Chen Ah-Si. Their faces were calm, as though nothing unusual had taken place.

Chen Ah-Si came to my side and muttered, "Don't look so shocked, Young Master Wu. Your grandfather, or your uncle for that matter, would have done the same thing. And if I had been in Lang Feng's place I would have expected Monk Hua to use me this way. You need to remember, in our business it's three steps before and four steps after."

I knew what he meant. I'd read this saying in my grandfather's notebook. Every decision a grave robber made when underground was a matter of life or death. It had to be thought about three times before doing it and four times afterward. Nothing was impulsively done; everything was remembered as a lesson in the future.

It was quite possible that Lang Feng wouldn't have gotten out of this place alive; he was in a coma and carrying his heavy body would have endangered us all. And yet his death still seemed barbaric to me and Chen Ah-Si's calm justification of it made me sick.

I can't think about this until we get to a place where ethics make sense, I told myself, and forced myself to be as outwardly emotionless as the old killer who stood beside me.

The fire from the explosion began to burn out and we walked to the pit, trying to avoid looking at any fragments that had once been Lang Feng. Fats grabbed me by the shoulder. "Forget about this," he whispered. "Who knows what Lang Feng had done to deserve this kind of death? These guys are all animals, even the monk."

A cold wind blew up from the pit, a strong gust of fresh air; it came from outside, we knew. And that meant that this hole could provide an exit that might have no centipedes, if we did some digging.

Without a word, Fats jumped into the crater, followed by Monk Hua. "Do you suppose it's safe to excavate here?" Fats asked and I replied, "We have no choice. Just be cautious. The explosion may have weakened this place to the point that the whole thing could collapse."

Taking out our rope, we tied one end to one of the hall's massive columns, with the other end tied around the waists of Fats and Monk Hua. We all made sure our packs were securely strapped to our backs so no matter what happened we wouldn't lose our gear. Then each of us grabbed onto the rope as if our lives depended on it.

Taking out his pickax, Fats began to tap on the rock beneath his feet. With the first tap, the stone cracked and gave way, engulfing Fats's left leg all the way up to his thigh.

"Shit," he yelled as he struggled to pull his leg back to the surface. He brought it up as far as his knee and screamed, "Something's pulling me," as his body began to slide away from us.

Monk Hua grabbed his hands and we all came down to pull him to safety but his foot stuck fast as though something held him from below. Ye Cheng directed his flashlight into the crack in the stone and there was a green hand, firmly attached to Fats's ankle.

19. THE CENTIPEDE DRAGON

CHAPTER TWENTY
THE MEZZANINE

Brandishing a shovel, Panzi shoved it into the crack in the rock and began to batter frantically at the green hand, as Fats kicked and squirmed within its grasp. "Careful, damn you, you're going to amputate my foot with your shovel," he screamed.

"Keep dancing around down there and I'll cut off your whole leg, you fat idiot," Panzi roared back.

"Can I please have a replacement here?" Fats yelled. "This guy has always hated my guts and he's taking this opportunity to kill me while pretending to be a hero."

Ye Cheng and Monk Hua both jumped down to help, but Ye Cheng broke through the rock and landed right beside Fats. Monk Hua reached out to grab him but instead hit my hand that held onto Fats. I lost my grip and Fats plunged down to the next platform, like a giant dumpling dropped into a stew.

Then everything around us began to quake violently. All of us slid down after Fats, landing on a floor below, with bricks and rock crashing around us. We were on a platform that had been built below the shrine, protruding from the side of the cliff. Only the rope we had secured ourselves to had kept us from plummeting to the ground far, far below.

We could hear Monk Hua calling through the darkness, "Fats, where are you? Is that green hand that still holding onto your foot?"

Fats was under a pile of bricks, rocks, and all of us. His groans were loud and pitiful. "It's still hanging on, but now it's clenched onto my thigh. Hurry up, damn it and get me free of this thing."

Those of us who were lying on the top of the pile hurled all the stones and bricks we could reach over the edge of the platform. At last we were able to reach Panzi, freeing him first, then Monk Hua and finally Fats, his face red with rage and pain.

"Having you guys sprawled on top of me was like Death by a Thousand Cuts, a slow and painful homicide. Be more careful next time, won't you?"

"Where's that thing that you had on your foot?" Panzi asked.

Fats shook his leg, and then felt it cautiously. "It's gone! Although with a fall like mine, that's not surprising. It's probably at the bottom of the mountain by now."

"It could still be nearby," Monk Hua warned. "Take out your flashlights and let's all have a look."

Ye Cheng was the first to beam a light on our surroundings. He pointed it in my direction and its rays nearly blinded me.

"Would you move that damned thing out of my eyes?" I grumbled, but then I saw the expression on Ye Cheng's face. Reluctantly I turned to see what made him look so scared.

Less than a foot away from my nose was a wrinkled face with a green and purple complexion, as though it had been badly bruised. Without thinking, I grabbed a nearby brick and smashed it into this thing, then scurried as far from it as I could.

By now everyone had pulled out their flashlights and I could see spaces like alcoves in the cliff, each one containing a shrivelled, green-and-purple-fleshed mummy. They were placed close together, all of them sitting cross-legged as though they had frozen to death while meditating. There seemed to be hundreds of them, all staring at me. I screamed and Ye Cheng crumpled into unconsciousness.

I glanced to where the face had been next to me; I saw a crushed and broken body of one of the mummies. Close to where Fats stood was a severed hand, dessicated and curved in the shape of a hook. "It's frozen solid, hard as any rock," Fats announced as he picked it up for a closer look.

"Terrified by a chunk of ice, were you?" Panzi asked. "Quite the grave-robbing hero, aren't you, fat boy?"

"If you'd been brave enough to go into that pit first, the way I did, you'd know for yourself what that damned thing felt like. But since you let me take care of you, you'll never have a clue of what it is to be a hero," Fats muttered. It was clear that he and Panzi weren't destined to become best buddies, at least not in this life.

We looked about, flashlights in hand, and Panzi asked Monk Hua, "Why are there so many dead people here? I've never seen anything like this before."

"By the looks of it, this should be the platform that held bodies to be sacrificed during the burial ceremony. But this...I don't understand it at all. No imperial tombs of any dynasty look like this one...what kind of people were these corpses?" Monk Hua replied.

The bodies made me sick but I suppressed my nausea and pointed my flashlight toward one of them. A layer of ice enclosed the green and purple corpse. His face was wrinkled but well preserved, eyes closed and mouth wide open to display long, sharp fangs.

"These things can't be human," Fats said. "Look at those teeth. If one of these guys kissed a girl, they'd tear off her face in the process."

"Not human?" Ye Cheng had regained consciousness but when he heard this, he looked ready to pass out again. "What are these things then? Monsters?"

"They could be yeti, abominable snowmen, except they don't have hair," Fats babbled.

"Bullshit," Monk Hua argued. "What the hell are you talking about? The teeth of these corpses were sharpened by hand; that was a crucial part of shamanism in ancient times, until people began to wear sharp-fanged masks instead. One thing is for sure. These men were neither Jurchen nor Mongolian—just look at their bodies. They were wrapped in linen for an ice burial."

I remembered the bodies entombed in the glacier ice that we had seen the night we had camped beside the Small Sacred Mountain. I said, "Could these be the corpses of previous generations that were dug out from the glacier burial site when Wang Canghai built this mausoleum?"

Monk Hua nodded. "Absolutely. This cave might have been a cemetery in the past where local ancestors performed their glacial burials, but then was transformed to a false sacrificial burial tomb by Wang Canghai. These corpses must have been discovered during the excavation stage of the project."

Fats asked, "If that's what happened then why didn't Wang Canghai burn the corpses? What role did he want these bodies to play here?"

"Who knows? You see how creepy these mummies are? There are many shamanist ceremonies that depend upon corpses. The arrangement here might be related to shamanic spells and witchcraft; eerie things might happen as a result. Maybe these corpses are why we couldn't get out of here a few minutes ago. We have to be very careful."

I thought of the array of corpses Lao Yang and I had found on our way to the bronze tree of death, and the piles of pale bodies we had seen in the cavern of the blood zombies. Expeditions in which the bronze fish were involved always seemed to lead us to places that held a multitude of dead bodies—was black magic to blame for this?

Shamanism isn't really a religion but a kind of aboriginal witchcraft combined with the worship of spirits, augmented by psychotropic plants and healing herbs. I knew very little about it, except what I'd seen in old movies about the Qing dynasty. But I knew that shamanic powers had gradually faded away into history, with some of them living on in the tantric practices of Tibetan Buddhism.

I had been taught that shamanism was evil superstition and I knew that it was part of the She people's Gu ceremonies. Could there be some link between the ceremonies at the bronze tree of death and the ones in this place?

Monk Hua saw the confused look on my face as I puzzled over what surrounded us and said, "This is all speculation, you understand. All I really am certain of is that we have to get out of here as soon as we can. Let's spread out to cover as much area as possible and start to look for an exit."

20. THE MEZZANINE

We all agreed and began searching for a way out of this corpse-laden cliff. I found nothing and was ready to turn back when I heard Panzi shout, "Damn you, Fats, what in the hell are you up to now?"

We turned to see what was going on and saw Fats squatting among the corpses. His mouth was wide open and his face had taken on a green and purple tinge; he almost blended in with the bodies that surrounded him. Weirdest of all was that for the first time since I had met him, Fats had absolutely nothing to say for himself.

CHAPTER TWENTY-ONE

THE CHANNEL

"Quit playing around, Fats," Panzi yelled again. "You're not funny, as usual."

Fats remained silent. Panzi scowled as he turned to us and said, "For once he's not kidding. There's something weird going on here. He looks just like one of the mummies."

"Why aren't any of the rest of us affected by whatever has Fats going on? Let's go take a look at him and make sure this isn't one of his little games," I suggested. We all walked toward him. As we came near, Panzi held up his hand to stop us, then motioned toward Monk Hua who nodded in response. Both of them unsheathed their knives and moved slowly toward Fats, who stayed as silent and unmoving as a display mannequin in a shop window.

When they were close enough that they could have tapped Fats on his shoulder, they stopped in their tracks and walked back toward us. "We're in trouble. There's something wrong with the mummy that's directly behind our fat friend. We all need to check this out together."

Again Panzi and Monk Hua approached Fats, with the rest of us right behind them. Panzi wasn't exaggerating; the corpse behind Fats had a head three times the size of any of the other mummies. From its mouth extended a long tongue that was coiled like a boa constrictor around Fats's thick neck.

"What in the hell is that?" I gasped.

"If this were a real tomb and not a trap, I'd say this was a corpse corral that is guarding the entry to the tomb treasures, but why would there be one in a fake tomb?" Monk Hua said. "Unless of course it's an interlocking chain."

This was a term used among grave robbers for something that is real which has been made to appear fake, and then to seem real again but with a few obvious flaws. Those who find the flaws will look through the "real" exterior to the internal fraud, without going further to discover the object is actually not a fake at all.

Chen Ah-Si snapped, "Of course! Wang Canghai almost fooled us. If this fat idiot hadn't blundered into his corpse corral we would have left here never knowing it was the entry point we have been seeking all along."

"What do you mean?" I asked.

"Don't you remember when we discovered the magnetic turtle and we decided our compasses had led us in the wrong direction, that this tomb was a fraud? Actually the magnetic turtle was fake; we were in the right spot all along. This corpse corral is the giveaway; it's not needed unless there's truly treasure somewhere nearby. The tomb is real but it's not a Three-Headed Dragon." Chen Ah-Si looked at me triumphantly as he finished his explanation. "It's all feng shui; do you understand?"

It wasn't completely clear to me but I had a faint glimmer of what he meant. I sighed as I realized how close we had come to being outwitted by a man who had been dead for a thousand years.

Panzi whispered impatiently, "Enough feng shui, damn it. What are we going to do about Fats? It can't be good for him to have that tongue wrapped around his throat. How are we going to rescue him this time?"

We all stood in silent frustration; none of us knew what to do.

"Look, he's moving!" Ye Cheng yelled. He was talking about the mummy, who had begun to crawl away, using its hideous tongue to drag Fats along with it. There was no resistance at all from Fats; it was as though he had been immobilized by a blanket of ice.

We began to run after him, and the mummy picked up its pace. It was heading for the edge of the platform, which meant certain death for Fats. The mummy scrambled onto the cliff beyond and it and Fats began to roll down the rocky slope. We followed, sliding down the surface of the cliff as though we were on a steep slide in a children's playground.

We skidded for thirty feet or more, with Fats in plain sight ahead of us. Suddenly he disappeared. Rushing to where we last saw him, we found a tunnel on the side of the cliff with Fats's legs protruding from its entrance, like two tree trunks.

Panzi leaped onto Fats, grabbing his feet and pulling with all of his strength. The rest of us joined him, Monk Hua holding a rope that he tied to one of Fats's legs. The only way this mummy was going to get Fats would be if it tore him in two.

We finally managed to pull Fats from the tunnel, popping him out like a champagne cork, but the tongue came with him, coiled so tightly around his throat that it had cut deeply into his skin. Fats was a shade of deep purple, his eyes were rolled up into his head, and his breathing was a series of shallow little whines that gave him little oxygen.

Pulling out his knife, Panzi stabbed swiftly at the tongue; from the tunnel below came the shrill scream of a woman. Split in two pieces, the tongue released Fats from its grip and slid in a stream of blood back down through the tunnel's entrance.

I began pushing on Fats's chest; his body began to move. He coughed and panted air back into his lungs while rubbing his neck with both hands.

"That thing could come back up," Panzi observed, peering into the tunnel. He swept the darkness with his flashlight for several long minutes and then announced, "It's gone; we're safe."

Only then did we begin to laugh, pounding Fats on his back. He looked pale and almost delicate as he croaked, "Thank you all," then turned to Panzi and muttered, "Especially thanks to you, hero."

"How did this happen to you?" I asked Fats. "You were as motionless as a statue of the Buddha."

"I have no idea," he replied. "First I felt a cool touch on my neck and all of a sudden I couldn't move at all. I could see and hear everything but I was paralyzed. I couldn't even fart. It was horrible, like being buried alive."

Panzi laughed. "From the sound of the shriek we heard just now we know this is a female mummy. Maybe she was lonely and when she saw you were her type, she decided to carry you off and keep you around for fun and games— that's the kind of woman who's truly the date from hell."

Fats smiled, reached out to give Panzi a slight shove, and said, "Bullshit—you're the one she really wanted. The two of you look exactly alike."

Laughing, Panzi took a step back to avoid Fats's push. None of us saw the mummy's head rise out of the tunnel, its injured mouth dripping blood, until it had already grabbed Panzi by the leg and dragged him down out of our sight.

21. THE CHANNEL

CHAPTER TWENTY-TWO
DOWN THE DRAIN

By the time we reached the tunnel's opening it was too late; we couldn't even see a trace of Panzi's shadow. I rushed forward, ready to leap down into the darkness, but Fats was already there ahead of me. Knife drawn, rope secured to his ankle, he hurtled down into the tunnel. Before I could follow, Monk Hua grabbed me. "Don't be foolish," he said. "There's only room for two guys in that space, especially when they're the size of Fats and Panzi."

I peered down into the tunnel, saw nothing, and could hear only the slithering noise of Fats making his way to the bottom. Then the rope stopped and quivered violently. "Pull!" Fats bellowed.

We all grabbed on tight and pulled on the rope as hard as we could; up to the surface came Fats and Panzi, with the monster's jaws still firmly clamped on Panzi's leg.

"Out of the way," Chen Ah-Si ordered as he moved inches away from Panzi, pistol in hand. He fired at the monster's head; it retreated back into its lair, shrieking in pain and anger, and we pulled Fats and Panzi to safety.

We all backed far away from the tunnel entrance, except for Monk Hua who stood waiting beside it with a shovel in his hand. When the monster reappeared he struck it hard, sending it screaming back into the darkness.

"You see," Fats grinned at Panzi, "she likes you best."

Panzi was shaking too hard to manage a smile. "Don't talk about it. We're even now, okay?"

Monk Hua waved his hand. "This tunnel is weird. What did you guys see when you were down there?"

Fats replied, "I didn't bring a flashlight so I didn't see anything. But I touched some rocks; I'd say this tunnel is man-made."

All of us looked at the entrance with less terror and more interest, pointing our flashlights into it for a better look. It was deep, and we could see signs of chiseling on the edges of the opening, which confirmed Fats's theory. There was no trace of Panzi's admirer.

"Looks a little like a cellar opening in the north," Fats remarked. "Could this be where the workmen kept their cabbages when they were building this place?"

Monk Hua ignored him. "There's a wind blowing out of this tunnel. The shaft goes through the mountainside to the outside world."

Fats asked, "Maybe this is the back door that goes to the Palace in the Clouds—like the secret passage that you guys talked about? Let's go down and have a look—and if we run into that monster, we'll send it to hell for you, Panzi."

"No," Monk Hua objected. "This tunnel is more complicated than it seems. I'm sure this was built as an escape route that the workmen made secretly, so they could save themselves when they were buried alive after they finished the tomb. I think this leads to nothing

22. DOWN THE DRAIN

but the world outside. The good thing is, if my theory is correct, this tunnel will contain no traps. No one would place deadly hazards on an escape route."

Monk Hua's theory appealed to me. I was more than ready to get back outside and resume our journey. If this tunnel could get us closer to the Palace in the Clouds without forcing us to retrace our steps, I was all for it. I no longer trusted Shunzi after what he had done to the man who had carried him on his back for hours; if we went back with him to his village for more supplies, he would probably betray us. I was certain that by now he had figured out that we were grave robbers, not sightseers.

Fats felt the same as I did, Panzi was still too shaken to make a decision, and Ye Cheng was terrified of encountering the monster again.

Turning to Chen Ah-Si, Monk Hua asked, "What's your opinion, sir?" There was no response. Chen Ah-Si sat, eyes closed, silent, and motionless.

"Come on, wake up," Fats said, tapping him on the shoulder. Chen Ah-Si swayed under the touch, but his eyes remained shut.

Monk Hua rushed over, grabbed the old man's hand, and looked stunned. Fats placed his hand on Chen Ah-Si's throat. "He's dead," he gasped.

We all approached cautiously. I touched the old man's wrist; I couldn't find a pulse. His arm was as stiff and unmoving as an ice sculpture.

"Is he dead or suffering from hypothermia? He's ninety after all; perhaps he's just in shock," I suggested.

Monk Hua frowned as he lifted the old man's eyelids and pointed the flashlight into his eyes. He shook his head without saying a word and sank to the ground, holding his head in his hands. And then we all knew Chen Ah-Si had died.

"My grandfather died suddenly, just like this," I said. "We were all at the dinner table; one minute he asked for some wine and then he was dead. My father told us that many grave robbers' hearts were damaged because they had been exposed to so much bad air within the tombs. When they grow old, many of them die this way, which isn't really so bad. After all, it's the most comfortable death."

Nobody replied. We were all lost in confusion. With Chen Ah-Si dead, what would become of our expedition? Without him, Ye Cheng and Monk Hua were under no obligation to stay with us. And as for Panzi, Fats, and me, we were leaderless. Qilin had disappeared, I was inexperienced, and the thought of being under the guidance of Fats or Panzi made me nervous.

My thoughts were interrupted by hands gripped around my neck. Standing before me was Chen Ah-Si, his eyes staring vacantly as he choked the breath out of me.

"Zombie!" Fats yelled. "Somebody get the black donkey's hoof to strip him of his power."

I tried to pull away but the old man's clasp on my throat was astoundingly strong, clutching me like a pair of pliers. "Get the damned donkey's hoof now," I choked.

With these words, I could feel the hands on my neck release their hold and then give me a hard shove. "What the hell are you talking about?" Chen Ah-Si asked.

I stared at him; he looked completely normal. If it weren't for the others looking as befuddled as I was, I would have thought the attack was a hallucination on my part.

Monk Hua broke the silence. "Old Sir, are you okay? What happened just now...?"

Chen Ah-Si glanced at him, lit a cigarette, and said coldly, "Don't worry. When it's time for me to die, I won't go that easily."

CHAPTER TWENTY-THREE

ENTERING THE TUNNEL

We gathered around the edge of the tunnel's opening and explained Monk Hua's proposal to Chen Ah-Si. "Let's do it," he agreed, "but give it some thought before we plunge in."

The angle of descent was very steep and when Panzi tossed a flare into the opening it rapidly disappeared. This seemed to bear out Monk Hua's theory that the tunnel led between two mountains and was built in a V shape, going sharply down and then back up in the same fashion.

Panzi wanted to be the first one to go down into the tunnel to recover his loss of face after being abducted by the monster. "Don't worry," he told us, "I have my knife unsheathed and ready so if that bitch comes at me again, I'll do away with her in a couple of seconds."

We tied a rope around Fats's thick waist and dropped it down into the depths below. Panzi spat on his hands and slid from view; soon we heard him bellow, "It's okay—come down!"

We climbed down one by one, with Fats securing the rope to a nearby rock and rapidly joining us. The only trace of the monster that we could see was a puddle of dark liquid, more like water than blood.

"Keep your eyes open. That thing could be anywhere," Monk Hua warned.

We continued our descent down a passageway that became more constricted and narrower the deeper we went. The darkness became almost absolute; it swallowed up the rays of our flashlights while revealing nothing. Suddenly the space ahead of us came to an end, leaving a gap just wide enough for a man to enter if he were standing sideways.

"What the hell happened to the secret escape route of the workmen? Were they all small enough that they could make it through this crevice without any trouble? And how am I going to get through that tiny crack without tearing off most of my skin?" Fats grumbled.

"It's a volcanic cave," Monk Hua explained, "and they always begin with an underground tunnel that leads to a larger passageway. This crevice will widen as we go further into it, don't worry."

We all squeezed our way through, sucking in our stomach muscles and sidling along like crabs, Fats cursing eloquently. The surrounding blackness was so thick that our flashlights were useless and my old fear of being in the dark crept into my thoughts once more. We moved slowly, placing our feet as carefully as dancers would, and in less than a quarter of an hour every muscle in our bodies screamed with pain. But as we went on, the crevice gradually widened as Monk Hua had promised, allowing us to walk normally again. In several more hours we reached the wide and spacious corridor that he had predicted.

When we stopped to rest, I calculated the approximate distance we had walked and the gradient of the slope, discovering that the altitude we had now reached was already below the snow line. We might even be at the bottom of the valley between the two peaks. If we had walked on the surface of these two peaks, it would have taken us at least eight hours even if we traveled in a straight line—we'd saved a lot of precious time by walking underground through this tunnel.

Crude stone steps were carved into the rock ahead of us, which indicated we had reached the second part of the V. Perhaps at the end of this primitive stairway was the Palace in the Clouds. We connected ourselves in a long line with our climbing rope and set off, trying to keep our excitement from interfering with the caution we needed. Slowly we began to scale the steep and narrow little steps.

Fats had feet like an elephant and keeping his balance on these tiny stone ledges was so difficult that soon his legs were trembling with strain. The rest of us weren't much better off. I felt as though we were mountaineering our way up Everest, and forced myself not to look down at the dark abyss from which we had come. For hours we moved upward, one foot on a rock the size of a girl's hand and the other dangling in midair. There was no place to rest and we climbed in a dazed stupor, with no idea of when this ordeal would be over.

As we climbed we could hear waterfalls around us and the dim beams of our flashlights revealed several splashing rivulets, all of them covered with steaming vapor. "Hot springs," Fats sighed happily. "Let's wash up a little, shall we?"

"Don't even think about doing that," Shunzi warned us. "Look over there."

At first glance we saw nothing, but then lines on the

rocks nearby that looked like volcanic patterns suddenly took on a familiar shape—house centipedes were everywhere we looked, all of them dead motionless.

"What's going on here?" Fats whispered. "Is this the nesting ground for these bloodsuckers?"

"Everything that's alive in these mountains congregates around the hot springs—even leeches. The house centipedes are in a dormant state at this time of year. Only a very strong stimulus will rouse them. Hurry up; we'll be safe once we get past this section of the stairway," Shunzi hissed back.

We resumed our climb; tiptoeing, Fats asked, "What do you mean by a very strong stimulus?"

"Shut up," Shunzi murmured. "And nobody move."

We all stood like wooden carvings as Shunzi stared into the void below; a familiar rustling sound turned my spine to a long chain of ice cubes. It was the sound of countless legs rubbing against the rocks as they approached us.

"Turn off your flashlights," Shunzi said softly.

The minute our lights went out, everywhere we looked was full of thousands of green lights, big and small, surrounding us like a sea of stars twinkling magically in the darkness. For a second I felt as though we were lost in a galaxy, adrift in the universe. Then I looked down, following Shunzi's stare. Below us was a long green glowing line of house centipedes, looking like emerald tassels on a gigantic curtain of blackness, millions of them, on every surface within sight.

CHAPTER TWENTY-FOUR

THE VOLCANIC CRATER

Out of the darkness came Shunzi's voice. "My people worship this insect as though it were a god because it can live for a very long time. After one of them dies, its dead body attracts many of its own kind. So be especially careful as you walk—don't step on any of them. Not only will squashing one be disgusting, it will lead to our deaths."

Then he turned on his flashlight and the sea of green stars immediately vanished into the darkness once again.

We continued to climb as calmly and slowly as we could; as we passed through the area with the hot springs, the centipedes became fewer and fewer until they were completely gone. Once we no longer had to worry about stepping on them, we picked up some speed, but still the darkness above us seemed limitless. Our journey stretched forward without an end in sight.

Fats asked as he climbed, "Grandpa Chen, let me ask you something. What is that Coffin Carried by Nine Dragons that you talked about back at the train station and that I haven't heard you mention since?"

Chen Ah-Si stopped and glanced at him. Then he looked at Monk Hua who explained, "We don't know what it is either. All the information we have is gathered from the bronze fish. It might be a long-forgotten form of burial. The original text seems to say that Emperor Wannu's coffin was carried by nine dragons that guarded his body so that no one could come near him. But the Jurchen dialect is so obscure now that I don't know if my translation really is at all accurate."

"Perhaps this is metaphorical and is really only something like nine dragons carved on the bottom of the coffin," Fats said. "If there really were a dragon, then we could make a fortune. We could catch it, bring it back, and put it in the Imperial Palace. I guarantee there'd be a huge crowd. The ticket sales alone would make us several million."

"All you can think about is money," I scoffed. "Only a Monkey King could really catch a dragon and I've never seen a Monkey King with a body as fat as yours."

Outraged, Fats bellowed, "So what if I'm fat? I rely on my body fat wherever I go. I shake my body a little and situations change in a split second. When I shiver, the earth moves—oh shit!"

A gust of wind billowed down from the cliff above and almost blew Fats over the edge; I grabbed him quickly, pulling him back to safety. As I stared ahead, I saw the steps had come to an end. Had we reached the world outside? In the pitch-blackness that surrounded us, it was impossible to tell.

Silently we clustered on the edge of the steps; Monk Hua lit a flare but we could see nothing.

He hurled the flare over the side of the cliff and we watched it fall straight down, becoming smaller and smaller. By the time it hit the ground we could barely see its tiny spark of light.

"Light a larger flare," Chen Ah-Si ordered. Monk Hua obeyed and like a shooting star the flare glided in a long arc for about five hundred feet before it began its descent. A sphere of dazzling white flame filled the air and illuminated the darkness before us. There was a gigantic volcanic crater at least a mile in diameter, looking like a mammoth stone bowl made of gray basalt. It was filled with a forest of trees, all of them dead.

"Holy shit, what's that?" Fats yelled. Monk Hua sent up two more signal flares. Under their blaze we could see a vast number of magnificent buildings in the middle of the dead trees, like a huge black fortress. Was this our destination, the tomb we had been seeking? Had the Palace in the Clouds been built in the middle of a volcano?

The scale of these buildings was enormous, beyond all imagination. If these buildings below were in fact the palace, it was the size of the Mausoleum of the Qin Emperor.

Based on the pictures we'd found in the undersea tomb, the real Palace in the Clouds should be above our heads, but after the avalanche that we'd seen in those paintings, the spiritual shrine might have collapsed into this crater.

The signal flares flickered and died; once again we were in the darkness with only our dim flashlights providing any illumination. All of our faces, except Shunzi's, were suffused with the greed and excitement that all grave robbers feel when confronted with the wealth of the dead. "Leave everything we won't need and get the ropes ready. We're going to travel light," Chen Ah-Si told Monk Hua.

We sorted through our equipment and left most of our gear on the steps. Putting on our gas masks, we began our descent toward the floor of the crater, using our climbing

24. THE VOLCANIC CRATER

ropes to scale the cliff walls step by cautious step.

Rising from the dead forest below was a strange smell, so strong that it penetrated our gas masks. As we reached the bottom, Panzi warned, "This is a pit of death. We have to hurry or we'll die from lack of oxygen. I heard about this when I was a soldier—not even birds can fly over this kind of place without plummeting to their deaths. It's poison gas from the sulfur of the volcano that does it."

Monk Hua lit a small flare that revealed a stone pathway paved with slate, wide enough for two cars to drive down it side by side. It led straight ahead without a bend or a curve, the Holy Pathway of the mausoleum that would lead us all the way to the main entrance of the tomb. We could dimly see a giant black shadow at the end.

"Where do we go from here?" Monk Hua asked.

"Along the Holy Pathway. We'll give it more thought after we enter the mausoleum," Chen Ah-Si replied.

Passing a number of fallen trees that littered the Holy Pathway, soon we came to a tall, stone door. This was Heaven's Door, the first portal of an imperial tomb. After passing through this, we knew we would see many stone carvings on both sides of the Holy Pathway.

After we walked through Heaven's Door, Chen Ah-Si warned, "Remember to walk backward when we leave here. Don't fall prey to the Door of Decapitation."

I had read about this in my grandfather's journal. The Heaven's Door serves an eerie function; it's here that the funeral team and the coffin bearers were killed. After the coffin had been placed in the mausoleum and all the required ceremonies had been performed, everyone who exited from this door had their heads sliced from their necks. So anyone who entered as we just did would have to leave walking backward when they exited, in order to dodge the blade of execution.

On the other side of Heaven's Door, we saw stone statues of humans and horses every fifteen feet on both sides of the Holy Pathway. In our haste, we made a beeline forward without giving them more than a glance, knowing they were too heavy to carry away with us when we left.

As we ran forward, Fats suddenly stopped; I slammed into him and fell flat on my face, nearly bringing him down with me.

"What the hell are you up to, fat man?" I spluttered.

"It looks like there's someone standing on the side of the road," he whispered.

The guys in the lead saw that we had stopped and they all turned back.

"What's up?" Panzi called to us.

Fats told them what he'd seen. Looking dubious, Panzi said, "It's probably just a statue. Are you seeing things again?"

Fats shook his head. "It flashed in front of me as I ran past. It looked like a woman, but I can't be sure of that. I was running too fast to get a good look."

We pointed our flashlights toward the statues behind us; we'd run past six or seven of them. None of them looked like a woman.

Monk Hua said, "Sir, should we go back and take a look? Maybe it's that woman from the other expedition."

"He means Ning," I said, "but how is that possible? Her group was coming in from the main entrance of the Palace in the Clouds; they ought to be digging a robbers' tunnel above our heads right this minute. There's no way they could have caught up to us at this point."

"It certainly wasn't her," Fats grumbled, "I'd recognize that bitch in one glance."

"You and the others keep on going," Chen Ah-Si commanded. He patted Shunzi on the shoulder. "You come with me and be my eyes."

CHAPTER TWENTY-FIVE

THE PALACE ENTRANCE

Shunzi looked perplexed, but he wasn't the only one. None of us had any idea of what Chen Ah-Si was up to. Maybe he wanted to divert our attention so he could do away with Shunzi? But when I gave this more thought it didn't make sense. For one thing, Chen Ah-Si was in his nineties; even in a sneak attack, he probably couldn't kill an ex-soldier who was still in his prime. And besides, we needed Shunzi to find our way back out of this place. He was still worth more alive than dead, even if he had killed Lang Feng.

There was no way to figure out Old Chen's thoughts; still I grabbed Shunzi by the arm and told him to be careful. He shrugged and followed Chen Ah-Si, while we turned to continue our race down the Holy Pathway.

Our flashlights revealed crumbling black walls and eaves; soon we came to the altar at the end of the Holy Pathway. At the top of sixty tumbledown stone steps behind the altar was the main entrance to the imperial tomb.

As seen from the top of the cliff, its scale seemed enormous and its majestic quality demanded attention, carrying an element of exotic mystery. But once we entered the tomb, that feeling immediately vanished. It looked desolate and dilapidated. If there hadn't been a large structure that looked like a temple still standing erect there, we would have been very disappointed.

The air here was still and there was no wind, sun, or rain. The tomb should have been very well preserved. Why was it in such a ruined state?

We climbed the giant steps and walked into the main entrance of the tomb. The huge mausoleum door had collapsed long ago and lay on the ground. We walked inside, and I could feel the inside of my mouth and my nose sting and burn as I breathed. "We have to hurry," I told the others.

The front door was the door to the palace hall, which was easily the size of two basketball courts. Copper carriages that had transported the emperor were on both sides of the hallway and two black statues covered with dust flanked the back wall, looking ferocious, merciless, and wrathful.

We headed down the hall toward the center of the imperial tomb, and had gone only a few steps when Fats slipped and fell flat on his back. Grimacing with pain, he picked himself up and walked back to see what had caused his fall.

"Do you see something or did you trip over a ghost?" Panzi asked. Fats shook his head, crouched down, removed one of his boots, and turned it over to examine it. There was the shell of a bullet stuck to a hobnail on its sole.

He pulled it free and Panzi grabbed it. "It's still warm—damned thing was fired just a little while ago."

"Someone got here ahead of us?" I asked in bewilderment. "Could Ning and her gang have been here already? But why did they have to fire a gun in this place?"

"Light a fire. Take a look and see what else we can find in the area," Panzi said.

Monk Hua immediately lit a small flare and we began to search. There was a long line of bullet holes in one of the columns, reaching from the floor up to the ceiling.

"It looks like something was coming along this column and the bullets followed it all the way down," Fats said.

Panzi went over and studied the bullet holes, probing at them with a finger. "No. It's just the opposite. Judging by the offset angle of this bullet, the shots were fired at something going from the bottom to the top of the column."

Fats pointed his flashlight at the bullet holes and moved it upward little by little till the light hit a crossbeam high above ground. A black shadow dangled from it. It was the corpse of a man wearing a small gas mask, with an assault rifle strapped to his shoulder. His face looked Russian, not Chinese. "He has to be one of Ning's group," Fats said.

Monk Hua began to climb up toward the corpse but Panzi stopped him. "There's something terribly wrong here," he said and Fats pointed toward other dark figures on the beam. "You're right," he agreed. "He's not the only one."

We looked up and saw seven more bodies, dangling above us like ghosts on a gallows.

These people all wore the same-colored clothing and all carried the same assault weapons. Why hadn't they used their rifles to their advantage, I wondered. What could have killed them? And who or what hung their bodies on the crossbeam?

"Let's get the hell out of here," I croaked. As I turned to

25. THE PALACE ENTRANCE

begin my retreat, I saw Fats climbing up toward the bodies on the beam.

"What the hell are you doing? Come down right now!" I yelled. "Why are you climbing up there? Where the fuck is your brain, you fat idiot?"

Fats ignored me. His movements were quick and agile; he reached the beam in a few seconds. He looked down at me and said, "Why panic? I'm not a child. I'll come down if something's wrong." Then he climbed along the beam toward the closest body.

I suddenly came to my senses and realized that Fats intended to get one of those assault rifles. He never could see anything that he didn't have without going after it. I fumed but unless I shot him, there was no way to stop Fats when he was in the grip of greed.

When he reached the corpse, the first thing he did was grab the rifle and toss it down to Panzi. Then he found the ammo belt and threw it over his own shoulder. Finally he began to remove the gas mask, inch by inch, from the dead man's face.

Behind the mask was a middle-aged foreigner with a pale and twisted face, his mouth wide open as though he were screaming at the moment that he died.

"Don't touch him," I yelled, "his face looks as though he might have been poisoned."

Fats nodded. He put on his gloves and went to check the rope that held the body in midair.

"What did you find?" I yelled.

"This goddamn rope looks like hair…"

"Hair?"

Fats nodded. "It's long too. Could these people all be

women?" He peered at one of the bodies. "Wait, that's not right...the hair's coming out of his neck." He pulled out his knife and tried to cut the strands but with no luck. "This stuff's like steel thread," he muttered. "I'll try burning through it with my cigarette lighter."

"Forget it. Stop poking around and come back down now. You'll be in a lot of trouble if that hair holds poison."

"Just one second," he shouted back as he scurried to grab another rifle from the closest body. He tossed it down to me, grabbed the ammo belt, and had just begun to remove the gas mask from the corpse when I saw the dead man's hand reach out toward Fats.

"Wait! This one might still be alive! Don't take off his mask!"

Fats placed his own hand on the body's throat, checking for a pulse. Then his eyes bulged with surprise; he took out his lighter and burned through the rope of hair, and the body fell from the beam. Monk Hua and I ran to catch it and laid the body on the ground.

"Shit. Fats was right," I gasped. "This guy does have hair growing out of his back. Is he really still alive?'

"He's not dead yet, but he's close to it. There's no point in trying to save him. We can't lug him around with us, after all."

I said, "But he's living—we can't leave him in this place."

Monk Hua laughed, unsheathed his knife, and grabbed the body by the neck. "He's been poisoned and he'll go through agony as he dies. I'm going to put him out of his misery."

Before I could intervene, the body twitched violently, his eyes opened, and he grabbed Monk Hua's hand. Then he stood upright, shrieking with pain. Monk Hua and I both hurled ourselves upon him to try to calm his convulsive motions but he threw us both off and fell to the ground, screaming something at the top of his lungs and frothing at the mouth.

"Fuck this," Panzi bellowed, "I wouldn't let a dog die like this." He aimed his rifle, hit the man in the chest with one shot, and the body lay still.

"What did he say just now? Did any of you understand?" Monk Hua demanded.

"It's the Hakka dialect. I didn't understand much of his screams but it sounded like he was yelling 'back, back,'" Ye Cheng said.

"Back. Could there be something odd on his back?" Monk Hua turned over the body to take a look.

There was blood everywhere and I started to feel sick. "Fats, get down here so we can leave this hellhole," I yelled.

Fats calmly squatted on the beam, smoking a cigarette as he watched the chaos below. "Stop rushing me. You're not my mother—I swear to Chairman Mao, I'll come down as soon as I finish this cigarette."

As I watched him take his time, a face emerged in the darkness, looking as though it was draping itself over Fats's back. We all saw it—all of us but Fats.

"What are you staring at me for? I said I'll come down when I'm ready."

Panzi aimed his rifle at the face and Fats turned to see what the target was. Face-to-face with that other visage, Fats dropped his cigarette and stared as though he'd been hypnotized.

Where did this guy come from? We had swept our flashlights around the entire place when we entered and we certainly wouldn't have missed seeing a man this size—shit, he was almost as big as Fats. How did he suddenly show up?

Could he be someone from Ning's group who became possessed by a spirit here? Or was he a ghost of one of the sacrificial victims who died in this tomb?

Fats made a gesture that urged Panzi to shoot, and then moved his head an inch or two away from that other face. Panzi took aim but stopped when Monk Hua murmured, "Hold on. What is that thing?"

He moved the beam of his flashlight so it struck the face full-on and we all choked at what we saw.

The face had a huge hole where his nose should have been; the sockets of his eyes were so deep it looked as though someone had scooped out his eyeballs, and his mouth looked like the beak of an owl.

Panzi hesitated and loosened his grip on his rifle. "Is that just a giant owl? It's so damned big, how could it stay alive in a place with air this bad?"

Fats's own face was so damp with sweat that it looked as though he were standing under a shower. He opened his mouth in a snarl of fear and as he did, whatever was near him began to snarl in return. Its open mouth was full of fangs that were at least two inches long.

"Shit! That's no bird!" Panzi gasped. He raised his rifle again but before he could shoot, we heard a whooshing sound and a strong gust of wind swept past me. An object struck the barrel of Panzi's gun and his bullets whistled past Fats's ears, missing their target.

"What the fuck are you aiming at?" Fats bellowed. "You nearly killed me."

Chen Ah-Si was suddenly beside us, shouting, "Drop

that gun." Shunzi was close behind him, looking as terrified as the rest of us.

The creature was poised above Fats's throat, ready to bite, but Fats twisted, butted the face with his head, and grabbed it by the head, trying to throw it away from his body. "Damn all of you—get up here and help me," he shrieked as he wrestled with his attacker.

Chen Ah-Si swung his arm forward and an iron ball struck Fats hard on the leg. Fats groaned, lost his footing, and fell toward us. As he hit the ground we saw he was alone; whatever had been on his back had vanished.

I remembered the line of bullet holes on the column and shouted, "That thing's still up there—watch out!" Then a shadow flickered above us like lightning and Shunzi fell to the floor, with three lines of blood oozing from his left shoulder.

Panzi's rifle was on the floor in front of me and I grabbed it, but Fats snatched it from my grasp and fired. We all pointed our flashlights toward the ceiling to help his aim, but when the gunsmoke faded away, there was nothing to be seen. The creature had escaped.

"What the hell was that?" Fats asked, his voice quavering.

"How can you expect us to know? It was crawling all over you and you didn't notice a thing. What the fuck is wrong with you?" Panzi yelled.

Fats lunged in Panzi's direction but stopped. There was the monster, clinging to Panzi's shoulder, staring at us. We backed away, as Panzi stared at us in confusion.

"Don't you feel anything?" Fats yelled. "I'm not the only one to be oblivious, am I?"

As Panzi turned in horror, the monster opened his gaping mouth, baring his fangs once more. Fats fired off a volley of shots, blowing the monster's head to bits. A stinking green fluid splashed around us, and then within what was left of the giant mouth I could see a tiny face.

"Damn it!" I heard Shunzi gasp; he swooped toward Panzi, stabbing wildly into the air behind his back. Nothing was there. "Who opened fire?" he yelled.

Fats immediately raised his hand. "I did."

"And so did I." Panzi's hand shot into the air.

"Those who opened fire—stay behind! Everyone else run! Run straight ahead! Don't look back!" There was a commanding expression on Shunzi's face that I'd never seen before and his tone of voice made it clear that he would accept no argument.

Yet I realized I would be the only one left of my original group if Fats and Panzi were left behind. Quickly I sent my hand into the air. "I fired too," I lied. "I'll stay here with the others."

As I spoke, the sounds of tiles breaking overhead filled the air, along with the thud of heavy footsteps on the roof of the palace hall. "Run!" Shunzi shouted. "It's almost too late."

Chen Ah-Si spat in our direction and shouted to the men near him, "Go now!" He, Monk Hua, and Ye Chen raced down the hall, leaving Shunzi behind.

25. THE PALACE ENTRANCE

CHAPTER TWENTY-SIX

UNCLE THREE'S ORDERS

As the sounds of footsteps and the crack of breaking tiles grew louder above us, Panzi and Fats reloaded their rifles. The four of us drew close together.

"What the hell is up there, Shunzi?" I asked. "What should we do?"

Shunzi replied in a low voice, "I don't know."

"Then why did you make the others leave?" Panzi asked.

"I had to separate you guys from that old man and his gang. It's not my idea—those are orders from your Uncle Three."

We all stared at him. "Who are you?" Panzi asked.

"Don't ask so many questions," Shunzi said. "I'm going to take you guys to see Master Three now. You can ask him yourself."

My chest tightened as I began to ask, "Is my uncle here in this tomb right now?" Suddenly a volley of cracking sounds rattled from overhead and roof tiles began to fall around us like hailstones. Pointing our flashlights upward, we saw countless shadows moving and shifting above.

Shunzi muttered, "Your gunshots echoed beyond the forest of dead trees all the way to the hot springs. Everything that's alive in this place has flocked to this spot to see what they can find."

"Then why aren't we running away too? Are we going to wait to die in this place?" Panzi asked.

"Wait until those other guys have gone a bit further," Shunzi replied, looking down to where we had last seen the back of Chen Ah-Si and his men. In a few minutes, he hissed, "Time to go," as he led us down the palace hall.

Farther down the Holy Pathway, we could see a second hall, just beyond a long, arched bridge made of flawless white jade, at least sixty-five feet long. Along the railing on each side of the bridge were carved two coiling dragons. As we drew close to it, a strong blast of wind struck us and we dropped to the ground to take cover. Fats fired aimlessly at nothing we could see and we heard a slight hissing in the darkness behind us.

We got up and raced toward the bridge, feeling as though something hovered over our heads. Fats continued to fire into the air as he ran. As our feet touched the white jade, I felt something on my back and I fell, rolled twice, and regained my footing. Fats aimed and fired, and immediately I felt a weight fall from my shoulders.

We looked back and saw a black shadow struggling to get up. Panzi raised his rifle and cut the thing in two with one shot. Fats squeezed off a long round of ammunition into the sky and the light from the bullets showed dark shadows clustered in the air above us.

"What in the hell are these things?" I yelled.

"There are too many of them, making a cloud overhead—I can't make out an individual shape. Where are we going?" Panzi shouted. "Where's Master Three?"

"Your Master Three should be waiting at the underground palace," Shunzi said.

26. UNCLE THREE'S ORDERS

"Underground palace?" Fats opened fire again and something shrieked as it fell. "That's just perfect. That clarifies everything. Where's the entrance to this mysterious palace?"

"I don't know."

We all stared at Shunzi as Fats cursed, "You don't know, but you said you were going to bring us to him. This imperial tomb is huge. How are we going to find your damned palace?"

Shunzi turned toward me as he said, "Your Uncle Three said that this is the place where the Black Tortoise lies. He said if I told you this, you would instantly know where the entrance to the underground palace would be. Think about it. Do you have any idea what he meant?"

I was dumbfounded. The place of the Black Tortoise is regarded as a joke that doesn't really exist. In feng shui theory, that's the place with the worst feng shui in the world. "Did he really say that?" I asked. "Did he say anything else?"

"That's all. Your Uncle Three seemed to be hiding from someone so he was in a rush. He arranged for me to help you guys in the village, bring you into the mountains, and deliver this message to you when the time was right."

I stood there listening to what he said, feeling flabbergasted. If this place was really where the Black Tortoise was, being buried here would cause the dead man's descendants to die out. Could there really be so much animosity between Wang Canghai and the Emperor Wannu?

But according to Chen Ah-Si, the feng shui here was supposed to be superb. Why would the place of the Black Tortoise be here?

Fats also knew something about this, much more than I did, and he interrupted with, "Bullshit. How could that be possible? Everyone knows the saying 'The Black Tortoise rejects the corpse.' The Mysterious Palace of the imperial tomb absolutely can't be located where the Black Tortoise is."

Panzi fired another volley of shots, pushing back the objects that were coming toward us. He turned around and said, "It's not entirely impossible. Feng shui only applies to humans. Don't you remember what that monk said? The corpse buried here isn't human. Perhaps the weird discrepancies within this tomb are because of that."

I knew Panzi was only speaking off the top of his head. Although Monk Hua said the bronze fish claimed that the Emperor Wannu was a hellish monster, I didn't think that could be taken literally. We'd only know the full story after deciphering the two fish that I carried with me.

"If you don't know anything, then don't pretend that you do," Fats replied angrily. "If it wasn't a man that was buried here, are you saying it's a dog? No matter what's buried in this tomb, you still wouldn't choose a spot with bad feng shui for its coffin. Besides, take a good look at the size of this place. It's like a city. Why would a mausoleum of such grandeur be built for a monster?"

Panzi wasn't as educated as Fats was and was at a loss for words. He fell silent, looking chagrined.

"I don't know what any of you are talking about, but it all sounds like nonsense to me," Shunzi said. "What did Master Three really mean? Whoever knows—speak up! We're wasting time here."

"This isn't easy to explain," Fats replied. "Haven't you ever heard of the Book of Burial? Do you know what it means when it says the earth has four types of terrain and the weather follows eight directions: the four celestial animals plus the Green Dragon on the left, the White Tiger on the right, the Red Phoenix in front, and the Black Tortoise in the back? The place of the Black Tortoise is in the back. Rejecting the corpse means that there is no corpse here. Put it together and it means there is no corpse in the back. Is this explicit enough? The corpse is in the front!"

"The scale of 'the front' is a bit broad, isn't it?" Shunzi asked. "What front are we talking about? We won't be able to find the entrance with only this information."

"That's only Fats's bullshit," I assured him. "Nobody else would ever interpret the Book of Burial this way. Since Uncle Three didn't directly give away the position of the Mysterious Hall's entrance, it must be because a plain description wouldn't convey the location. We can't interpret what he said from the literal meaning. It's pointless to make guesses like that, Fats."

"What ideas do you have then?" Fats asked, obviously in a huff.

"I have none at all; I need to think about this first. Uncle Three is a master of ancient codes and ciphers, which should be the direction our thoughts fall into. And since he thought that I could understand it, it can't be too complex. However, I don't have time to sit and ponder this, do I?"

While we talked, we had neared the end of the jade bridge. Soon we'd reach the plaza of the imperial tomb. In the dark we could dimly see two monuments erected side by side at the end of the bridge. Both were about thirty feet high; one of them was broken. Under the monuments were two large, black stone turtles. Not far behind the monuments was a towering shadow.

The monuments I knew were the boundary markers of the mausoleum. Behind them were the Longevity Steps that led to the Resurrection Hall, which was also the door to the world of the dead.

The boundary markers are truly the dividing line between the living world and the world of the dead, because not even the tomb guardians can go beyond them. From the moment that the imperial tomb was sealed thousands of years ago, no man had ever set foot in the area beyond the boundary stones. The minute I saw them I knew something ominous waited for us in that massive shadow behind the monuments.

Fats, who was in the lead, suddenly stopped and stretched out both arms to block us from going further. I came to his side and saw the end of the jade bridge had collapsed. Between where we stood and the mausoleum markers, there was a black abyss about twelve feet across.

"What should we do?" I glanced at Panzi.

He raised his eyebrows and snorted, "What do you think? Jump across, one at a time—let's go!"

Fats had already handed his gun to Shunzi; he took a few steps back, ran to the edge, and leaped over the chasm. Shunzi followed and Panzi yelled at me, "Your turn now— I'll come after you."

Shit, I'm no athlete, I thought, but at least if I die, it's going to be a quick death. I gulped, stepped back, began to run, and then I heard Panzi yell, "No—stop!"

It was too late; I was in midleap. Turning back to glare at Panzi, I saw a large black shadow soar down upon me, clutching my shirt with its talons. It smashed me into the side of the abyss and loosened its grip, and I plunged down into the chasm.

My mind went into slow motion. I saw Fats rush over, trying to grab me as I fell, and I felt his hand grazing against my neck as he missed. Panzi raised his rifle and fired three shots above my head. Then I lost sight of them both as I fell into the darkness. In seconds, my face struck the ground hard and I could feel every bone in my body become filled with pain. My ears buzzed and I passed out.

CHAPTER TWENTY-SEVEN
THE MOAT

I coughed myself back into consciousness. My mouth and throat were filled with bile, and blood gushed from my nose. It took me a few minutes to realize where I was or why I was there. It was too dark for me to see anything but I could feel rocks and sand under my body.

Had I fallen into a moat that the jade bridge had once spanned? If so, I was lucky that it was dry and that the rocks beneath me were flat, not jagged.

My gas mask had broken into four pieces that hung loosely and uselessly from my face. Without its protection I smelled the sharp, acrid burn of sulfur, but after a few breaths I barely noticed its stench. Maybe Panzi was wrong about the toxic air in this place.

When I looked up, I could see the beams of flashlights above me, perhaps as high as forty feet. I thought I heard some faint sounds but my ears still rang from my fall. If my companions were calling me, I couldn't tell.

I tried hard to yell to them, but when I opened my mouth, I felt an excruciating pain spread from my chest all the way over my entire body. Instead of yelling, all I could manage were faint moans. Picking up a piece of my gas mask, I pounded the rocks with it, hoping that would let my comrades know that I was still alive. The sound echoed from the bottom of the moat; if I were lucky, it would rise to the top.

Something struck me on the arm; it was a signal flare dropped from above. I looked up and was sure I could see Fats leaning over the side of the jade bridge. Picking up the flare, I waved it at him and saw him raise both arms in response. He tossed a rope over the side of the moat; it dangled toward me and Fats began to climb down, rifle slung over his shoulder.

He was at the bottom in a minute, crouching beside me. "Holy shit. Are you okay?"

My answer came out in a weak croak. "Why don't you try to do what I just did and find out for yourself?"

"If you can joke, you're going to live," he told me. "Hey Panzi and Shunzi, come on down. Bring the gear with you. We have a broken man to take care of here."

They slid down, picked me up, and placed me on a flat rock. Then Panzi took out the medical kit and started examining my injuries. "No broken bones," he said as he bandaged the larger cuts. "Damn you, I told you not to jump. Good thing it's not your turn to die yet—how would I ever explain this to your uncle?"

"What are you talking about? I was already in midair when you told me to stop. Was I supposed to go into reverse?" Then a horrible pain erupted in my chest and I contorted in silent agony.

"Don't move!" Panzi yelled. He grabbed me and held me still as I tried to break free, gasping with pain.

Fats handed me a bottle of water, "You're lucky, you know. You could have been paralyzed by this fall, if not killed."

I sipped the water and rinsed the blood from my mouth. "What the hell slammed into me up there?"

"The weirdest damned bird I ever saw, big as a man with a huge head. It looked a lot like that owl monster that grabbed Fats. I took a shot at it but I missed," Panzi said.

"Don't you think it's weird that those things aren't flying down here to get us?" Shunzi asked. "There's nothing at the top that I can see now. Could it be that there's something dangerous here and they don't dare to come down?"

"Why don't I just take a look around?" Fats suggested. "If there's any potential problem that I can see, we'll go back up immediately. You guys stay here. Young Wu, rest, damn you."

"I'll go check the other side," Panzi said, and the two of them walked off in opposite directions.

Soon Fats whistled. "I've found something," he called.

We looked in his direction; just beyond the beam of his flashlight, we could see a large black shadow as if many people were standing together in the darkness.

"What is that?" Panzi shouted, raising his rifle.

Fats shouted back, "Come over and take a look. You'll find out."

"Can you walk?" Shunzi asked. "Want to go and see what he's discovered?"

I nodded and he and Panzi helped me limp over the rocks toward the spot where Fats was standing. The shadows became clearer as we drew close and then we could see—in the floor of the moat was a ditch, three feet deep and sixty feet wide, filled with statues. The figures of men and horses, life-size and corroded, were crowded together, some still standing, others lying in a heap. Many of the human figures held pieces of bronze ware in their hands, as though they were making an offering.

"What are these?" Shunzi muttered.

"These look like sacrificial statues, welcoming the emperor and his party, but why are they here in this place? Shouldn't they have been put in the underground palace or the sacrificial pit?" I was so confused I was stuttering. "You can't put sacrificial objects out in the open like this—it's taboo. Wang Canghai built this place, he would never have done such a thing."

Fats held his rifle in firing position as he climbed down into the ditch. Shining his flashlight toward a headless statue, he said, "Looks like this is clothing from the Yuan dynasty—tribal minority garments." He reached out to touch the fabric.

"Don't fuck around with this," I warned. "This place is eerie—there could be a trap somewhere."

"What are you afraid of? It's not like these things are going to come back to life." But my words had some effect; he drew back his hand. Poking at the statue with his rifle barrel, he observed, "He's stone all right, all the way through."

Panzi climbed down to join him and I felt uneasy. "Be careful, you two."

Fats waved his hand dismissively and tried to pick up one of the figures. "Do you suppose these are worth anything?"

I nodded. "A lot. There are buyers for even fragments of these kinds of statues, let alone one that's intact. A terracotta head by itself is worth two million U.S. dollars. The horse heads are even more valuable, but I can't tell you how much."

27. THE MOAT

"Shit, we'll never manage to carry these out. Too bad," Fats complained.

"The real issue is why are they here? There has to be a reason," I said. "When this place was built, there was water in this moat. These statues were submerged in water; nobody could see them or even know they were here. What was the point to them being here? Were they defective statues that were dumped like garbage into the moat? They're too neatly arranged for that to be the case."

"Look," Fats burst out. "Did you notice that the statues are all facing in the same direction and sculpted to appear as though they're walking? I've never seen sacrificial statues like these before."

I turned my flashlight to see what he was talking about and frowned. "These figures all look like soldiers, marching together. And the horses too—they're all moving in the same direction. Look at the men's clothing; these are troops of the emperor."

We looked in the direction where these statues were marching. They formed a long line that extended far into the darkness. Who could tell where their destination might be?

CHAPTER TWENTY-EIGHT
THE BURIAL TRENCH

Still throbbing and shaky after my fall, I peered into the darkness, knowing we should go where the line of soldiers took us, but reluctant to voice that idea. I should have known Fats would do it for me. "Let's follow the line of soldiers and see where they're headed. We should go now."

Panzi shook his head. "No. We can't take any more sidetracks. Young Master Wu is hurt, and if we blunder into any more trouble, he isn't going to be able to get away. Let's not spend any more time and energy here. We don't even know the meaning of Captain Three's message—instead of complicating things, it's better to take some time. Let's think about where the entrance of this underground palace is that Captain Three talked about, especially now that those damned birds aren't attacking us anymore."

It was a long speech for Panzi and it suited me just fine. I grinned in approval, nodded, then coughed a few times to show that I was indeed seriously injured. Shunzi was silent, as usual. Fats looked sour and shrugged. "Fine, just terrific. Whatever you say."

We went back to the place where I'd fallen. Panzi took out a lantern from his backpack and lit it for warmth as much as for light. As he pulled out some packs of dried food, I realized I hadn't eaten for almost a day. My stomach growled in protest as we all sat down to eat.

"We're in big trouble," Panzi announced. "Most of our food is still in the bags of Chen Ah-Si and those other guys. Fats and I were loaded down with most of the heavy gear so what we have now are ropes, grappling hooks, emergency flares, and that sort of thing. That's all well and good except we have most of the equipment and they have the bulk of the rations."

Shunzi interrupted, "Instead of worrying about what can't be helped, why don't we think about the meaning of Master Three's message?"

"What kind of situation was going on when Uncle Three came to you? Can you tell us in detail? That one sentence alone is way too vague," I said.

Shunzi sat down, frowning. "It was about a month ago. I was taking some tourists up the mountain, but of course we didn't go as far as we are now. We walked around and the tourists did some sightseeing; your Uncle Three was in that group. Later when we were spending the night in the mountains, he took me aside, told me he was going to climb the mountain, and asked me not to tell anyone. Then he gave me some money and told me when a fellow named Wu showed up to take him and his companions into the mountains. When I brought you guys to him, then he would give me another chunk of cash. It was then that he gave me this clue, and he stressed that you would understand it immediately."

"He really said that?" I asked.

Shunzi nodded emphatically.

This whole thing was bizarre. My uncle seemed to be stressing the person who was the recipient of the message rather than the content of the message itself. If I heard it I would immediately understand—what was it about me that made me able to decipher this riddle?

"Then how did you know you should tell us this only after we were separated from Chen Ah-Si and those guys?" Fats asked.

"I'm not a fool." Shunzi smiled. "Master Three told me how many people would be in your group, and if the number wasn't right, I should only deliver the message to you and you alone. I felt there was something wrong the moment I saw you—you were two separate groups so I played dumb."

So it turns out that he was faking all that simplicity and honesty from the start, I thought. This guy really can't be judged by his looks. No wonder the farther we traveled, the calmer and more self-assured he became. He's really only showing his true colors right now. I can't trust him.

Although Panzi wasn't the best-educated guy in the world, when it came to sizing people up he was brilliant. His brow furrowed as he said to Shunzi, "This isn't as simple as you make it out; I think you know more than you're telling us."

Shunzi grinned. "I served as a soldier here before I retired. I've walked all over these mountains. My parents were Koreans who fled across the border during wartime, and they lived in these peaks. I know ancient legends about this area and about the weird creatures people have encountered here. I've seen all kinds of people come here for all kinds of self-serving reasons and I'll tell you:

If it weren't for the deal I made with Master Three, you guys would never have gone beyond the spot where the avalanche took place."

After observing a moment or two of silence, Panzi took out a cigarette and held it toward Shunzi. "Brother Shun. We failed to recognize a master. Now that we're all together on the same team, let's have a smoke together as friends."

Shunzi looked past the cigarette. "I'm a practical person, so let's cut the bullshit. I'm helping you not because I like you but because I'm seeking a fortune. Your Master Three promised me enough money to keep me comfortable for two lifetimes, so I need to bring you guys to him safely, no matter what. Your job is to figure out what his message means as fast as you can, so get to it, won't you?"

"Will you repeat Uncle Three's exact words to me?" I asked.

Shunzi thought for a moment and said, "It was something like this, 'When Wu arrives, tell him that the entrance of the underground palace is at the place where the Black Tortoise rejects the corpse.' And when I asked him what it meant, he told me if the person were really and truly you, you would definitely know the meaning."

"Still unclear," I sighed. "The key of it all is me but I don't get it. Since when did Uncle Three have so much confidence in me all of a sudden? Is he trying to make me look stupid?"

Seeing my confusion, Fats asked, "Could it be that this message is related to something that happened in your family in the past, something that only a Wu would know?"

"I can't say," I said. "I know my uncle and he's not the type of guy that would come up with a supercomplex signal and then let us guess blindly what it means. Since he used Shunzi as a messenger, the meaning of this sentence has to be very clear. We must have branched off somewhere and taken our thoughts in the wrong direction."

"But since Master Three emphasized that you would get it once you hear it, then it's something that we may not get when we hear it. It must be a common signal between the two of you," Panzi said. "Why don't you think about expressions that you two have in common?"

I didn't think this would work, but I couldn't think of any other solution at this point, so I stared at my hands and concentrated hard on things my uncle and I had said to each other.

Truthfully, Uncle Three and I didn't have much in common at all, let alone anything shared by just the two of us alone. If it were something that Panzi and the others also knew or had in common with my uncle, then I had to eliminate that from my thoughts.

The only thing that came to mind is we both now make our homes in the same city, Hangzhou. And then an idea popped into mind—"The Black Tortoise rejects the corpse"—Uncle Three's hint—Hangzhou—I will definitely understand—

And then suddenly I did understand as it all became clear to me.

CHAPTER TWENTY-NINE

THE SECRET MESSAGE

The Black Tortoise rejects the corpse—what horseshit—
it was all a misunderstanding. Uncle Three hadn't said that
at all. Because we knew about the Book of Burial, we were
the ones to add that meaning once we heard the message.

Just as I had thought, there was nothing really secretive
about these words. Uncle Three had made his message
sound very straightforward so that he could pass it on to
me in front of other people. But only I would know what it
really meant.

It seemed that Uncle Three had already thought that
people might come to the imperial tomb with me who
were not part of his plan.

"Listen," I explained to my companions. "We really
started from the wrong direction. The most important
reason why Uncle Three said I was the only person
who would get what he said is not because of the
commonalities we share, but because I was born and
raised in Hangzhou and I speak the dialect fluently. That's
the key."

"It's the pronunciation?" Fats asked.

I nodded. "And that's what threw me off. Shunzi
repeated the message using the wrong tones."

"Fuck me, I didn't think of that. So what does it mean when you say 'the Black Tortoise rejects the corpse' in the Hangzhou dialect?" Panzi asked.

"Let me explain it. Uncle Three's message actually included three more words—'the place where.' Putting everything together in the right dialect he said, 'It's along the water at the bottom of the river canal'!"

Fats nodded, "Fine interpretation—good work."

"Master Three is truly a master," Panzi agreed. "If Chen Ah-Si heard this phrase, he'd ponder the meaning of "the Black Tortoise rejects the corpse" until his head split open."

"River canal water?" Fats said after thinking it over for a while. "But there isn't any canal here eh? Could there be a river in the imperial tomb?"

I said, "Not in the tomb. There can be a spring in a tomb, but not a river, because the water level of a river is uncontrollable. If it's too high, the tomb would be flooded, and if it's too low, that would be destructive too. Besides, a river would expose the location of the tomb. The river in the message is probably this moat."

"So we blundered onto the right track?" Panzi asked.

"Can't say for sure." I shook my head. "After all, we haven't entered the imperial tomb yet, and we have no idea what the situation is inside. But according to what's in front of us and all the information we've gathered so far, I'm pretty certain I'm right."

"If the river is the moat, then would that be the canal over there?" Fats stood up and looked toward the sacrificial ditch filled with sacrificial statues.

"But," Panzi was a bit unsure, "there isn't any water in that ditch."

I shook my head. "Uncle Three might not have entered this tomb before he left the message. What he said is probably based on some tip that he obtained from somewhere, perhaps an ancient book or a map, made by someone who never imagined that someday there would be no water in this moat."

"What the hell are we waiting for then? Let's go!"

"Wait a minute, Fats," Panzi pulled him back. "You see how badly injured Young Master Wu is? And he hasn't even rested yet. Do you want to go alone and leave him here to die?"

"All right, all right." Fats grabbed Shunzi's arm and said, "Well then, the two of us will go and test the waters first. Panzi, take care of Young Wu while we check things out."

Shunzi pulled from Fats's grip. "My job is to bring him," he pointed to me, "safely to your Master Three. I don't care a damn about the rest of you or what you want to do. I'm staying right here."

I laughed. "Okay Fats, now you know who's important here, don't you?"

"Fine. You guys stay here and I'll go alone. And whatever I find is mine—I'm not sharing with any of you bastards." He picked up his rifle, took a few steps, and stopped.

"Chickened out already?" I scoffed.

Fats groaned as he sat near the warmth of Panzi's lamp. "Of course I'm not chickening out. You guys actually want me to go, but I'm not that stupid. If I do find something, the three of you might come and snatch it out of my arms—maybe even kill me to get it. I'm not going to do something idiotic like that."

"Don't think that we're all like you," Panzi taunted.

"All right, stop bitching at each other," I yelled. "It's around midnight right now. Let's get some rest while we can."

Panzi glanced at his watch and nodded. He turned up the lantern and the air around us grew warmer.

Fats lit a cigarette. "I'll take the first watch."

I glared at him. "I'd better not wake up in the middle of the night and find you gone to loot whatever you can find. You can have whatever you want once we enter the tomb but right now you have to take it easy and listen to me."

"Who the hell do you think I am?" Fats blustered. "You can trust me."

Knowing full well that I couldn't, I was too exhausted to argue with him. When I finally woke up, Panzi was keeping watch and Fats was snoring like a hundred bullfrogs. Checking my watch, I saw I'd slept only for five hours. My body ached so badly that I knew further sleep was impossible. "Let me take watch for a while," I offered, but Panzi told me he didn't need a break. We sat quietly while I had a cigarette and waited for my brain to wake up.

"Do you suppose Master Three is all right?" Panzi suddenly broke the silence. "I'm really worried about him."

I glanced at him, feeling humbled. Panzi was a soldier who had seen his friends die before his eyes in battle, yet he still had loyalty to spare for my uncle, a man who seemed to be a liar and a killer. What had Uncle Three done to deserve a friend like this, I wondered.

"Don't worry. My uncle is a tough old man; he knows how to take care of himself. Right now we need to worry about ourselves, since we don't know what we're doing or why we're here."

Panzi sighed. "Unfortunately I'm not smart enough to

figure out the things that Master Three does. Otherwise, he wouldn't have to do all these dangerous things alone. He could send me instead."

I smiled without answering him. What Uncle Three does isn't necessarily dangerous, I thought, it's actually more dangerous for us. We're always following after him, trying to understand his little plots while he leads us by the nose. So far we've been lucky but sooner or later we'll fall into some trap we can't get out of.

One thing seemed certain, Uncle Three wasn't being held captive by Ning and her group; he was probably already within the palace. Whatever information had led him there was probably something he had found within the undersea tomb, and that information was why Ning, her company, and my uncle had gone to Xisha in the first place. Their goal had never been the undersea tomb but the Palace in the Clouds. They had gone underwater to search for clues to the site of this tomb in the Changbai Mountains.

Ning had been separated from us for a long time in the undersea tomb. While we were on the run and plagued by traps, she could have found the same information that my uncle had—that was probably how the bodies we saw hanging from the beam had managed to get here before we did. They had entered through a secret way that only they, and perhaps my uncle, knew about.

This was the difference between them and us—we were completely ignorant and they had all the information they needed. We had no idea of what lay ahead, but we had no choice but to continue.

I couldn't talk about this to the others. For Panzi, Uncle Three was almost a god; he would do whatever my uncle said no matter what. Shunzi was a complete outsider; for him this was a business deal and he cared only about the money. For Fats it was even simpler; he was here for treasure, and my uncle to him was only an annoying pronoun—oh him. The only one who cared about my theory was me. I was the only one who was puzzled and confused; everybody else lived a much simpler life and suddenly I envied them.

"How are you feeling?" Panzi asked. "You need to get some more sleep—who knows when you'll have another chance to rest."

"Not much chance of that with Fats snoring the way he is—listen, he's jabbering in his sleep right now in some incomprehensible dialect—sounds like he's making a deal with someone."

Panzi snorted, tossing a rock in Fats's direction, which stopped the snoring and mumbling long enough for me to fall asleep for another couple of hours.

We packed up and walked into the trench once again, among the black and broken statues that stretched into the darkness. Fats beamed his flashlight to both ends of the trench. "Your Uncle Three told us to follow the flow of the water, but there isn't any water here. So which way should we go?"

Panzi approached one of the statues, pointed toward the direction that the figure was facing, and said, "Judging by the water stains on the stone, downstream should be in that direction."

Carefully, we began to walk toward the darkness, following the statues. The trench was rugged and uneven; in some parts the statues were badly damaged as if a giant had crushed them underfoot.

The farther we walked, the darker it got. As we walked on, the towering walls of the moat disappeared. Surrounded by absolute darkness, we slowed down. Then Fats, who was in the lead, came to an abrupt halt. I came to his side and followed the beam of his flashlight.

We had come to the end of the canal; the statues had disappeared. Before us stood a large stone wall, with something carved upon it that looked like a Buddha figure. There was a rectangular opening beneath the bedrock of the wall; many of the rocks had been removed, revealing a dark hole inside. It looked like another escape tunnel, secretly excavated by the builders of the tomb.

"Another tunnel?" Panzi exclaimed. "How could the opening be here? That's impossible."

"What makes you think so?" Fats asked. "You didn't dig it."

"This was all underwater when this was built," Panzi replied. "Do you think those workmen were fish?"

"Hey," Shunzi interrupted. "Shut up and get over here. There's something you need to look at."

Peering at a rock next to the rectangular opening, we could see that someone had carved a few words. And the words were in English.

CHAPTER THIRTY

THE DRAINAGE TUNNEL

The letters were crooked, carelessly hacked into the rock with a pickax, and had been recently carved. They were jumbled in a weird fashion and made no words that I recognized. Could Uncle Three have left it as a signpost showing us that we were on the right track? I dismissed that thought immediately; my uncle knew very little English.

Fats crowded in beside me and yelled, "Look Young Wu— it's almost as though we've seen this sort of writing before."

"No," I replied. "Not as though—we really have seen this writing before." It was the same as the odd words Fats had discovered in the undersea tomb, the ones that made Qilin remember what had happened there twenty years before. Why were the same sort of letters, done in the same fashion, here?

Since they were carved with a pickax, I was sure it had to have been done by Uncle Three, Qilin, or Ning; they were the only people who would be carrying pickaxes with them. Whoever it had been must now already be within the tunnel.

"What's going on here?" Panzi demanded and I told him what Fats and I had seen in the undersea tomb.

"Interesting," he observed. "But I've worked for your

uncle for ten years; together we've robbed more than fifty tombs, some of them enormous. But never in that time have I seen your uncle carve messages into the rock—besides, he doesn't know one letter of the English alphabet, I swear. He didn't leave this."

"So it's either Qilin or Ning," I decided. "Anyway, it looks like we're on the right path, and that someone else has already entered the tunnel. The entrance of the underground palace should be down inside. Should we go in?"

"Yes!" Fats immediately said. "Why are we wasting time?"

Panzi asked me, "How are you holding up?"

I nodded to say I was okay. "Fats is right. We can't delay anymore. Don't worry."

We prepared the gear we needed to take with us, hanging signal flares, flashlights, and explosives on our belts while leaving lanterns, fuel, and food behind. Fats and Panzi loaded their rifles and we all made sure our knives were close at hand.

Fats led the way and climbed into the rectangular opening. We followed behind in single file and moved forward into a new subterranean world.

The farther in we went, the more I saw the traces of other people's footprints, and odd little caves in the walls above us, every thirty feet or so.

These caves weren't big, just large enough to hold one person, and were bent in an angle of one hundred and eighty degrees. They went straight up for a bit and then would make a big turn downward, forming a shape curved like the number nine.

Since I had become involved in this kind of work, I'd climbed through many tunnels, yet I'd never seen any like this. The work that it would have taken to dig these weird little caves was nearly as much as digging this entire tunnel. There had to be a good reason for them which was eluding me at the moment.

Panzi asked me from behind, "Young Master Wu, did you notice that this tunnel looks a bit familiar?"

"Familiar? Why?"

Panzi said, "Wasn't the canal that passed through the carcass cave when we were at the cavern of the blood zombies in Shandong built just the same as this tunnel? Didn't that old man hide up there in the caves above the canal when he tried to kill us?"

I thought about what he said and looked closely at the caves above. I had been in a mad panic when I was in Shandong and didn't pay much attention to the caves on the ceiling of the carcass cave. But since Panzi mentioned this, it was probably accurate.

"Are you sure?" I asked.

"I just remember hearing the old man saying there were caves on the ceiling of the canal. It was so dark when we were passing through that I didn't notice."

I stopped, carefully studied the caves above us, and suddenly understood why they were there. "The carcass cave was probably also a water robbers' canal then?"

Panzi nodded. I continued, "So these small caves were probably used for breathing. You see, when water was poured into this drainage channel, there would be air in these weird caves because of their curved structure. The escapee would only have to swim for a section, stick his head into one of these caves, take a breath, and then move on."

30. THE DRAINAGE TUNNEL

Panzi exclaimed, "How clever! In that case, this tunnel was really underwater back when the tomb was being built?"

I answered, "I think so and it looks like the water robbers' canal in the Temple of Seeds could also have been dug by Wang Canghai's workers." I thought for a minute and realized that couldn't be right. That robbers' canal was extremely ancient; Uncle Three had said that it was dug during the Warring States period. Could it have been excavated when the tomb of the Ruler of Dead Soldiers was built? Could Wang Canghai have been to one of those caves and then copied the ancient techniques that he saw there? That was quite plausible.

The tunnel became wider and wider, and after a long time we finally reached its exit. Climbing out, we discovered an extremely deep, dry canal before us.

On both sides of the canal were river dikes that had room for no more than one person at a time to walk on, and a stone bridge crossed the dry bed. We carefully walked over to the other side. "Now which way should we go?" Fats asked.

I said, "This canal here and the canal outside are connected and should be considered as one. We'll follow the direction of the water flow."

Panzi crouched down, and then pointed to one side. "That way."

We continued to move forward. Before long, a square opening appeared on the stone wall of the river dike in front of us.

Fats lit a small flare and we saw a black stone slab on the floor beyond the opening. Obviously this was the sealing stone of the underground palace. Fats made his way through and motioned for us to climb out of the ditch.

The place we climbed to was a coffin chamber built from black rock. It wasn't high—we could barely stand up straight—but it was wide and spacious. There was a large number of crockery vessels placed neatly around the chamber that looked like wine jugs, each of them about half the height of a normal person. At a rough estimate there seemed to be more than a thousand of them. It looked as if Emperor Wannu might have been a drunk.

There were two stone gates on the left and right sides of the chamber walls, behind which we saw two dark tunnels.

"You aren't feeling well, Young Master Wu. Take a break," Panzi told me. Exhausted, I sat on one of the wine jugs, gasping for breath.

"I wonder if these jugs are worth something," Fats said, examining one of the containers.

"The workmanship is too crude. Don't give them a thought. Not even the market vendors who sell sheep kidneys and chopped pickles would take that jug if you gave it to them for free."

"Who said that I was interested in the jug? I'm not just looking for treasure, you know." Fats broke open the seal of the jug with his knife and an odd smell, neither good nor bad, immediately filled the air.

I had read about tomb wine cellars in many ancient classics before, but this was my first time to see one with my own eyes. I went over to take a look.

The wine in Fats's jug was pure black; much of it had evaporated, leaving only half a barrel. The thought of drinking it was tempting but who knew what its shelf life had been.

30. THE DRAINAGE TUNNEL

Fats dipped his knife in the wine and was about to taste it. But I stopped him. "Don't you want to live? It could have gone bad."

Fats said, "You know nothing; wine can be stored for thousands of years without spoiling. I heard that you might even become immortal if you taste this sort of wine—some of our ancestors actually got into the grave-robbing business just for that reason. It's okay to take a sip. At the worst you'll just get diarrhea."

Before he finished speaking, Panzi kicked over the wine jar and the black liquid spilled all over the floor. A rich scent filled the air.

"Don't be angry with me," Panzi said. "Take a look at what's on the floor, Fats."

Fats and I peered down and saw many dark red flecks in the black liquid. Poking at them with his knife, Fats muttered, "That's flesh and bones in there. Think it came from a human?"

"This wine is called Monkey Head Brew. It's made from the body of a baby monkey," Panzi explained. "This is a kind of wine from Guangxi. It could very well be the wine offered as tribute by the Southern Song dynasty when the Daiken of Jurchen was still at the height of its power." He picked up some of the red particles with his knife and held it to Fats's mouth. "I don't know whether you'll become an immortal after eating it, but I heard that it can strengthen your manhood. Please help yourself."

Disgusted, Fats turned away. "How do you know about this? Did you try this goddamn wine yourself?"

"I've seen it before. Big Kui and one of our other guys found a big barrel and started guzzling it—I thought it was disrespectful and wouldn't touch it, but they didn't care. They didn't find the stuff at the bottom until they were almost done, and Big Kui was in the hospital for two months afterward. You know, I was actually pretty kind to you. I could have knocked it over and told you what it was only after you'd downed a few swigs."

Fats picked up his rifle and pulled the bolt to try to hide his embarrassment. He looked at the grave tunnels on both sides and asked, "Which way should we go?"

We all paused. Shunzi pointed to the left. "This side looks safer."

"Why?" Fats asked.

Shunzi pointed his flashlight to the ground of the tunnel opening on the left. We saw a few more words carved on one side of the tunnel. "I just saw this a moment ago. I think someone's guiding you."

30. THE DRAINAGE TUNNEL

CHAPTER THIRTY-ONE

A SIGNAL

I crouched down, trying to read this strange signal carved in the English alphabet, but once again the letters were all over the place, in no intelligible order. I was beginning to wonder if it was even written in English.

"Are you sure your uncle didn't do this?" Fats asked.

Panzi looked outraged. "Captain Three isn't this elaborate—if he were to leave a sign, he would just dig a big hole. He definitely didn't do this. I think we should be careful—signs aren't always meant to show the way."

"You're right," I agreed. "This could be a warning signal."

But when we saw the same kind of sign back in the undersea tomb, nothing particularly dreadful happened. Besides, there were only two tunnels—if one wasn't right, there was always the other.

Fats continued to lead, I followed close behind, and we entered the tunnel.

It was wide enough to accommodate two of Mao's Liberation tanks side by side. Fats said that it had to be a road for the mules pulling carts of supplies at the time of the construction. He was probably right; I'd never seen such a wide tunnel in a tomb before, and I could see some traces of ruts left by the carts.

But the strange thing was that the tunnel was surprisingly cold. The temperature had dropped and a chilly wind blew toward us from the inside as though the tunnel went straight through to the outside world. We all knew that the construction of any ancient tomb was particularly airtight. Where was the wind coming from?

"This is called a mystery wind," Panzi said to me in a low voice. "Our ancestors called it ghost breath—happens often in large tombs, but it's not dangerous."

"Is there any explanation for it? How is it produced?" I asked.

Panzi shook his head. "It's just an expression passed down from the older generations. No one has ever studied this, and it's best not to."

The beginning of the tunnel was flat, but as we went further in, we discovered signs that the ground had been wracked by earthquakes. Many black stone slabs were in upheaval on the floor, making our pathway difficult. There were arched beams reinforced by cracked columns that were wrapped with the carving of a dragon.

None of us said a word for quite a while until Fats stopped abruptly and said, "A door here?"

A black door appeared at the end of the tunnel; as we came closer we found it was locked. However, a large hole had been blasted into the left-hand side, which was where the cold wind was coming from.

"This isn't a door," I pushed it and continued. "It's a sealing stone made to look like a door."

Fats crouched down to look at the hole on the slab. "So, okay, it's a sealing stone and that means this tunnel might be quite important. It could lead to the center of the underground palace. It looks like we're on the right track, and that sign was put there to guide us in this direction. Plus, the tunnel is all excavated and ready. Someone's already gone in." He stuck half his head through the opening, shone his flashlight inward, and examined what lay beyond.

"What do you see? Is there anything inside?"

He replied, "Just a tunnel. There's another sealing stone up ahead. It looks like Emperor Wannu had a deep-seated sense of insecurity."

I said, "Bullshit. Don't you have a triple security lock on the door of your house? There are at least three sealing rocks in an imperial tomb. It's all based on Buddhist cosmology—don't you know that?"

Fats ignored me and sucked in his massive gut as he went through the hole in the door to the other side. I heard him muttering, "Fuck this place—why is it so damned cold?"

We all followed him. There was another tunnel behind the sealing rock, and the temperature was much lower on this side. And Fats was right about there being another sealing stone; this one was cruder and simpler than the other. A hole was blown into the stone here too, larger than the first had been.

We kept going; the tunnel extended before us, leading to a third sealing stone that also had an opening blasted through it.

"Shit. It still isn't over yet," Fats muttered.

As we talked, we passed through the last sealing stone, and a crossroad appeared in front of us. Another tunnel went across the one we were on at a perpendicular angle. It was wider by half than the previous one, and it went much higher.

We came to the intersection and found that the walls of the new tunnel were red, not black like the first. They were covered with murals that extended farther than the beams of our flashlights could reach—even the tunnel's ceiling was filled with paintings.

"This has to be the main tunnel that links directly to the Coffin Hall. It's the central axis of the entire tomb. Otherwise it wouldn't be so magnificently decorated," I said.

"Still the same old question: which way do we go?" Fats asked. "Look around. Is there any sign to guide us?"

Having passed through several narrow tunnels, we had lost our sense of direction. In order to make out which side of the main tomb tunnel would lead to the center of the underground palace or the main entrance of the tomb, we would have to rely on the hints and warnings handed down by our forefathers. Otherwise, our only hope was to toss a coin and guess.

We drew our flashlights across the tomb tunnel in order to find another sign, and as we did, a light glowed from the murals. They were painted in the same style that we had seen near the hot springs before we entered the mountains. They all showed spirits in their celestial horse-drawn carriages ascending to the clouds and riding on the mist. None of them seemed particularly meaningful. Of course, scholars and archaeologists would be able to explain these paintings, but we saw only decoration, with no symbolic significance.

We'd only been searching for a little while when Panzi let out a yelp. "Get over here."

We crowded around him and sure enough, there was something carved in a corner of the tunnel that was different from the signs we'd seen before.

"This isn't the same kind of sign as the other words we've seen. I can't decipher this one either. It's a symbol of some kind, not a word in another language. It's different from the first two signs that were at the bottom of the moat and the opening of the tunnel. Assuming they were meant to tell us that those places were safe to enter, a different sign carved here right now would suggest that the message is different. This could be a warning."

Let's try to figure out who left this here and why," Panzi suggested.

"I don't care who left the sign," Fats complained. "And do we really have to guess why it was left here? Of course it's intended to guide us in a particular direction."

I shook my head and said, "I thought so too before, but not now. If the signs were really left for us, they would be something that we could understand. Yet the carver used such an obscure medium for the messages, it doesn't seem that they were left for us. These signs were left for someone else, and we simply were lucky enough to blunder into them."

"Then who would they be carved for?" Panzi asked.

"There are many people on Ning's team. They're probably operating in small groups. The words and this symbol might be a secret code that they all use to communicate," Fats said.

"It's useless to think about the reasons for this right now," I interrupted. "The important thing is the information contained in this sign. This type of symbol is similar to the keys in international explorer maps, which indicate different levels of danger marked by different symbols. Other than acting as a guide, a symbol can also tell what to expect on a particular trail. We need to pay attention to this symbol because its form has suddenly changed. Could it mean that there are zombies in this tunnel, for example?"

"That's not right," Panzi objected. "I don't think the message of this sign could be a hint of any danger ahead. Think about it. The carver would have to walk through the entire tunnel in order to find out about its dangers. It would be crazy to face the same hazard again by coming back to carve this symbol after reaching safety. This was put here right before the carver entered this tunnel to tell people following him that he went in this direction. As for what's inside, he couldn't have known at the time he carved this. This kind of thing actually has been studied before. It's called 'tracking language.'"

"How do you know all this anyway?" Fats asked.

Panzi said, "I learned about it when I was in the army."

"So can you read this symbol?" Fats asked.

Panzi shook his head and said, "This is completely different from anything I studied, so I don't recognize it. But I believe it's a form of tracking language. There's no need to decipher it. It might say nothing more than that the carver just twisted his ankle here."

Fats sighed. "This is bad—it means the person who left this sign wasn't sure he was going to survive this tunnel. He was leaving information for the group that came after he did because he wasn't confident that he'd come back out alive."

"Exactly." Panzi smiled. "We might as well act like we haven't seen this sign at all since it wasn't left for us. Our goal is to find Master Three. He didn't carve this, so he didn't necessarily take this path. Even if it's safe, it's pointless to follow it; we'll take our own path. We've robbed a lot of graves before. It isn't like we've never come across a situation like this. We're not so stupid that we can't even explore a damn tomb tunnel without help."

Fats liked this way of thinking. "That's more like it, Old Pan. Why don't we split into two groups—you and Young Wu can go that way, Shunzi and I can go this way. We'll see who's luckier. It's a straight road anyway. If we get to the end and find out something's wrong, we can just turn back. The pair that takes the right path should wait for the others outside the Coffin Hall. Hanging around here isn't the answer."

I didn't think this was a good idea and argued, "What you said is true, but I'm afraid the main tomb passage isn't such an easy route. Look at the four-foot-thick slate on the ground. It's likely that this tunnel is filled with traps like arrows and trap doors. Your two teams might be dead at the two ends of the tomb tunnel. We might part for good once we separate."

Fats scoffed, "If you're going to be such a pessimist, then you shouldn't have come. If you're stuffed from a good meal, why look for more food? Now that we're in the underground palace, we shouldn't let fear keep us from our goal."

"Did you think I wanted to come?" I yelled. "I only wanted to become prosperous and an upstanding citizen. But with the luck I was handed this year, I'm always running into zombies and murderous insects. I'm not afraid of that kind of thing anymore, but what's the big problem with trying to be careful?"

"Young Master Wu is right," Panzi agreed. "I'll give you another reason for caution: Ning's team is definitely close by. Even if we don't have to guard against zombies, we still have to be alert against people. The firepower of two guns is stronger than one. Besides, if one team suddenly vanishes the way Poker-face did, then what will the other team do? We'd better stick together. At least we can coordinate efforts that way."

Shunzi, who had been silent for a long time, spoke up. "I have to deliver Young Master Wu no matter what. I'm following him."

Fats raised his arms as though he was surrendering. "Go ahead—work against me. Fine, that's my bad luck; whatever you say, I'll do. The worst that will happen is we'll all die together."

Panzi said, "We'll go in the direction of the carved sign and if it isn't right, we'll turn around. And we need to be careful on the way."

We all got to our feet and Panzi took out a folding walking stick similar to the white canes used by the blind. As he tapped it on the ground, we walked in the direction where the sign had been carved.

I thought we'd spend at least half an hour walking through the tunnel but it turned out to be a very short passageway. In less than two hundred yards, the tunnel suddenly widened and a giant jade door appeared at the end.

I recognized at first glance that this was the main entrance of the Coffin Hall, for any other door in a tomb tunnel wouldn't be made of such a precious stone. The lower half of the door had been blasted, creating a huge empty hole. Someone had gone in there—who knew if it

31. A SIGNAL

was Ning's team or someone else.

I was secretly delighted. This meant that we had gone the right way. Behind the door was the core of the entire underground palace. Many classic tomb structures immediately emerged from my mind. Although this was a Dong Xia imperial tomb, it had been built by a Han Chinese. Presumably it wouldn't be very different from the graves of the Central Plains. What would we see after we enter?

We bent over and climbed into the chamber behind the door one by one. Fats lit a flare and we all gaped like idiots, too surprised to move or to speak.

CHAPTER THIRTY-TWO

BEYOND OUR WILDEST DREAMS

The size of this tomb chamber was nearly ten times larger than the chamber that had held the wine jars. Four giant columns stood in each corner of the room. Piles of treasure lay in heaps all over the floor, mounds of gold and silver dishes as well as glasses studded with pearl, jade, and gemstones. Their gleaming colors almost blinded us.

"Holy shit—" Fats's eyes were wider than a cow's and his face was twisted with surprise and greed.

I couldn't believe that there were so many treasures in the imperial tomb of a tiny border kingdom. It looked as though we would be rich for the rest of our lives if we came away with just a few of the objects here.

Fats rushed toward the gold and silver, but I grabbed him. "Don't get carried away. There was often poison sprayed on the gold vessels found in tombs. It would be silly to come all this way and be poisoned to death—better to stay back until we know for sure that it's safe to touch these things."

But Panzi had already rushed to the pile of gold and grabbed an armful of it, staring in open-mouthed wonder. His whole body trembled, he lost his grip, and the treasure slipped through his fingers, sending the sounds of clanking metal into the air.

And even I, conservative and proper on the outside, I felt my heart thunder when I saw what was lying before us. I had to be honest with myself; I wanted that wealth as much as anybody.

Lost in avarice, we ran from heap to heap of the precious objects, staring, choosing, and making our own piles. Everything in view would be the prized highlight of any museum in the world and it was all ours for the taking. Fats was the first to dump all his gear from his backpack, filling it with treasure, pouring it back out, and then putting in new objects. He moaned softly as he rushed from heap to heap.

But soon we discovered that no matter how hard we tried, we couldn't choose the things we wanted to take away. Always something more beautiful and precious would come to light and we'd grab that and then something else would replace it, until exhaustion cooled our frenzy.

I shook my head to clear away the greed and stood up. There was Shunzi standing on the top of a mound of gold, staring fixedly into emptiness.

"What are you looking at?" I asked him.

Silently he pointed downward. There in the middle of a pile of gold and jewels several people lay motionless. They were dead.

Fats and Panzi saw us standing in shock and thought we found even more exquisite treasures. They dashed over to have a look, only to see several corpses sprawled in the gold.

We went down to get a closer look and found the bodies had been dead for a long time. Their skin was dried to the point that it looked like orange peel and their clothing had rotted away.

32. BEYOND OUR WILDEST DREAMS

"What's up with this?" Fats asked. "Who are these people? They're from this time period, not from ancient history. Do you suppose they were in our business?"

I shook my head. The corpses wore clothing in the style of the 1980s, which country people still wore even now. Judging by their state of decay, they could have been here anywhere from five to twenty years.

Panzi asked, "Could they be herb collectors or hunters who went into the Changbai Mountains, got in here by mistake, and then died here because they couldn't find their way out?"

"That's unlikely." I tore the fragments of clothing off one of the corpses. She was a female, wearing some old-fashioned earrings and a rusted wristwatch.

"Look. This is a Titoni watch from the eighties. Not even a village mayor could buy one back in those days. This woman came from a pretty influential background; it doesn't look like she was someone from a rural area."

"Then could they be lost tourists?" Panzi asked. "Do you think they carved the words we saw on the way here?"

I shook my head. They couldn't have carved the words. I had seen the same kind of language before in the undersea tomb, which meant that it was certainly carved by people who had been there as well as here. If the words in this tomb weren't carved by someone on Ning's team, then they had to have been done by Qilin. It was possible that these corpses were lost tourists, but how could they have ended up here if they were really lost? Without considerable courage, no average person would dare to go down a tunnel of an underground tomb.

But since this woman wasn't an ordinary citizen, her

disappearance might have caused a local stir. Shunzi wasn't young; he might have heard of something like this at that time. I turned around to ask him about it but he hadn't followed us. He still stood on the pile of gold, his face pale and expressionless, his body trembling violently.

"What's going on?" Fats taunted, "Are you afraid of dead people?"

Shunzi ignored him and walked toward us, his footsteps heavy. He crouched down beside one of the bodies, shaking so hard that I thought he'd topple over. Then I knew.

Fats asked me in a low voice, "What's wrong with him? Is he spellbound?"

"No," I replied. "He's looking at the body of his father, who disappeared ten years ago in these mountains."

CHAPTER THIRTY-THREE
THE EXPEDITION TEAM OF TEN YEARS AGO

I told Shunzi's story to Fats and Panzi, while realizing there was so much I didn't understand. This group got in, so why didn't they get out safely? Would we have the same difficulty when we were ready to leave? And what were these people doing here? They obviously weren't the sightseers that Shunzi's father had thought they were.

We rummaged through the rotting backpacks, finding a lot of gear and three notebooks that contained lists of names and phone numbers. There was no clue as to who these people were; none of them carried an ID card.

"Look at their equipment," Panzi said. "They had everything they needed to get out of this place. Why did they die? Were they too reluctant to leave all of this treasure?"

Fats had been staring at the objects before us. "Comrades, did you notice there's something missing here? Look. There isn't any food in any of these bags. "

"You're right," I said. "Could they have run out of food and starved to death?"

But this didn't make sense. As long as there was water available, a person of normal body weight would be able to live without food for a month before dying of starvation. If this group had wanted to get out, they wouldn't have died from lack of nourishment. There was only one reason why these people had died in this place—they were unable to leave.

I remembered the disappearing doors that had held us prisoner in the undersea tomb and quickly ran back up to check our entrance. The door was still there, it hadn't vanished.

Fats knew what I was worried about. "Don't be frightened. If we encounter that same problem again, we can blast our way out. We have dynamite, remember?"

Panzi touched Shunzi's arm gently. "Do you know how many people there were on the expedition team that your father guided?"

"My mother told me that my father had set off with seven people."

"There are…one, two, three, four, five, six—six bodies here. There are at least two missing," Panzi said. "Could evil thoughts have come up in the minds of those two when they saw the treasure? Could they have killed their companions and then left on their own?"

"No," I argued. "Do you see any signs of violent death here? These bodies are all huddled together—nobody tried to flee, they aren't contorted by poison, and they all have the same expression on their faces, calm and despairing. I've never seen a group of corpses look like this before. Nothing simple and easy to explain caused their deaths."

The more I thought, the more uneasy I felt, as though something in this chamber was watching us, waiting.

"You know," Fats observed, "this isn't the end of our search. Yes, there's treasure—the richest array of burial objects that any man was ever given—but where's the coffin? We need to go back and travel down along that

33. THE EXPEDITION TEAM OF TEN YEARS AGO

second tunnel to find that. But what are we going to do with all this loot? We can't abandon it."

I said, "Just choose something—one piece from here will keep you comfortably for the next half of your life. Don't be so fucking greedy. Besides, we can always come back for more."

Fats grabbed a couple of golden platters and Shunzi picked up his father's wizened corpse, carrying its light weight on his back.

We filed out of the chamber, taking one last look at our gold mine, and then I heard Fats gasp. "Shit," he said. "The murals out here have changed color. They were red—now they're black. And look at those shadows—my God, they have gigantic heads."

"Holy shit," Panzi muttered. "What happened? Did we leave through the wrong door?"

"No!" Fats and I had gone through this before and knew immediately what was going on. "The tomb tunnel has shifted! When we were in that chamber, the old tunnel moved to another spot and a new one moved here."

"Is that really possible?"

"Yes!" Fats and I both nodded. "And it can get a lot worse than this," I added. "Anything can happen in a tomb designed by Wang Canghai, so don't think this will be the only trap we're going to find in here. At least now we know why those other people starved here. The shifting of the tomb tunnel means that the crossroads we passed by when we came doesn't exist anymore. It's impossible to get back that way. Although we don't know what's at the end of this new tunnel, our fate will be the same as the group of corpses if we stay in this place. My guess is we're heading toward a dead end, which is why the corpses have such hopeless looks on their faces."

"Maybe we're stuck in a Rubik's cube and we'll never find our way out," Panzi said.

"I doubt that, to be honest. Wang Canghai's biggest trick was using psychological warfare. Most of his victims died because their nerves failed them. We have to explore this new tunnel and find our way out. If we can't, then we'll blast our way out with dynamite."

I led the way into the tomb tunnel, with Fats and the others following closely behind.

When we reached the tunnel's end, there was a jade door, identical to the one we first saw, right down to the hole blasted into its bottom.

Once again, we climbed through in a single file. We turned on our flashlights and there was a room just like the one we'd left—heaps of treasures, a column in each corner of the room.

As we all stared in surprise, Fats yelled from where he stood, perched on a pile of gold. His mouth moved but no words emerged from it. I ran to his side and saw several corpses huddled together, and a carefully arranged line of equipment—the very same objects we had just sorted through a few minutes ago.

"Oh hell," I muttered. "We're right back where we started from. Look, here are our footprints. But how did this happen? The tunnel was straight, without a curve or a fork in the path. We walked down it for twenty minutes. We couldn't have gone in a circle."

"Then we're under a curse," Fats said. "Shunzi, is your old man fucking with us?

33. THE EXPEDITION TEAM OF TEN YEARS AGO

"Keep talking and I'll kill you," Shunzi replied.

"Both of you shut up," I ordered. "There's only one thing to do. We'll go back to the tunnel and walk down it one more time."

All I could think of was the hopeless expression on the corpses' faces. Could they have been trapped here in the same way? No matter how many times they walked through the tunnel, did they come back to the same place? This was completely inconceivable. But my intuition told me that I guessed right. The occurrence that caused their deaths had now befallen us.

The thing that I needed to do right now was to prove my hunch, or perhaps I was trying to deny this terrible premonition deep in my heart. I rapidly walked back into the tunnel while the others followed.

Because we had walked through it once before and knew there weren't any traps, we went quickly this time. I basically jogged the whole way, my eyes locked on both sides of the road, making sure there was no fork to deceive us.

Within ten minutes we completed the entire course. When I felt that we were almost at the end, I found myself constantly praying that my hunch was incorrect. But when I saw that same jade door, I knew we were in trouble.

As we went through the door, Fats rushed up to the gold mound. Then he covered his face and fell to his knees. There were six bodies and the objects we had laid out earlier...we had returned.

Catching his breath, Fats said, "We're cursed, we're definitely cursed. We're going in a circle. Both ends of this tunnel lead to the same place. We're going to meet Shunzi's father for sure."

"Calm down! Stop it!" Panzi yelled. "Be sure not to panic. Young Master Wu, didn't you say that Wang Canghai's little tricks can only create psychological stress at best? With this knowledge, we definitely can't fall for his scheme. We have to stay remain calm and figure this out."

Panzi's words pulled me together. I nodded. "You're right. This is only a trap. We already learned in the undersea tomb that there's no such thing as being cursed. Wang Canghai is good at using clever tricks to create an uncanny atmosphere. If we didn't know his ins and outs, we'd be doomed—but we know. We just have to figure out his ruse."

Because it felt so real when we were in the tomb tunnel just now, I really couldn't imagine what trap had been used to create this effect. The first thing that came to mind was that either the chamber or the tunnel was moving. But I immediately rejected that idea. We had been running; and if the chamber really could move, how fast would it have to be? It wasn't likely that the tunnel had moved either; we'd been walking in it and would have noticed if there had been any kind of vibration. But if it were neither the chamber nor the tunnel that was the trick, then there was really no explanation for what was going on.

"Whether it's a curse or a trap, we still have to solve the problem. What do we do now? Should we walk through it again?" Panzi asked.

"Yes, God damn it," I said. "Let's do it again. We'll go slower this time and get a good feel of any motion in the walls or under our feet. I don't believe we can't find a flaw in this."

So we walked into the tunnel again, this time taking

forty minutes, but before we got to the end, we knew we had failed again. The tomb door looked exactly the same, and we didn't feel a thing along the way.

We did this again several more times, each ending in failure. I started to feel the despair we had seen on the faces of the corpses, and our own faces turned pale.

"This isn't working. Since we've walked the tunnel so many times now, we've basically ruled out everything. The trap must be set up in a way that we hadn't expected."

Disheartened and frustrated, Fats sat down and said, "Are we going to die? These people here must have done everything they could. What's left for us to try?"

Panzi said, "Stop. If you think like that, you might as well kill yourself. We'll turn to despair only after we've done everything we can. While we're still physically able, let's think of other ways to get out."

I thought of the corpses and asked, "Should we ration our food? We have to prepare for a long-term battle. The longer we live, the greater the chance we'll get out."

Panzi shook his head and sighed. "Young Master Wu, to tell you the truth, we're actually not any better off than the corpses were. We don't have much food left. I think we have two more meals at most, and they won't even fill our bellies. I don't think we should ration anything now. We'll eat whatever there is and maintain our energy. If we can't get out within two days, then we'll use the explosives. And if the explosives don't work, then we'll just wait for someone to remove our corpses."

Two days…How long had these bodies been in here before they died? Could we make it out in two days?

Fats's stomach was growling so loudly we all could hear

it. He asked Panzi, "Well, can we have an early dinner then? I'll resolve the hunger problem first. Then I can put all my effort into thinking about other things."

Once Fats mentioned food, we all started feeling hungry. Our bodies warmed up after we ate, and our energy returned to thoughts of escape. There must be a purpose for Wang Canghai's design of this tomb. What could it be?

Fats suddenly shouted, "I got it!"

33. THE EXPEDITION TEAM OF TEN YEARS AGO

CHAPTER THIRTY-FOUR

FAT'S SOLUTION

When Fats announced he had the solution, we all braced ourselves for more of the bullshit that he specialized in.

"Listen to me," he continued. "It's a waste of time to think about this problem without organizing our thoughts. Why don't we write down all the possibilities, group them in categories, and then try verifying them directly ourselves? Look, this is what I mean."

He grabbed a stick and wrote the numbers from one to four on the ground.

"Everyone make one suggestion about what has us so confused—nothing specific, just a general idea is good enough."

"There's a trap," Panzi said.

Fats wrote down the word "trap."

Then Shunzi said, "There might be something affecting our sensory perception. I've seen this on television before. It's like something has hypnotized us and makes us come back to the starting point involuntarily."

Fats wrote "illusion" under number two and then looked at me for the next suggestion.

I said, "In theory, it might be related to space-folding."

"What the hell is that? I don't understand you," Panzi said.

Fats said, "It doesn't matter. We don't understand any of what's happening, do we? We'll count it in."

He wrote down the words "space-folding" under number three. Then he said, "I think there are ghosts." And he wrote the word "ghosts" under number four.

"What's the point of writing them down?" Panzi asked.

Fats replied, "You guys are educated but I'm not, so I have to write every goddamn thing down. But there are advantages to this. For instance, if you have a few things on a schedule you can place them in order in advance. This can save you a lot of time. Don't we only have two days? We've got to use our time wisely. Oh yes, is there a fifth idea? Anyone?"

None of us responded so Fats said, "Okay. Let's verify the first and second points. These two can be dealt with together."

He looked very pleased with himself as if he had something up his sleeve. I immediately felt there was something wrong here; what crazy scheme did he have in mind anyway?

Fats picked up his rifle and said, "This tunnel is about a thousand to two thousand yards long. My assault rifle can kill at a range of four hundred yards, but the bullet can travel three thousand yards. I'll fire a shot here and see what happens."

Suddenly I felt a surge of admiration for Fats. Though human senses can be fooled, bullets are inanimate. The tunnel might affect us, but it couldn't affect a bullet. If this situation fell under the rules of common sense, then the bullet would disappear at the end of the tunnel.

The most flawless part of this experiment lay in the speed of the bullet. In such a short tunnel, the bullet would be able to travel the entire distance in a couple of seconds. No trap could ever take effect in such a short period of time.

But if the situation went beyond the scope of common sense into the area of metaphysics, then the bullet would transcend space and make a 180-degree turn in the straight tunnel, just as we had.

It was a simple and beautiful solution; I was a bit ashamed that I hadn't thought of it myself.

Fats pulled his rifle bolt and was about to shoot into the tunnel.

I quickly shouted, "Wait!"

"What is it?" he asked.

"Don't do it that way," I said. "If, and I'm saying if this is really that wicked a scheme, you might die in an instant if you fire the gun in that position and the bullet comes back this way."

Nodding, he shifted the gun slightly to the side. If the bullet did come back in our direction, it would hit somewhere close to the lower side of the muzzle.

We all hid behind the door, and Fats opened fire. A loud bang was heard from the tunnel, followed by a series of echoes. Then the tomb door shook violently, sending a cloud of dust into the air.

Fats still stood poised in shooting position, the smoke from his gunshot still hanging in the air around him. A couple of inches below the barrel of his rifle was a bullet hole in the tomb door. Clearly what we were facing was neither a trap nor hypnosis; our problem was in some way supernatural.

We went back into the treasure chamber once again and sat down.

"We're fucked," Shunzi gasped, casting a glance at his father's corpse. I knew what he was thinking. I had the same thing on my mind. Now we all knew why the dead bodies here bore expressions of desperation and hopelessness. We might soon be in their company, with the same miserable expressions on our own dead faces.

We were silent for a long time before Fats finally said, "Well, we all saw it with our own eyes, so let's skip the bullshit and move on to the third one? How can you explain space-folding so we can understand it, Young Wu?"

"No! We don't have to understand it," Panzi burst out. "There are six bodies here. Assuming that there were eight people that entered this place, two of them must have gotten out, even though we have no idea how they did it. But if Young Master Wu's third assumption was true, then no one would have gotten out. So there's really no need to consider it, unless we want to give up and die."

"How do you know that eight people have come in? There might only be six."

"The number of people that came in here is completely irrelevant to our situation right now, but it's still very important for our morale. If two people did make it out, then our mind-set would be completely different, enabling us to think over their method of escape. At least that would give us a little hope," I explained. "Let's examine the dead people's notebooks. Maybe one of them kept a journal that will provide us with a clue."

But when I flipped through the pages of the notebooks, I could find nothing that looked useful.

I wondered why these people would be writing anything at all when their deaths were so imminent. And then I suddenly realized they probably didn't even have any source of light before they died. The batteries of their flashlights must have failed, and they had nothing to warm themselves, which explained why they huddled close together as they died.

If eight people came in, when did two of them get out? It certainly wasn't when the others were conscious, because then they would have followed. Could they have gotten out under cover of darkness while the others were unable to see them? Was the key to our escape found in darkness, leaving the chamber without using a light? I shuddered. I would hate to walk down this tunnel in the dark.

"Turn off your flashlights," I told the others. "We need to save the batteries. If we light Panzi's stove, that will give off enough light for us to look carefully at these notebooks. Here's one for each of us—and look, this guy had a novel. Shunzi, take a look at that for any handwriting."

We clustered around the stove, turning pages, hoping to find a clue as we carefully read every word.

The penmanship in the notebook I held was delicate and graceful, written by a woman. I turned over several pages, finding only names and phone numbers, followed by a guest list for a dinner party with the address of the Changbai Mountains Hotel. There were even a few simple maps drawn in some places with addresses and short memos.

The following pages were empty, but still I flipped through the pages one by one in hopes that she might have written something else. As I did this, Fats suddenly said, "Here's a clue. 'Sold the last one brought up from the ocean today. Got three thousand yuan for it. Gave one thousand and five hundred back to Old Li and paid off the debt.' Looks like my guy was a fisherman."

I shook my head and smiled wryly. Then I turned to Panzi. His notebook was the thinnest of all, with barely anything written in it; he had already finished it. I looked at Shunzi, who was absorbed in his novel.

Fats was upset and quickly took it over. He cursed, "What the hell?" Fats cursed. "We asked you to look for clues, and there you are reading for the fun of it. Give me that book!"

As he tugged the book from Shunzi's hands, it fell to pieces, pages flying all over the floor. As we gathered up the scattered paper, Panzi yelled, "Hey. There's a photo here." He held a faded black-and-white photograph for us to see.

I grabbed it, peered in the dim light, and my breath caught in my throat. In the photo were my Uncle Three, Wen-Jin, and the archaeological students at the pier before they went to the site of the underground tomb.

CHAPTER THIRTY-FIVE

PEOPLE FROM THE BOTTOM OF THE SEA

"What's this doing here?" I sputtered. "Holy shit, it's my uncle—and Poker-face—look! How did this photo end up in here with these corpses?"

For once, even Fats was speechless and Panzi looked as though he was going to puke. My brain whirled dizzily— could these dead bodies somehow be connected with the disappearance of Wen-Jin and the others? Could they be the bodies of my uncle's lost love and her group? Had they found something in the undersea tomb that lured them to this place?

I suddenly thought of Uncle Three and Poker-face. Almost everyone that had been in the undersea tomb was here today. These dead bodies had come here ten years ago, and now Uncle Three and Poker-face were here too. What the hell was going on?

The mysteries that had faded in my memory suddenly came back to life and a thousand questions roared through my head.

I explained my thoughts to Fats and Panzi, and Fats responded, "No way. Hold on a second. I have another idea. It seems like everyone who has been to the undersea tomb, including Ning and us, has also come here. Could there be a curse in that place that compelled all who have been there to climb the Changbai Mountains?"

I knew what he said was nonsense but it still gave me goosebumps. What was clear to me now was that the undersea tomb wasn't important after all. The key to the puzzle was here; the undersea tomb was merely a springboard.

I rummaged through everything I could find on the bodies, but I didn't find any other clues. There was no way I could find out who these people were. Confused and troubled, I turned and walked toward the tomb tunnel without even taking a flashlight with me.

Fats quickly pulled me back. "Calm down, damn it— where do you think you're going?" I sat on the ground, barely able to speak. "I have to get out," I muttered. "I have to find Uncle Three and get him to explain everything or I'll carry the mystery with me until I die."

Fats said, "But we still haven't found any clues that prove anybody has successfully gotten out. Who knows? This might be an enclosed space and we'll never escape it. What difference does it make what's on your mind when you die?"

Nobody could respond to this cheery thought. I began to cough and what I spat up was blood. "You aren't well yet, Young Master Wu," Panzi remarked. "You need to stop thinking and rest so you can heal. We could all use a good night's sleep so we'll be more clear-minded and less panic-stricken."

"How can I fall asleep?" I asked. "It's better if I keep thinking until my brain shuts down."

Fats lit another cigarette, released a haze of reeking

smoke, and said, "In fact, now that I think of it, we shouldn't have followed that sign. It would have been so much better if we did what I suggested. At least if one group was trapped, the other bunch of us could still find a way out. You know, I think the sign was left by these bodies here. Maybe they did what I had suggested—split into two groups at the very beginning, and the two missing guys walked in the other direction."

I shook my head. "Who's to say that the side that didn't follow the sign was any safer? There might be something unknown waiting for us in the other direction that's worse than the hell we're in now."

"Look at it this way," I continued. "The mere existence of this tunnel isn't logical in the first place. Wang Canghai was no god. He couldn't create rules of physics to suit himself. What we're faced with here has nothing to do with Wang Canghai, and these people here didn't die because they were trapped. The reason we're caught as we are is because," and I carefully pointed my finger to the fourth word that Fats wrote down. Without speaking I mouthed the words, "There are ghosts in this place."

"Are you sure? What should we do?" Fats responded, so quietly that his lips barely moved.

"What we see and hear right now is an illusion—and what could produce an illusion so strong that four people all experience it at the same time? What we have gone through right now defies all rules of nature and of logic. Only a ghost could defy all natural law the way this place has. But a diabolical ghost whom we can't see is an adversary we can't fight. We have to make it become visible and I'm going to ask you to sacrifice something you treasure, Fats."

"Are you going to kill me and make my soul negotiate with the ghosts? I'm not going to do it. If you guys kill me, I'll join forces with these ghosts and put you in a more miserable place than we're stuck in now."

"What sort of bullshit are you thinking about now, fat man? I just want to use that charm you always wear around your neck."

"What are you going to do with it?" Fats covered his throat with both hands. "This is the real thing, it's a pangolin bone. Can you afford to replace it if you destroy it?"

"Don't worry about it. It's fake," I told him.

"Fake?" Fats took it off and looked at it carefully. "Are you sure?"

"Of course. This is made of rhinoceros horn. How do I know? Because the longer you wear something made of pangolin bone, the darker its color becomes. Look at your charm. It's already begun to turn green."

Fats handed me his charm. "How are you going to use it?" he asked.

I said, "There's a legend called 'Psychic Channeling Through Burning a Rhinoceros Horn.' Have you heard of it before?"

"Is that one of those Hong Kong movies that came out a few years ago?"

"Something like that. It's the same idea," I nodded. "Once you burn this stuff, you can see ghosts under the glow of its flame. Of course I've never tried this before, so I don't know whether it works."

I lit our camp stove and stuck the charm into its flame. At first it refused to ignite but soon a strange smell filled the air and a peculiar light displaced the stove's flame.

35. PEOPLE FROM THE BOTTOM OF THE SEA

I lifted the stove to illuminate as large an area as possible. We looked around but saw nothing unusual.

"Maybe the ghost has retreated to another place," Shunzi suggested.

"No. Legend has it that if a ghost is really casting some sort of spell or curse, it needs to cling to the back of one of its victims."

We checked each other's backs, but there was nothing to be seen. Fats muttered, "Told you legends are bullshit—you destroyed my charm for nothing."

Panzi was discouraged. "It looks like there's a fifth possibility here, one that can't be explained. What should we do now?"

I sighed. Just as I was about to say something, Fats suddenly gestured for me to shut up. I followed Fats's gaze and looked up; there above us on the ceiling of the chamber was the black, indistinct shape of a huge baby.

The rhinoceros horn burned brighter and the child became clearer and more distinct. I looked at it carefully. This thing was familiar—it was the big-headed baby, the Kunlun Embryo in the ice that we had seen earlier. How did it get here? Could it have been following us?

"Damn it! So it's this thing that's playing tricks against us!" Fats roared. Then he loaded the gun and raised its muzzle. The anger that he had no place to vent immediately broke out. He sprayed the ceiling with gunfire and the monster was hit repeatedly, black liquid from its body splashing all over the place. Then it fell straight down to the ground.

We backed away as the ghost baby whimpered like a hungry infant. It lashed out with one small fist, knocked over the stove, and crawled toward the darkness with lightning speed.

"Don't let it get away! Otherwise we'll stay in its trap forever!" Panzi cried out. "Chase it!"

We began to follow the ghost and as we ran we noticed that the murals had returned to their original color. The spell was broken.

"We're out!" Fats shouted. "We're not going to die!"

CHAPTER THIRTY-SIX

AN UNEXPECTED LETTER

The ghost baby crawled rapidly into the dark tunnel and we knew we had to follow it to keep from falling under its spell again. We ran with desperate speed and soon reached the tunnel's end, just in time to see the ghost disappear down a long flight of stairs. We continued the chase but ran more slowly down the stairs than we had on level ground. As the ghost disappeared into the darkness at the end of the stairs, my legs became tangled and I lost my footing, rolling down the steps to the bottom. My flashlight flew into the air and I felt a warm stream of blood pour from my scalp.

I cursed as I struggled to my feet, and the sound of gunshots echoed through the darkness, but not from behind me. It's not Fats or Panzi, I thought, what the hell is going on here?

My question was echoed by my companions, but as soon as I saw them, I had one to ask them. "Where's Shunzi?" I demanded.

"He's gone," Fats told me. "When he found his father's corpse and the treasure too, he decided he'd had enough of this adventure. Now tell us, who's shooting?"

We swept our flashlights across the place and discovered

a tower at the other end of this staircase with a long platform outside. This was called a Sky Veranda, the platform holding the equipment that lowered the coffin into its chamber below, which was where the volleys of gunfire were coming from. Could the ghost baby have leaped down there? Is that what the guns were aiming at?

The three of us went up a staircase into the tower in single file. When we looked down, we saw a huge circular chamber below. Ning and her group stood inside it, all firing their rifles without stopping.

"Shit, look at that, will you?" Panzi breathed. Surrounding the people below were their targets, an ocean of centipedes, each one the size of my foot.

In the middle of the chamber was a coffin well the shape of an inverted pyramid, with eight enormous black coffins at the bottom. Between the columns was a colossal coffin of translucent jade which had been pried open—and that was where the centipedes were coming from.

Could this be the Coffin Carried by Nine Dragons that was described in the text on the bronze fish? Was this really the coffin of Emperor Wannu? And how did these jerks manage to trigger the centipede attack—had they stepped on one of them and maddened the rest?

"Should we help them?" Fats asked me.

Panzi shook his head. "Let a few of them die first."

Fats laughed. "You might as well shoot them. They'll die faster that way."

I had no idea of what to do. This wasn't an issue of saving or not saving them, but what they would do to us after we saved them. Ning had been ready to kill us in the undersea tomb, and we only made our escape due to blind luck. And that was after I had already saved her once; you'd think she would have been grateful. But after seeing so many people die, my conscience would haunt me for the rest of my life if I didn't save her now and her group too.

I wasn't sure whether a rescue could be carried out at all. Opening fire from above wouldn't really make a difference. If we were to save them, we'd have to throw down some ropes and pull them up.

As I was trying to come up with a plan, I suddenly caught a glimpse of a foreigner carrying a man who was very familiar. Unsure of whether I could believe my eyes, I pointed this out to Panzi, who immediately shouted, "It's Captain Three!"

"Are you sure?" I moved a few steps closer to get a better look but instead what I saw was the ghost baby. I had stepped on it. It instantly grabbed my foot, pulling me off balance, and I fell flat on my face, shouting for help. Panzi and Fats opened fire, blowing its head to fragments, but the weight of its body pulled me along with it as it fell from the tower.

I landed right in the middle of Ning's group. As I got to my feet, I saw the centipedes racing off in full retreat, with only the dead ones left behind. A small crowd of people encircled me, looking at me as though I were some kind of apparition. Ning stared as though she had no idea of who I was, recognition only slowly coming to her eyes as she gazed.

Nobody moved. I began to walk toward the man who looked like my uncle and as I did, the people surrounding me backed away, their hands on their guns. Fats and Panzi raised their own firearms as they saw this but I beckoned for them to put their rifles down.

Ning waved her hand and said to her team, "Drop your guns. I know this man; we worked together in the past." Although they obeyed, they continued to eye me with distrust.

Ning frowned, looked at me, and asked, "You guys… why are you here?"

Fats smiled as he and Panzi jumped down to join us. "This is legendary fate coming to pass. As the poem says, 'Separated as we are thousands of miles, we come together as if by predestination.' If I told you we were just passing through, would you believe me?"

Members of Ning's group seemed to recognize Fats and several of them cursed as he appeared. "Terrific," one of them muttered. "We find a nightmare while we're trapped in hell."

I laughed at the remark while Fats glared at me and the speaker. Ning began to question him as Panzi and I ran to the man we thought could be Uncle Three.

He was being held by a foreigner, who placed him on the ground as we approached. I looked down at an emaciated face covered with a scruffy-looking gray beard.

"Shit, it's my uncle! He looks twelve years older than he did when I last saw him. I thought finding him would mean our rescue, but Panzi, look! This isn't the man who led us in the past. Could this really be Uncle Three or is it just another illusion?"

Uncle Three opened his eyes, squinted, and twitched in response to my voice, but he remained silent. Suddenly I was both relieved and furious—here was my uncle and now what in the hell was I going to do?

Panzi began to examine the old man; there was a

badly infected wound on his chest and a large number of centipedes buried under his pus-covered skin.

Face reddened with rage, Panzi lunged for the foreigner standing nearby, yelling, "What the fuck did you people do to Master Three? How did he end up like this?"

Grabbing Panzi and holding him still, I asked, "Where did you find my uncle and why didn't you take care of his injuries?"

"We just found him right here, right now. At first we thought he was dead. Ning said this old man knows a lot and that he had to come with us. She told me to carry him but I wouldn't have done it if I'd known he had all those bugs in his flesh."

"It was definitely you people who did this!" Panzi was furious. "I saw this in Vietnam. The Vietnamese used this trick to torture prisoners under interrogation— I'm going to kill you all!"

I held Panzi tighter. "Calm down. This has nothing to do with them. If they had put the centipedes on my uncle's body, that would mean they knew how to handle them and they wouldn't have been in such a panic just now."

Ning walked over to inspect my uncle and looked as though she was going to throw up. "Get over here now, Doctor," she commanded, and some of her men brought Uncle Three into a sitting position. As he rose, I felt him drop something hastily into my pocket and with a surge of relief I knew my uncle was still in charge. I squeezed his shoulder to let him know I'd noticed and his eyelids flickered slightly in response.

The doctor found sixteen wounds on my uncle's body, cleaned them, and removed all of the centipedes that had burrowed into his skin. When the excisions were finally stitched shut, Panzi asked the doctor about my uncle's condition. He sighed and said, "I've done everything I can. His wounds are badly infected. I'll give him a shot of antibiotics later but he's running a high fever and I don't know if he'll make it. It all depends on how strong his will to live is. Don't disturb him, let him sleep."

I stood up to move into a corner where I could discover what my uncle had given me, but I tottered and fell.

"You're in bad shape too," the doctor said. He bandaged my cuts and told me to stay still.

I looked around me. Fats and Ning were talking together, too far away for me to hear what they were saying. Panzi was a wreck; he sat miserable and silent beside my uncle's unconscious body. There seemed to be sixteen people in Ning's group, some resting nearby, others exploring the area where the coffins lay.

I wanted to be where nobody would pay attention to what I might do, but there was no place to hide. I went to the body of the ghost baby, which was so battered and disgusting that nobody else drew near. Carefully I pulled out what my uncle had put in my pocket. It was a slip of paper, crumpled into a small ball. I stealthily unfolded it and began to read.

I'm going down.

This is the end. You guys hurry back. Further along is not a place you could handle.

Everything that you guys want to know is written on the Bronze Fish with Snake Brows.

Zhang Qilin

It was from Poker-face and it ended with the

indecipherable English alphabet letters that had puzzled us earlier. What in the hell did he intend for them to mean?

Below this was a line of words in my uncle's scrawled handwriting:

"We are only one step away from the truth. Give the fish to Ning's assistant Wu Laosi, and have him decipher it. Don't worry about them. The most important thing is still in my hands. They won't dare do anything to us."

Apparently when Uncle Three got here, he had discovered Poker-face's note, and then wrote this message for us. It seemed as though Poker-face wanted to stop us from going down among the coffins, and judging by the words in his note, he had gone to a very dangerous place via a tunnel somewhere. And Uncle Three clearly didn't appreciate that kind warning.

This is really killing me, I thought. What the hell does this guy want to do? And what on earth is the important thing that is still in Uncle Three's hands? Since Poker-face didn't want us to go down, who were the carved symbols left for? Could he have left them…for himself?

I suddenly found myself traveling in the outer space of my imagination, and more and more clues began to surface. But because the previous mystery was way too complicated, the emergence of a new idea plunged me even deeper into confusion. I remembered the letters in the undersea tomb that let Poker-face know when he saw them that he had been there before. Was he carving new symbols because he thought he would lose his memory again? Did he write the letters in advance so he would again remember everything the next time he came here?

It's all too confusing, I thought, and my head began to

ache again. Ning and Fats shouted to me; startled, I turned around and saw them beckoning for me to join them. So I simply stopped thinking, stuffed the note back into my pocket, and approached.

Ning handed me a glass of water. As I took a sip, she said, "I talked over this with Mr. Wang. Let's cooperate from now on, okay?"

Cooperate? I remembered everything that she had done in the undersea tomb to throw us off the track and I thought of the words I'd just read. What should I say to this woman? Now that we found Uncle Three, I felt much more at ease, but there was also a bit of selfishness in this comfort, as I was thinking I could finally get out of this place. But as Uncle Three mentioned, we were very close to finding the truth.

It seemed as though my uncle was somewhat puzzled himself. If we rescued him and brought him out right now, we might find out he was as ignorant as we were. It would be fine so long as we put all of this out of our mind. But if we didn't, Uncle Three would definitely come here again, and would I be able to sit back and do nothing to help him?

I thought about this, gritted my teeth, and asked, "How can we work together? Why don't you tell me? Honestly, I really have to think hard about cooperating with you again."

She looked at me, smiled, and shook her head. "Oh that. I didn't have time to say goodbye to you on the island. Now I'm thanking you for saving my life. When we were under the sea…it was a really hard time for me. I didn't mean to hurt you."

How can I believe you? I asked silently. I lit a cigarette and said, "If you really want to work together, tell me what this is all about. What were you looking for at the bottom of the sea? And what are you doing here?"

Fats chimed in, "That's right. Everyone has to be frank and honest before any cooperation can take place."

Ning was surprised. "You guys don't know? Didn't your Uncle Three tell you anything? You guys have no idea and you still dare to risk your lives like this?"

I smiled. If Uncle Three had told me the truth about this, I probably wouldn't care now if he were dead or alive. I shook my head and said, "He didn't say. I've been an aimless pawn all along."

Ning frowned as she stared at me for a long time. "No wonder. I've always thought you played a particularly powerful role because I could never tell if you were lying or not. And now it turns out that you really don't know anything at all."

I felt there was something wrong here all of a sudden— why did this woman want to work with us? She had so many helpers and adequate supplies of food and gear; there were only three of us, without anything at all. Why did she need us? Even if it were because I could scare the centipedes away, she could simply tie me up and bring me along as a captive. Was it because she was in a hopeless situation or did she have some compelling reason to want us with her?

Ning stared at me, and sighed. "In fact, we play a minor role in this ourselves so we don't know too much either. We're merely working for our boss." She motioned for us to sit down and then called to a foreigner. "This is Kirk, a Sinologist specializing in the Dong Xia dynasty. He knows more than any of us so ask him your questions."

"Unfortunately I can't tell you our boss's motive," Kirk said, looking me straight in the eye. "To be honest, I'm just the team leader. Ning and I only know that we have to get to a place, take something out, and then our mission is over. We had two objectives in the undersea tomb—an imperial jade seal, a ghost seal, which was rumored to possess the capability of summoning troops from the world of the dead; and a map of this palace. Unfortunately we found neither."

"Ghost seal?" I almost jumped out of my skin when I heard what he said. "Are you talking about the ghost seal that belonged to the Ruler of Dead Soldiers? Are you saying that was in the undersea tomb?"

Kirk nodded and said, "That's correct. I believe you guys know a little about it, right? After Wang Canghai robbed the tomb of the Ruler of the Dead, he replaced the ghost seal with one of the Bronze Fish with Snake Brows. We'd always thought he had taken the ghost seal into his own tomb, but we couldn't find it after numerous searches. And the map of this place is probably in the hands of your Uncle Three. We don't even know how many times this old fox has fooled us, but we have to cooperate with him because he has so much more information than we do."

I nodded and grimaced at his words about my uncle. I knew just what he meant. Fats had been listening and interrupted, "So when Ning went undersea with us, what did she bring back up?"

Kirk was just about to answer when Ning cut him short. "Just say what you're allowed to say. That's all."

"What do you mean?" Fats retorted.

Kirk seemed not to care about Ning's warning. He

laughed. "Even if you don't tell them, you'll still have to take it out sooner or later. Besides, it's useless now."

Ning glanced at us and stamped her foot in the way Fats and I remembered so well. "I worked so hard to get this. What a bargain it is for you guys to get it so easily now."

She handed me a stack of paper and I saw a group of photos, all of murals, none of which I'd ever seen before. "Where did you take these pictures?"

Kirk replied, "They were taken in the main chamber of the undersea tomb; they're very important narrative murals. Take a close look at the pictures."

There were fifteen murals. They appeared to be related but there was nothing sequential in what they depicted. One showed a group of people climbing a snow-covered mountain; one showed a single climber surveying the peaks; another showed rock climbers; and another, soldiers fighting in a battle. Nothing seemed linked in any way.

Kirk saw my confusion. He held out one of the photos and asked, "Look at the first picture. What do you see?"

The mural depicted several people dressed in Jurchen clothing tying up a man who was clearly Han Chinese. "Is this a prisoner of war?"

"You could say that. But guess who the prisoner is?" Kirk smiled mysteriously.

I looked again and saw the prisoner looked a lot like the paintings of Wang Canghai on the porcelain vessels I'd found in the undersea tomb. "Is this Wang Canghai? Did the Jurchen catch him and hold him prisoner?"

Kirk answered, "That's right, and that's the first image in the series. What does a picture like that say? It suggests that Wang Canghai might have been held as a captive and forced to build this tomb."

I looked at several other photos. "What about these?"

"These are all the things that happened after Wang Canghai was taken captive and fell into the hands of the Dong Xia people. Although we don't entirely understand all of it, we can make a pretty close guess of what happened based on the other photos."

I carefully looked at one of them and suddenly realized something wrong. "This one…"

Kirk looked and nodded. "Your eyes are very sharp. This is a very important photo. Do you see that this is the imperial tomb inside of the volcanic crater? When Wang Canghai was captured, the imperial tomb was already built but it was very badly damaged."

"Ah!" I said in response. "Was it possible that he didn't build the imperial tomb above our heads?"

Kirk explained, "We've done some research and found that the overall style of the imperial tomb above was from the Yin and Shang dynasties, but Wang Changhai was forced to transform it into the Ming dynasty style. The people of Dong Xia didn't capture him to build an imperial tomb, but to reconstruct one, because this tomb was really very old and could no longer be used."

"So the palace here already existed before that?" Fats asked.

Kirk nodded and replied, "We found the old road that leads to this place by studying these photos. But there are still some pictures that we can't figure out. Like this one."

The third photo counting from the end was a mural of countless evil spirits scurrying from a rock. Another showed a black mollusk of some sort climbing up a precipice where people were pouring something down from above.

I was feeling shaky as I looked through the photos. I sighed and was about to sit down and take a closer look when Ning suddenly grabbed me by the hand. "Okay, we've told you our story. You can look at the photos again whenever you want. Aren't you going to tell us something now?"

"Tell you what?" I asked, baffled.

"I didn't hold back on the things I know. Now, what's going on between you guys and Wu Sansheng?" Ning glanced at me and continued, "You can't be more uncharitable than a woman like me, can you?"

Instead of replying, I asked, "Is there someone by the name of Wu Laosi on your team?"

Ning nodded and asked curiously, "Why? Do you know him?"

I removed the two bronze fish from my pocket and flashed them into her face. "Everything that you need to know is right here. If Wu Laosi isn't dead, bring him to me."

Kirk almost passed out and Ning's gaze froze. Stuttering, she said, "My God! You actually have two... two of them..." Her eyes followed the fish as I moved them into the light.

CHAPTER THIRTY-SEVEN
SECRET OF THE BRONZE FISH

I really didn't want to reveal the bronze fish, but since my uncle told me to, I did. I certainly didn't expect such a dramatic reaction.

After a long silence, Ning asked, "Where did you get these? They hold the secret text of the dragon fish, the arowanas! I thought there was only one, but..."

"Is there anyone here who can read it?"

Ning called out "Wu Laosi!" and a man rushed to her side.

"Can you translate this?" I asked. He nodded and reverently picked up the fish as if they had been handed to him directly by the gods. He pointed his flashlight at the scales, and a huge portion of Jurchen writing was instantly reflected onto the ground. A few others in the group immediately came over to write down the text.

Ning's team was really something. These men could translate as they copied; they made Monk Hua look like a schoolboy. As I read what they had written, everything that had been a mystery became clearer to me.

The text was very simple, explaining in the beginning that the secret hidden in the coded text was very significant. Wang Canghai had recorded it in hopes that it would never be read, but if it were, he hoped that it would be discovered by a Han Chinese instead of a Jurchen.

What followed was a record of what he went through after he had been captured by the Jurchen people of the Dong Xia dynasty. Then he explained that in order to obtain some of the treasures that the Dong Xia wanted, he had robbed graves, one after the other. He secretively placed the bronze fish in places which were of great spiritual importance, giving someone in the future a chance to discover this secret.

Ah! Turns out it all started from here, I thought. As I read on, the text became unbelievable—it said that, while he was in the process of reconstructing the imperial tomb, Wang Canghai gradually discovered a bizarre secret about the Emperor of the Dong Xia.

During the ten years that Wang Canghai was held captive, he was taken to what was called the Miracle Door to the Underworld. Legend had it that the throne of the emperor was not hereditary. Instead, the royal successors crawled out from the Miracle Door to the Underworld as soon as the previous monarch had passed away. This Door could only be opened by the emperor just before he died. If anyone else opened it, he would be consumed by the fires of hell, and the whiteness of the Changbai Mountains would disappear forever. As I read, I had a feeling that this might refer to a volcanic eruption. Could Emperor Wannu have climbed out from a volcano? I wondered.

Wang Canghai had the honor to witness the transfer of the throne once. He was terrified when he saw that the new emperor who emerged from the Door to the Underworld was a monster, not a human being.

The Door to the Underworld was located underneath

the imperial tomb that we had been searching for. It dated back to ancient times and was probably made during the Xia dynasty. The tunnel that led to the Door was guarded by birds with human heads.

My mouth turned dry as I thought about the freakish-looking birds that had attacked us, but the most bizarre disclosures were yet to come.

The second fish held the story of Wang Canghai secretly sneaking through the Door to the Underworld. Apparently he was incoherent after he returned and the text was difficult to understand, but it was clear that he had seen something horrible.

Fats was listening as I read this aloud and interrupted, "Didn't the text say that whoever opened the door would be burned by the fires of hell? So how come Wang Canghai was able to enter and return unscathed? This is bullshit."

"He must have used some method we don't know in order to get out," I replied. But the text at this point was too confusing for any of us to understand it.

"Wait," Ning broke in. "One of my men has just discovered a weird symbol near the coffins. Come and see."

We went over to look; the lids of several coffins had been opened and everything they had contained was spread out beside them. Nearby was an open trapdoor with a symbol scrawled on its inner wall.

"Did one of you put this symbol here?" Ning asked.

"No. We have no idea of what this could be or who might have written it," I lied, as Zhang Qilin sprang into my mind.

One of the workers called, "These are shadow coffins—all fakes. The corpses in them are jade statues; the real coffin isn't here. When we opened these coffins a while ago, we set off a trap that launched the attack of the centipedes. Now that we've explored more carefully, we've found this secret tunnel; someone has already made his way in. It looks like this is a double-layered tomb and the real coffin lies somewhere below."

I looked beyond the open trapdoor. It led to a very unusual tunnel, steeper and deeper than any I'd seen before. This had to be the place Qilin had warned me not to explore.

CHAPTER THIRTY-EIGHT
THE ONLY WAY OUT

Fats and I pointed our flashlights down into the steep darkness below the open trapdoor. We could see nothing but blackness.

I started to panic as I thought about how far we'd traveled; we were already deep inside the Changbai Mountains. If we kept going, where would we end up? The center of the earth?

But even if it would be the center of the earth, we had to keep going because the guiding symbols that Poker-face left unmistakably indicated that he had gone in this direction. Every step we took moved us an inch closer to the truth.

We had no choice but to enter the tunnel. Relying on the light of our flashlights, we moved forward for almost twenty minutes. Fats suddenly said, "Young Wu, did you notice that it's starting to warm up a little in here?"

I nodded and replied, "Maybe our destination is close to a volcanic area. There might be lava or hot springs somewhere nearby, so the temperature is gradually rising as we go further."

We continued moving forward for a while when Fats asked again, "Tell me the truth. What kind of special relationship is there between you and that Qilin fellow?"

"What in the hell are you asking?" I sputtered and then realized I'd misunderstood the question. Fats just wanted to know why Zhang Qilin and I both had blood with the power to repel carnivorous insects.

According to what Liang had said when we were at the bronze tree, the peculiar power in my blood was because I'd eaten the dried blood of the legendary beast, the qilin. Since I had no idea if this was true or not, I kept quiet, thinking it over.

When I didn't answer, Fats continued with his theory. "He's probably a long-lost brother or cousin of yours, or maybe he's the illegitimate child of your father. No doubt everyone in your family is genetically bequeathed with this special power."

"Stop the bullshit. I'm my father's only son. If a stick-in-the-mud like him had an illegitimate child, then there's no man in the world who could be considered faithful. We have more to worry about than this nonsense of yours. Save your breath for something important."

We walked on for a long time and finally came to the end of the tunnel. As we emerged, a warm breeze touched my face and I felt unreasonably happy.

I looked around and saw we were standing on a platform, built on huge pillars that made it jut out over a cliff, like the one we had found in the ice dome.

A huge black three-legged pot stood in the middle of the platform. One of its legs had already sunk through the stone floor, looking as though it was about to topple over. Obviously we would have to be careful while walking on the platform, as the rocks that supported it were no longer solid.

Beyond the edge of the platform was yet another cliff with its end lost in darkness.

"Why have we come to an end again?" Fats whined. "There's nothing more ahead, yet there's still no coffin. Where is this Emperor Wannu hiding?"

"That's not even the strangest part," I said. "We followed Qilin's symbol but as you can see, there's no one here at all. Could it mean that when he found that it was a dead end, he turned back? Or…" I said as I looked toward the darkness, "could he have flown away?"

"Maybe we can climb down the cliff here," Fats said. He took out a signal gun, loaded a flare, and fired a shot into the darkness.

We walked to the edge of the platform as the signal flare burst into flames high up in the air, looking like a small sun in this immeasurable night. It lit up everything before our eyes and under its glow I could see that this was actually an enormous crevice in the mountain; the platform that we stood on was built on cliffs projecting from one side of the crevice. About six hundred and fifty feet across were cliffs on the opposite side, and below us was a flat expanse that looked like a huge African rift valley.

The signal flare gradually dropped below the platform, revealing another breathtaking sight. Crossing the space above the valley were layers of bronze chains as thick as the diameter of a bowl, connecting both sides of the crevice and continuing downward to the earth below.

As it fell, the flare shone on a countless number of these chains, from which were suspended many objects that looked as though they might be bells.

"I found a rope," Fats yelled. "Look, it's tied to one of

38. THE ONLY WAY OUT

those chains and it looks like it goes all the way to the bottom. It must have been left here by our poker-faced friend. It looks as though he's climbed down—shall we follow and give him a little surprise or should we go back up and tell those other guys where we're going?"

"We don't even know if we'll be able to get back up here after we climb down so we might as well bring them along with us. Ning's equipment is better than ours so it'll probably be worth going back. Besides, Panzi is still up there, and Uncle Three too. We can't leave them behind."

Once Ning heard about the bronze chains, she quickly took out her photos and pointed to one of them. The mural she'd photographed was a painting of many Dong Xia warriors carrying bows and arrows climbing on a precipice, and the background illustrated many chainlike objects. Clearly it was a drawing of an exploration of the valley that Fats and I just found.

I said, "So apparently these chains weren't put up here by the Dong Xia people."

Fats said, "Could the chains have been put there as some sort of defense to prevent something climbing up from below? Something like the giant black mollusk thingy shown in that other mural?"

I nodded and said, "Could be. Which mural is this, Ning? What's the next one?"

"This is the sixth. There are five more after that. Here they are in order."

Ning spread out the five photos as I looked at the mural in the last one. It was a scene of many Dong Xia warriors shooting their arrows as if in fierce battle, yet their enemies weren't visible and I couldn't tell what they were shooting at. I remembered the strange birds we'd seen earlier and I felt my heart squeeze painfully tight. Could there be creatures like that waiting for us below?

The next one was of many evil spirits coming through the rocks. I gasped.

Ning asked me, "Do you see something wrong, Superman Wu?"

"It's nothing really. You see, the battle scenes come after the mural of the soldiers coming down the cliff. I think perhaps they're telling us that we'll encounter some sort of danger after we get down to the valley, and those with weapons should be ready and alert."

Everyone seemed eager to go even after viewing the cautionary warning of the photograph. We picked up our bags and walked down the tunnel, into the depths of the Changbai Mountains.

I followed at the end of the team to check on Uncle Three, but he was still unconscious. "Don't worry, Young Master Wu," Panzi assured me. "Even if we have to climb and crawl to safety, I'll get your uncle out of any hellhole we come across."

Soon we reached the platform. Fats shot another signal flare in the air and let everyone take a look at the spectacular scenery surrounding the valley. Panzi and I took out some ropes and got ready to climb down.

It was a risky decision. We had no idea what was down there, and Ning's team wasn't exactly on our side. After I took out all the ropes we'd need, I pulled Fats over. "Be careful," I warned him. "Watch out for that little bitch turning against us again, once we find what she wants."

Fats grinned without a word and pulled up a corner of

his shirt. Tucked against his bare skin were ten sticks of dynamite, tied to his belt.

We tested the rope that Qilin had used; it seemed strong enough. Panzi climbed down first. After he landed on the chain, he hung down full-length like an athlete on a horizontal bar, smoothly jumping onto the chain below. He repeated the same motion five or six times, getting about thirty feet down before giving us a go-ahead signal.

Kirk put on a headlamp and, turning himself into a moving lightbulb, he climbed down next. Using him as our illumination, we all climbed down from the platform one by one and came to the world of suspending chains.

The breeze didn't seem very strong when we were on the platform, but the wind blowing from the bottom of the valley seemed particularly sharp and piercing now. Standing on the chains, I felt like I was sailing, and while the boat moved, so did the sail. I grew more and more nervous by the second.

But the chains were placed close together, and the descent was easy. Regardless of whatever their original purpose might have been, they made a convenient ladder for us. As I climbed down, I felt more and more secure, showing off a trick or two as I descended. I felt like Spider-Man.

But it was a long trip to the valley. Four hours passed; the platform above us had become much smaller when we looked up at it now. What Fats and I had thought were giant bells hanging on the bronze chains now appeared before us. Ning handed me her night-vision binoculars and in their eerie green light I saw the "bells" were actually corpses. Strands of black silk, each as thin as a hair, extended from the back of their necks, suspending them from the chains.

Wang Canghai's account had described strange birds with human heads that couldn't be seen in the air but were only visible when they alighted on the ground; before eating their kill, they hung it from branches to air-dry. Could the number of corpses here mean that there were bird nests down below?

No wonder Qilin was so determined to keep us from following him. But there was no other way out. If we didn't take this risk, we'd still be dead in the end. "Come on. Keep going," I hissed and we continued our descent.

38. THE ONLY WAY OUT

CHAPTER THIRTY-NINE
NESTS OF THE GUARDIANS

The corpses we passed were clad in fragments of armor, some mummified by the dry air around them and others completely skeletal. We were surrounded by them as we made our way down; their empty eye sockets seemed to watch our every move. The silence was particularly ghostly in this place but at least there was no trace of the predatory birds.

Fats pointed to the hanging corpses and whispered, "They're all long dead. There's nothing for those damned birds to live on here. Could they have deserted this place?"

I shook my head and told him to keep quiet. But his remark gave me some hope. If there had been birds living here and they had left to find new hunting grounds, there might be an exit somewhere that could serve as our escape route. Of course it was also possible that they were only gone for a little while; they might have flown out of here like bats in caves, going to hunt in a flock. If so, we needed to hurry out of here ourselves. I urged my companions to pick up speed.

But Kirk and Panzi, in the lead, had come to a complete stop and Panzi beckoned for me to join them. I took several leaps down, came to the spot where they were, and looked down. We had almost reached the floor of the valley.

It was an immense, black area; we could see nothing but a few fuzzy green shapes through the night-vision binoculars.

"Drop a flare and make it count, Fats. We don't have many left," I ordered. He obeyed and we watched its fluorescent dot plunging like a shooting star all the way to the bottom. It rolled along the floor of the valley and came to a stop.

Fats picked up his rifle and fired three shots that hit the nose of the flare below. Immediately it began to blaze and the entire valley was filled with light as bright as the sun at high noon.

Below us were many black, jagged volcanic rocks, and skeletons that had fallen from the chains above. Piles of bones and layers of black excrement that looked as though they'd been left by giant birds covered the rocks. On one side of a cliff that enclosed the valley was a huge bronze double door, about one hundred feet tall and two hundred feet wide, grander than anything I'd ever seen before. It stood as tall as a ten-story building. Who could have created such a marvel and who could ever open it?

Ning said, "This must be that Miracle Door to the Underworld where Emperor Wannu appeared. Each time that the new ruler took his throne, legends say the door was resealed with the skin of sacrificed corpses. What do you think could be inside?"

I barely heard her, preoccupied with my own thoughts. How could the emperors have emerged from this place? Were they gods with the power to move rocks weighing thousands of tons? I murmured, "No matter what's behind this door, there's no way we're able to enter it."

The door reminded me of the bronze tree I'd seen deep in the Qinling Mountains. Could these mammoth works in bronze, which were beyond human ability to cast in ancient times, somehow be related? Could things like this exist in other immense mountain ranges like the Kunlun Mountains or the Himalayas? I had a vague feeling that I was approaching one of the wonders of remote antiquity, and it made me feel as insignificant as a flea. I was worth nothing compared to the miracles of these ancient mysteries. How could I ever hope to understand their secrets?

The flare gradually died, and the valley returned to darkness, yet I still stood motionless, paralyzed by my thoughts. Panzi grabbed me by the arm, said, "Let's keep going," and brought me back to the task at hand.

We climbed down the chains one after the other and soon reached the bottom of the valley. Carefully stepping on the bones beneath our feet, we walked to the giant bronze door. Immediately my feeling of awe grew stronger and I had to fight off the impulse to fall down on my knees.

That a person as modern as I felt this way made it even more difficult to imagine how shocked Wang Canghai must have been when he found this door with the Dong Xia warriors. No wonder he recorded everything that happened here, hoping to pass on their journey through hell and its aftermath to the generations to come. I could even feel Wang Changhai's pain and sympathize with a man who thought he thoroughly understood the laws and secrets of the universe and then found out he really didn't know anything at all.

As these confused speculations went through my mind, I was suddenly jolted by a shout from Fats.

39. NESTS OF THE GUARDIANS

He was pointing his flashlight into the middle of the valley, where heaps of gravel looked like small hills. He walked toward a pyramid-shaped boulder that had been carved into a platform. A long stone staircase ran up the side with lamps placed on both sides of every step.

Fats was headed toward the object placed on the platform, an enormous white jade coffin the size of a limousine with nine stone-carved dragons coiled at the base in the shape of a lotus. At each corner of the coffin was a black stone statue in human shape, as if all four were worshipping the coffin on bended knees.

A mammoth three-legged vessel had been placed before the coffin. Behind that was a wall with carved murals which we were unable to see clearly.

I gasped, "Could this be it? Emperor Wannu's Coffin Carried by Nine Dragons—is this the one in Wang Canghai's secret text?"

"Absolutely," Fats replied. "Didn't someone say Emperor Wannu's coffin was guarded by nine dragons? Look. Aren't there nine dragons there? And I thought Chen Ah-Si was just bullshitting us."

As her group began to run closer to the coffin, Ning cried out, "Don't go over there. It's dangerous!"

Her men stopped and she continued, "Can't you see the dragons under the coffin?"

"My dear old grandmother, they're made of stone," Fats sneered. "What kind of danger could they present? What in the hell is wrong with your eyesight?"

Ning's face flushed up with rage. "What in the hell is wrong with yours? I'm not talking about the stone dragons. Take a good look at the side of the platform!"

"I don't see anything," I told her. "What are you talking about?"

I followed the beam of Ning's flashlight as she pointed it into the darkness and still saw nothing. Then a slight motion shifted in the light—there was a huge centipede camouflaged in the rocky wall of the platform. It was easily eight feet long—and it wasn't alone. Spiraling around the platform were eight more of those monsters. This truly was a coffin carried by nine dragons.

Ning explained, "Those are volcanic centipedes, carnivorous insects, vicious and very quick. They'll bite a man in two before he even knows they are nearby. Humans are their favorite prey."

"This is too weird," I heard Kirk mutter. "The general life expectancy of these centipedes is usually only about two to three years. They should have died after growing to the length of a man's finger. Could these huge monsters have been alive for thousands of years? But don't be too nervous. It's winter and these things are still in hibernation. They won't wake that easily."

Ning said, "Not easily woken means there's still a possibility that they can be roused. People like us would make a perfect hibernation snack."

Fats was ready to kill. "Let me go over and shoot a few bullets in their heads; they'll die no matter what size they are. Then we'll go and find out whether this Emperor Wannu was a man or a monster."

"Absolutely not," Panzi argued. "Don't you remember Shunzi saying that dead centipedes will awaken their dormant companions? Can you imagine how many centipedes there are in this valley? There might be an even bigger one hanging around here to guard and protect its brood."

I raised the night-vision binoculars in hopes of discovering that these centipedes might only be fossilized ancient insects. As I looked through the lenses, I saw a lot of Jurchen text painted on the mural behind the coffin. Could this perhaps be the most valuable information that an ancient tomb could contain—the last will and testament of the tomb's occupant?

I quickly called to Wu Laosi, handed him the binoculars, and asked him to read what was written on the mural. "I can't tell," he said. "That isn't written in the Jurchen language. I can't read these characters at all."

"Damn this emperor—he was way too slick. He didn't give away anything for free," I cursed. No wonder not even Wang Canghai, after being directly involved with the renovation of the ancient tomb for twenty years, could discover the core of the secret that the Dong Xia dynasties concealed.

Different ideas whizzed through my head every minute, and I had no idea what I was thinking. Then I heard Panzi calling, "Fats? Are you all right? Do you want me to take your place?"

Looking up, I saw Fats and Kirk had climbed up onto a chain and were cautiously approaching the area above the coffin. Fats was tying a rope around his waist, probably trying to imitate a superhero by hanging down from the chains and suspending himself over the coffin. But no one tried to stop him; some of the men were even giving him hints on what to do next.

"What in hell is going on here?" I asked Ning. "Are we

really so eager to watch Fats feed the Nine Dragons?"

"It's all right. I discovered just now that the centipede tails are tethered with bronze chains to the stone posts under the platform, so their range of activity is limited. Only those who walk close by them are in any danger. We've all come here to find out what's in this coffin. Now that we've found it, why should we hold ourselves back?"

"Even if Fats can reach it, he'll never open the lid of such a gigantic coffin. He's just making a fool of himself," I protested.

"He's not going to open the lid. He's only going to slip a hook into a crack in the coffin. We'll hang a pulley over that bronze chain above and then lift the coffin lid up from there."

I felt very uneasy. Ning was just doing what she'd been hired to do—finding one specific object in the coffin. And even though we were in a desperate situation, she still hadn't given up. Although I didn't know what she was trying to find, I saw no reason why anything should make her feel as if this was more important than her own life. Besides, Wang Canghai couldn't have missed any grave-robbing trick when designing this tomb, and the sheer number of bronze chains hanging above the coffin surely meant there was some trap involved. Fats had foolishly volunteered to spearhead this operation so he could take advantage of being the first person to open the coffin. I had to stop him.

Before I could move, the first disaster occurred. Kirk, who was standing above Fats, suddenly plunged down from the chains and fell on top of the coffin. We heard a dull thud as his head cracked open and his brains splattered over the lid.

39. NESTS OF THE GUARDIANS

Fats had already plunged downward when this happened. Thanks to the ropes around his waist which were stretched to their limits, his head fell short of the coffin, and he hung in the air just above Kirk's dead body.

What's going on? I thought. Could something be pushing them onto the coffin?

"Panzi," I yelled. "Send up a flare right now."

As the flare burst into light, we could see numerous shadows hovering above us. Several of them were hanging upside down on the chains, curiously watching us. It was the time for the giant birds to return to their nest with their prey.

"Don't fire your rifles," I called to the men who had raised their guns to shoot. "I don't think these birds see very well but they seem sensitive to sounds. Earlier in the front hall they found us because of a rifle shot."

But as I spoke, someone opened fire—not just one gunshot, but a rapid volley of them that echoed through the valley. The outbursts reverberated through the skies, setting off a rumpus in the air; countless hovering shadows began diving down like lightning flashes.

I angrily turned around to see which son of a bitch had ignored me and there was Fats on the stone platform, holding Kirk's rifle and raking the coffin with gunfire.

I looked again. The giant coffin had opened a tiny bit and three purple arms protruded from it, their long fingers waving in the air, reaching for Fats.

CHAPTER FORTY
KWAN YIN WITH A THOUSAND ARMS

Panzi's flare went out and darkness quickly engulfed us again. He rapidly set off another and everyone opened fire, shooting up over a dozen tongues of flame toward the heavens. Soon, several flying shadows plunged lifeless from above.

Strong light could apparently confuse these creatures, just as a bear is unable to tell for a short period of time if a man is human when he pretends to quack and walk like a duck. But this was only temporary, and we had just fired our last flare. With so many of these strange birds, we faced a merciless slaughter in the dark once the flare went out.

The birds were pressing lower and lower by the minute, with some even sweeping right past our heads. We simply didn't have enough bullets to kill them all, and soon a few of our guns were useless. Fats was in deep shit of his own; no matter how tough he was, he would soon be finished if no one went over to help him.

I had no idea of what to do when Fats suddenly fired a shot at my feet, scaring me stiff. I looked up and as I read his lips, I realized he was telling us to run.

Then I knew what I needed to say. "Panzi, take Uncle Three and the others and run toward the end of the valley.

This is the nesting ground for those damned birds, and they've got to fly away from here to find food. Find out which direction they're flying from, and run every step of the way. Don't worry about me. I have to go help Fats."

Panzi grabbed me. "Are you going to be okay? Why don't I go help Fats and you take Master Three with you?"

"I can't carry that old man." Lifting up my arms and showing him my bleeding cuts, I said, "Besides, I have my blood as protection—there won't be any problem."

Panzi nodded as he threw me his rifle. "Be careful. We'll wait for you outside." He tossed my uncle over his shoulders and shouted to the others, "Follow me!" as he began to run toward the end of the valley.

Everyone chased after him except Ning who stood motionless, her face pale and white.

"Run, you stupid little bitch," I yelled at her, but she cocked her rifle and raised it into firing position. I knew from past experience that it was useless to try to persuade her to go against her own wishes so I left her as I ran toward the stone platform.

The coffin lid was already partially open, and half the body of what looked like a huge black spider was squeezing its way out. Rushing up the platform, I saw Fats had climbed back up onto the bronze chains and was firing volleys at the birds that kept diving down at him. He was paying no attention to the monster below.

"Fats, throw me some bullets," I yelled.

He tossed some down and I began to shoot at the birds, giving Fats the cover he needed to come and join me. He slid down the chains, yelling, "Come on—run!"

I turned to look for Ning but she was nowhere to be

seen. I had no idea whether she had run toward safety or if she'd been carried off by the birds. I looked at the coffin; the lid was completely open. A large black male corpse stood up from inside. He had twelve arms that were twisted together behind his back and I thought immediately of the corpse with twelve arms we had seen in the undersea tomb. What was this thing? Could this twelve-armed corpse be Emperor Wannu?

As Fats fired at the diving strange birds to push them back, he yelled, "Why the hell are you in a trance?"

Ignoring him, I said, "Look...what is he doing?"

The corpse showed not the slightest interest in us. He jumped down from the stone platform and headed straight toward the giant bronze doors.

"Does he think he can open that door?" Fats gasped.

I immediately thought of the last sentence in Wang Canghai's record: If the timing wasn't right, the person who opened this door would cause fires to rise up from hell, setting the entire mountain range ablaze. When I first read this, I thought this prediction was a crazed fantasy that Wang Canghai came up with after he went through the door and saw the interior of a volcano. Now I realized it was also possible that whoever built this bronze door had created an extremely powerful trap to guard whatever secret the door concealed.

Now Fats and I were following in Wang Canghai's footsteps. If there was a trap nearby, we would probably be its first victims. We had to stop the corpse from opening the door.

I ran toward the twelve-armed creature, firing a long string of bullets, but they hit the body as though they had struck rubber, and the corpse seemed to feel nothing. He continued to walk toward the door and I screamed at Fats, "The dynamite!"

Fats rushed toward the corpse, leaped on its back, and stuffed a stick of dynamite in its mouth. As he jumped off and rolled away, I fired and hit the fuse of the explosive. It went off with a roar, blowing the head of the corpse into fragments that rained down around us. The force of the blast sent us to the ground and continued to echo in my ears. I could see Fats yell at me with a look of panic on his face but I couldn't hear a word that came from his mouth. Above us the shadows of frenzied birds came closer and closer.

Fats and I stood back to back. Untying the bandages on my arms and exposing my raw, open wounds, I prayed that my blood would be effective against our attackers.

One of the birds landed about a hundred feet in front of us. It was taller than I was. Its ugly mouth opened to show yellow fangs as it stared at us blankly as if trying to decide what we were. I raised my bloody arms in its direction but it didn't seem to care.

Two more of the birds landed, one on each side of us, then more and more, until we were completely surrounded. They stood like silent gargoyles, poised to attack.

None of them made a move and yet I knew we would soon be at their mercy. My blood seemed to have no effect upon them and Fats and I were out of ammunition.

A bird suddenly swept past above us and dropped a body from the sky. It slammed on the ground in front of us, splashing blood all over the place—it was Ye Cheng. His neck had been bitten almost in two. Another blood-covered corpse soon joined him but I had no idea of who it might have been. Its head was gone.

40. KWAN YIN WITH A THOUSAND ARMS

More bodies rained around us, members of Ning's group. Neither Panzi nor Uncle Three were among them.

"What in the hell are these birds going to do to us?" Fats asked.

"It looks like they're planning their next move but I'm no expert. I don't know what they have planned. Do you have any dynamite left? We could always blow ourselves up."

Fats shook his head. "I used it all on the emperor. You didn't tell me to keep a little in reserve."

"Shit, I never thought I'd die this way," I groaned. There were birds everywhere with no visible gaps between them. There was nowhere to run. Was I going to die here and become bird shit?

"Don't give up! Look, here's a crevice. We can hide inside and fend them off. Even if we're doomed, we can't let these damned birds win so easily!" Fats shouted.

He was right, there was a gap the width of a person between two gigantic rocks close by. Both sides of the crevice were open and unhindered. Although we'd have to squeeze in and it would be difficult for us to move once we were inside, it was an excellent place to stand and defend ourselves.

To die immediately or to die after a good fight—Fats and I took the second choice. We quickly grabbed the cartridge belts from the corpses and jammed ourselves into the crevice. The interior space was very small but I managed to fit inside it easily; Fats had more trouble squeezing in. "At least there's no room for the birds in here," he wheezed as he settled in beside me.

He immediately made a pile of rocks to serve as a blockade at the entrance. Then he turned to me and said, "They can only come at us one at a time, and we'll only have to kill a few before the entrance is blocked with their bodies. That way we can hang on a little longer."

I grimaced. We didn't have many bullets, and there would be no time to reload when the birds began to attack. Once we used what we had in the chambers of our rifles, we were finished. But Fats had the gift of contagious enthusiasm, and we weren't dead yet. Maybe we had a chance to survive after all.

Then the birds began to howl. Through the crevice I saw the bird closest to me open its mouth to a horrifying width, showing an impressive array of fangs. It spat out a creature that looked like a macaque, which leaped to the ground, ran to the pile of corpses, and then started tearing the flesh from the bodies, gobbling it down. I looked again carefully and saw that the monkey had no skin. It was covered with blood and seemed to be an internal organ of the bird it came from.

And then other birds began to spit out these creatures which all swarmed to the pile of corpses and ate ravenously. The ground was soon covered with flesh, blood, and bones as the scavengers stripped the corpses down to skeletons.

Fats's eyes were red with rage and fear. "You plan to savage us next, you fucking little bastards? If you want any of my fat flesh, you'll have to fight for it."

As the monkeys rummaged through the bare bones looking for more to eat, one of them caught sight of us. They crowded around our shelter, peering at us hungrily.

Their mouths had no lips and their fangs were as plentiful as those of the birds that were their hosts. Around each of their necks hung a bronze hexagonal bell that made no sound in spite of the rapid motions of the monkeys. I was too frightened to be surprised at this weird coincidence.

As the monkeys inspected us, Fats and I raised our guns to shoot in case they decided to leap in upon us. But when the first one did, it took us by surprise and Fats almost missed him when he opened fire. His rifle jammed as the monkey's dead body landed among its companions, and his unaimed volley of bullets swept out toward the closest monkeys, killing several of them.

The largest of the pack let out a shriek and all of them rushed toward us. Two squeezed into our space, snarling as they came. I kicked one of them hard and killed the other with two shots. Another took its place and I began to fire blindly, my vision obscured by the haze of blood that filled the air. The monkeys didn't seem to notice, surging forward in a never-ending wave of pure evil, even though the ones in front kept falling under our bullets.

Fats and I were both drenched in blood, firing nonstop with no hope of success. There were just too damned many of these little monsters. Then my bullets ran out and I had no chance to reload under this onslaught.

Then Fats emptied his gun, but he was too maddened with bloodlust to stop killing. Throwing his rifle aside, he took out his machete but six monkeys were on him in a heartbeat, fangs bared. Fats killed two with his bare hands but the other four went for his face.

Before I could draw my own machete, I felt savage bites on my legs and shoulders. Obviously my blood didn't bother these damned things one bit. This is it, I thought, So long, fat man.

CHAPTER FORTY-ONE

THE GAP BETWEEN HEAVEN AND EARTH

Although a crowd of monkeys leapt on my body and ripped away layers of my skin, I was determined to fight until my strength was gone. I knew there was no hope left for Fats and me but at least we'd kill as many of our attackers as we could.

Then the ground shook beneath us. We fell to the ground and felt the monkeys release us as they all rushed to the exit of our shelter. Fats and I poked our heads to see what was happening outside. The monkeys all climbed back into the mouths of the birds, the birds all took flight, and they disappeared into the sky, as if something had ordered their departure.

Fats reloaded his rifle as I cautiously stuck my head outside. We were alone in the midst of total silence which was almost more frightening than our near-death experience had been. We stepped back out into the world, and I asked, "What were they afraid of? Could there actually be something more deadly than those devils?"

Fats gulped and tried to speak but his lips moved without sound. He pointed frantically and I turned to see what he was attempting to show me. The bronze door had cracked open.

My own voice died in my throat. How did this happen? What had opened the door? Who was inside?

The earthquake must have been caused when the door opened, I thought in a burst of silent hysteria, could a demon from hell be coming out to walk his dog? Is it worthwhile to run or should we stick around to see what happens next?

But nothing came out, nor did the door open any wider. "Should we go take a look?" Fats asked.

I thought about the mystery locked behind this door. Wang Canghai had seen it with his own eyes, and he came back out crazy but unscathed, which showed that there was no direct, life-threatening danger beyond the portal. All of our questions could be answered if we only walked a few steps closer. But what if we entered and then the door swung shut, trapping us inside forever?

I weighed the matter carefully and decided I had to investigate. Fats nodded when I looked at him; he felt the same way.

The door was so big that the tiny gap we saw from a distance turned out to be one that a truck could have driven through, I smelled a strange aroma blowing out from the gap and I felt a strange mixture of excitement and terror.

Fats pointed his flashlight inward, but when the beam entered the door, it was swallowed up in darkness. What's the point of going in if we can see nothing, I wondered silently.

Then a few lights suddenly appeared in the darkness as though someone was coming out. Fats pulled me away from the door. A stream of light blue haze began to emerge from the rocks in the valley; forming a cloud, it rose with electric speed. Almost instantly a layer of haze veiled our eyesight as the cloud rose higher.

The sound of trumpets echoed from the other side of the valley and a row of shadows faintly appeared near the horizon. Fats turned gray with fear. "The Soldiers of the Dead," he whispered. He dragged me with him to hide behind a huge boulder.

The troops walked in rows of four, in a precise and synchronized march. They walked as if they were floating, rapidly and without a sound. I looked up to see them and almost bit off my tongue. They all had bizarrely long faces, with the length of their heads two times longer than that of a normal person. They all looked exactly the same with pallid, dead white, and expressionless features, as if they had been made of papier-mâché, each one dressed in the armor worn by soldiers of the Shang dynasty.

The procession moved past us like ghosts, paying us no attention as they marched straight through the gap in the bronze door.

Fats and I stared in horrified silence, hoping these apparitions would disappear as quickly as possible. Then the hand Fats had clapped over my mouth suddenly shook. There was Qilin, walking in the middle of the ranks, wearing the same armor as everyone around him.

I almost screamed. Had he died? Was his soul taken captive by the Soldiers of the Dead?

I took a second look. Poker-face walked as though he was moving of his own volition, in a way that was completely different from the robotic stride of the Soldiers of the Dead He's still alive. What's he doing? Oh shit, he's sneaking in through that door—is he out of his mind? My

41. THE GAP BETWEEN HEAVEN AND EARTH

pulse began to race and I started to hyperventilate. I tried to get up in an attempt to stop him but Fats clutched me tightly and wouldn't let me move.

I saw Qilin's eyes catch our movements. He turned, saw Fats and me, smiled, and moved his lips silently to say "Goodbye."

Then he walked through the giant bronze door and disappeared, along with the entire procession. The ground shook beneath us and the door closed as the last man walked inside.

There was no time for us to think about what we had just seen. The mist began to clear and we could hear the shrieking of the birds growing louder and louder by the second.

"Hurry up! Those birds are coming back again," Fats yelled. "We won't be so lucky next time they attack."

His warning was like a bucket of ice water poured over my head and I snapped out of my daze. The two of us began to race toward the other end of the valley, where Panzi and others had gone.

The boulders in the valley were like hills that were extremely difficult to climb. We hadn't gone far when the calls of the birds approached. I found myself praying in silence. It would be too cruel if we died in this place after our narrow escape from those damned things.

Our wounds had gone from painful to numb. I could hardly even feel my legs, and I couldn't run any faster no matter how hard I tried. Fats and I urged each other on. If we stopped even for a second, we'd never muster up the strength to move again. Clawing and scrambling over the rocks, we ran blindly toward the end of the valley.

There in the cliff ahead were three huge cracks in the wall. What do we do now? Which one should we take? Where is Panzi?

"Look," Fats gasped. There on the cliff's wall was a crude image of an arrow pointing toward one of the cracks. "What a lazy son of a bitch, you are, Panzi—couldn't you carve a better-looking arrow than that," he taunted.

"Who gives a shit about the artwork? Come on," I panted as I ran into the opening that the arrow pointed to.

Soon we saw the beams of flashlights in front of us and I knew we were all in trouble again. "They should have gotten in a lot deeper than this by now," I said to Fats. "This doesn't look good."

Within a few more steps we saw Panzi and a few of Ning's group. When Panzi caught sight of us, he broke into a huge grin that changed to concern as he asked, "Just the two of you? What about the others?"

"Leave it alone. It's a tragic story," I told him. "We need to hurry on; those birds are on our trail. Listen—can you hear them? "

"Follow me," Panzi beckoned us and we retreated further into the crevice. The shrieks of the birds faded away; apparently they decided chasing us was too much trouble. For the first time in days I felt we just might make it out of here alive.

CHAPTER FORTY-TWO
THE END OF THE TRAIL

The doctor on Ning's team was one of the survivors and he took care of Fats and me, while Panzi fixed us something to eat. "Don't worry about anything," he told us. "Feel that breeze. We'll follow it out of here as soon as you guys regain some strength. Your uncle's doing better; he's still unconscious but his temperature is back to normal. Ning made it here safely a couple of days ago. And there are hot springs so you can have a bath tomorrow and wipe off some of that blood."

I was too exhausted to respond. The next day Fats and I rested. Then we all set off in search of the source of the fresh wind and a way out. We walked for almost a day when Fats suddenly yelped, "We've been here before."

There was the double-layered mural stretching before us and beyond that was the sealing stone where we took shelter from the blizzard so many days ago. The supplies we'd left behind still waited for us and we stared at them in disbelief. We had come full circle.

"Shit," Fats remarked. "If we had only found this crevice when we were here before, we would have found that damned coffin in a day or two."

"Maybe that was Wang Canghai's biggest trick," I said.

"Or perhaps it's just a horrible little irony that we have to live with. In any case, we're done with all that now. Let's get outside."

The sunlight blinded us when we came out of the mountain. We slowly made our way down below the snow line where a mountain rescue team found us and took us to the closest hospital.

Uncle Three had a severe concussion and needed a long recuperation period before he would return to normal. Fats and I quickly recovered from our injuries, with a few scars as souvenirs. Ning immediately disappeared without saying goodbye to anyone. Panzi went back home to Changsha and Fats returned to Beijing.

I stayed with my uncle, trying to make sense of the nightmare we had just emerged from. Without Uncle Three to help me, I had an incomplete picture but a few things were clear.

I knew now that the Palace in the Clouds wasn't built by Wang Canghai; he had only repaired the original structure. But the original builder of this amazing place was still a mystery to me.

I also knew that Wang Canghai had been captured and had constructed a secret escape tunnel that had saved him from being killed with the other workmen after the project was completed. But what he had seen behind the giant bronze door I had no idea. His recorded narrative on the bronze fish became incomprehensible to me when he tried to tell that part of his story.

Wang Canghai had looted many tombs in the service of the Dong Xia Emperor and had hidden two of the Bronze Fish, the coded arowana, in important grave sites. He kept the third and placed it in what he planned to be his own grave, the undersea tomb.

Had his body been interred within the undersea tomb? I had no idea. Nor did I know why the group of students, including Uncle Three's lost love, Wen-Jin, had made their way from the undersea tomb to die in the Palace in the Clouds. Had two of that group survived? Where did they go?

For that matter, why did Qilin disappear through the giant bronze door? Why did my uncle make this expedition to the Palace in the Clouds? And what was the connection between the mammoth bronze tree; the bronze door; and bronze hexagonal bells that had turned up in the cavern of the blood zombies, the undersea tomb, the site of the bronze tree, and around the necks of those damned monkeys that had almost killed Fats and me?

The answer to all of these unsolved mysteries lay in what had happened in the undersea tomb twenty years ago, and with my uncle who was imprisoned in a coma. Or was the coma actually his refuge? With Uncle Three, who knew?

Coming Next:

Uncle Three remained unconscious for over a month after we returned from the palace of doom, but even though the old guy was comatose, I still didn't trust him. I stuck close to his side, sleeping on the next bed, my eyes glued to every twitch he made. The nursing staff thought I was crazy, but they didn't know my uncle the way I did. That old bastard was healthy enough; he just refused to come out of his coma.

"His wounds were terribly infected and your uncle is no longer a young man. Who knows? His central nervous system may be so badly damaged that he'll never wake up," his doctor told me.

I waited as patiently as possible. I kept myself busy by thinking over our expedition, especially the part involving Qilin's march with the Soldiers of the Dead through the bronze door into a mystery I might never solve. Then there were the two people in the earlier expedition who had disappeared long before we made our way to the same place. Had they too found their way through the bronze door never to return?

And why did the undersea tomb lead all who entered it to travel to that damned palace? I looked at my uncle, sleeping peacefully, with all the information I needed locked away in his dreams, and I wanted to kick him.

As I stared at my uncle one morning, his doctor entered the room, "I need to talk to you," he said, "Please come to my office."

"What's the matter?" I asked as I followed him out of the room. Standing in the hallway was one of Uncle Three's shop assistants. "Why are you here?" I demanded. He stared at me and I knew something was going on. I rushed back to my uncle's room. His bed was empty.

TO BE CONTINUED...

Note from the Author

Back in the days when there was no television or internet and I was still a poor kid, telling stories to other children was my greatest pleasure. My friends thought my stories were a lot of fun, and I decided that someday I would become the best of storytellers.

I wrote a lot of stories trying to make that dream come true, but most of them I put away, unfinished. I completely gave up my dream of being a writer, and like many people, I sat waiting for destiny to tap me on the shoulder.

Although I gave up my dream of being a writer, luckily the dream did not give up on me. When I was 26 years old, my uncle, a merchant who sold Chinese antiques, gave me his journal that was full of short notes he had written over the years. Although fragmentary information can often be quite boring, my uncle's writing inspired me to go back to my abandoned dream. A book about a family of grave robbers began to take shape, a suspenseful novel.... I started to write again....

This is my first story, my first book that became successful beyond all expectations, a best-seller that made me rich. I have no idea how this happened, nor does anybody else; this is probably the biggest mystery of The Grave Robbers' Chronicles. Perhaps as you read the many volumes of this chronicle, you will find out why it has become so popular. I hope you enjoy the adventures you'll encounter with Uncle Three, his nephew and their companions as they roam through a world of zombies, vampires, and corpse-eaters.

Thanks to Albert Wen, Michelle Wong, Janet Brown, Kathy Mok and all my friends who helped publish the English edition of The Grave Robbers' Chronicles.

Xu Lei was born in 1982 and graduated from Renmin University of China in 2004. He has held numerous jobs, working as a graphic designer, a computer programmer, and a supplier to the U.S. gaming industry. He is now the owner of an international trading company and lives in Hangzhou, China with his wife and son. Writing isn't his day job, but it is where his heart lies.